ENTICING

He whisked her into a nearby guest room and shut the door, leaving the dark room lit only by moonlight.

"What—"

"Shh," Scott said, putting a finger to her soft, luscious lips. He backed her gently against the wall by the door, murmuring, "She might hear us."

"Who?" she whispered.

"Marta—she's making her rounds." He placed his hands on both sides of Nicole's shoulders in a protective gesture, then leaned into her, letting his senses fill with her enticing essence.

BOOK YOUR PLACE ON OUR WEBSITE AND MAKE THE READING CONNECTION!

We've created a customized website just for our very special readers, where you can get the inside scoop on everything that's going on with Zebra, Pinnacle and Kensington books.

When you come online, you'll have the exciting opportunity to:

- View covers of upcoming books
- Read sample chapters
- Learn about our future publishing schedule (listed by publication month *and author*)
- Find out when your favorite authors will be visiting a city near you
- Search for and order backlist books from our online catalog
- Check out author bios and background information
- Send e-mail to your favorite authors
- Meet the Kensington staff online
- Join us in weekly chats with authors, readers and other guests
- Get writing guidelines
- AND MUCH MORE!

**Visit our website at
http://www.kensingtonbooks.com**

CAUGHT IN THE ACT

Pam McCutcheon

ZEBRA BOOKS
KENSINGTON PUBLISHING CORP.
http://www.kensingtonbooks.com

ZEBRA BOOKS are published by

Kensington Publishing Corp.
850 Third Avenue
New York, NY 10022

All Kensington titles, imprints and distributed lines are available at special quantity discounts for bulk purchases for sales
promotion, premiums, fund-raising, educational or institu-
tional use.

Special book excerpts or customized printings can also be created to fit specific needs. For details, write or phone the office
of the Kensington Special Sales Manager: Kensington Publishing Corp., 850 Third Avenue, New York, NY 10022. Attn.
Special Sales Department. Phone: 1-800-221-2647.

Zebra and the Z logo Reg. U.S. Pat. & TM Off.

First Printing: March 2005
10 9 8 7 6 5 4 3 2 1

Printed in the United States of America

Chapter One

The noise that shouldn't have been there made Scott Richmond freeze with his hand on the railing and one foot poised to take the next step up the staircase. It was midnight, the mansion was dark, the servants had all been given the night off, and his mother was away for the weekend. So what, exactly, had made that noise? Or who?

He half-turned to go back downstairs. Had he imagined it? No, there it came again. It sounded like the scrape of furniture against a polished wood floor.

Could it be a burglar? Not likely. Not with the state-of-the-art security system he'd just put in last year. Then again, furniture didn't usually move itself. Maybe it was an inside job. One of the servants, perhaps?

With that thought, Scott relaxed a little. It was probably just the housekeeper who had returned to perform some forgotten chore. And she wouldn't expect him to be here. He was supposed to be at a charity ball, but the event had bored him, so he left early.

He didn't want to frighten anyone, but then again, what if it wasn't a servant . . . ?

He cat-footed his way back down the staircase and

slipped off his tuxedo jacket and tie. Hanging them on the newel post, he glanced around, wondering where the noise had come from. Light striped the floor of the dark foyer, emanating from the partially open doors to the drawing room. *There.*

He made his way silently across, along the way picking up a heavy brass candlestick from the hall table. *Better safe than unprepared.*

Holding the candlestick at the ready like a base-ball bat, he edged his head around the door, his eyes blinking in the bright light. The family portrait above the marble fireplace had been swung out on its hinges to reveal the safe hidden behind it, and the thief was standing on one of his mother's or-nate Louis XIV chairs with his hand in the safe.

For a moment, Scott cursed the whimsy that had caused him to use the old movie cliché of hiding the safe there—it had made it too easy for the thief to find. He was about to tiptoe away to call the police when the burglar's appearance suddenly registered.

Black leotard and tights, slender curves . . . and sassy, curly blond pigtails? The thief was a woman! A little slip of one at that. And judging from her tight-fitting clothes, it was obvious she didn't have a weapon.

He stifled a laugh of disbelief. It appeared the evening wouldn't be a total bore after all.

As she continued to pull velvet jewelry boxes out of the safe and tuck them into a black tote bag, he slipped in and locked the double doors. Setting the candlestick aside, he came up behind her and peered into the safe, saying, "I think you have them all now."

She shrieked and jumped, dropping the bracelet

case she had been about to put in the bag. "You scared me," she accused in angry tones.

As he got a good look at her face, he revised her age downward. She wasn't a woman. Not yet, anyway. The thief was a teenaged girl. Intrigued, he pointed out, "Well, you are burgling my house, you know."

Her eyes widened as if she had just realized what she'd been doing. Immediately, she jumped down and tried to make a break for it. He let her run and watched as she tugged fruitlessly at the locked doors.

"You can't get out that way," he observed. Then, when she ran to the windows, he added, "Or that way. The windows are barred for security." Who knew they'd be more effective in keeping a thief in than keeping her out?

She whirled to glare at him. "Let me out of here."

"No," he said with a casual smile.

She looked confused by his expression. "Why not?" Her eyes narrowed, and she brought her hands up in a martial arts stance. "I warn you—I know karate."

He grinned. *Karate? More likely ballet, given that getup.* "Don't worry, I won't hurt you. I just want to know what you're doing here."

She relaxed her posture and rolled her eyes. "Duh, what do you think? I'm here to have tea with the queen."

Smart-aleck kid. But he liked her spunk, even if he had seen a little fear behind the bravado. "No, I mean, why my house?"

"You weren't supposed to be home," she blurted out, then looked as though she wished she hadn't.

"Who told you I wasn't supposed to be home?" he asked softly.

Dismay flickered across her face. "No one. I, uh, I saw you leave all fancied up like that. I figured a slick guy like you would be gone for hours."

She didn't lie very convincingly. But he wanted to know who had given her this idea. "So you thought you'd just run in and make off with a few jewels?"

She raised her chin in defiance. "Why not? It's the least you owe me."

He raised an eyebrow. He'd been afraid this was some sort of gang initiation or something. Instead, it appeared to be a personal vendetta. "Owe you? What do you mean?"

She shrugged, looking sulky. "What do you care?"

"I care because you're stealing from me."

"Stealing from your mother, you mean," she shot back. "I can't see you wearing a diamond tiara or a ruby necklace."

So she knew the jewelry belonged to his mother and what some of the pieces were. That was interesting . . . especially since he hadn't seen her open any of the boxes. "True, true. But you see, they don't go with the tux."

She stared at him in disbelief. "Are you drunk?"

"No, are you?"

"Of course not." She drew herself up in a righteous manner. "I don't drink."

"That makes sense. You're not old enough. It'll probably be—what?—six years before you're old enough to drink?"

"No, a little over three years. I'm seventeen—almost eighteen," she said in indignation. "And the reason I don't drink is because it's wrong."

"So is stealing," he pointed out, wondering how she rationalized that.

The teenager looked uncertain for a moment, then said with a sniff, "You're rich. You can afford it."

They were well off, perhaps, but he wouldn't say rich. It had taken him years to rebuild the family coffers after his father had run their jewelry business into the ground, then died to leave his family with crushing debts. "So are the Kennedys across the street," he said. "In fact, they'd be a better target. She has twice as many jewels and half the security system. Or maybe you could try the Elliots' house on the next block—"

"Are you crazy?" she asked in disbelief.

"No, are you?" he inquired, hiding his simmering amusement behind a polite facade.

She rolled her eyes again. "I must be, to talk to *you*. Let me outta here."

"Not until you tell me why you're here." In firm tones, he said, "Sit."

"I'm not a dog," she protested.

He sighed. "If you don't sit down and tell me why you're here, I'll call the police."

That seemed to surprise her. "You haven't already?"

"Not yet, but I will if you don't sit down. Please."

"Oh, all right." With a pout, she crossed her arms and flopped down on his mother's antique fainting couch as if it were a cheap futon.

"That's better." He sat down across from her and regarded her with curiosity. "Why us?"

"Why not?" she challenged.

Scott sighed. "I'm not letting you leave unless you tell me."

She gave him a wary look. "You'll let me leave then?"

"If I believe you, I might."

She frowned, obviously considering his offer. "All right." She crossed her arms in a defiant motion. "It's because you owe me."

Oh, yeah. She'd mentioned that before. "I do?" Scott repeated in disbelief. "How? I've never met you before in my life." He certainly didn't play around in the kiddie set, and if he'd met her somewhere else, he would have remembered this dramatic child.

"I mean your family does," she said impatiently.

"Oh, I see. My mother gambled away her jewels in a game of craps and wouldn't pay up?"

The little thief gave him a disdainful look. She must have seen his mother then. Grace Richmond, arbiter of Denver society and hostess to the elite, was not the craps-playing type. "Of course not. It's your father's fault."

"My father lost to you in a game of craps?"

"Don't be ridiculous," she snapped. "We both know he's been dead for years."

"Then how can he owe you?"

"Because right before he died, your father fired *my* father. For no reason."

Scott frowned. He didn't doubt it, but there had been a reason, though not a good one. His father had laid off quite a few employees just before he died, hoping unsuccessfully to stop some of the Richmond money from going down the drain. "Couldn't your father get another job?" And hadn't Scott tracked down everyone his father had fired and compensated them?

She rolled her eyes again. "Oh yeah, like there are lots of jobs for valets out there."

Scott winced. No one could do sarcasm like a teenager. "Dreyfuss was your father?" he asked in disbelief. There was no resemblance between that dour ascetic and this smart-aleck kid.

"Yeah, and after working for your father for twenty years, he didn't even get a pension or severance pay or . . . or anything. He died a few years ago, and what little money he saved is gone now. So, we have no money." She held her head up in a self-righteous pose. "See? You owe me."

Hell. He did. Though in his own defense, Scott had attempted to make restitution but failed. "Why didn't you just come and ask me for the money instead of resorting to theft?"

She snorted. "Yeah, right. Like you'd give it to me."

"I might . . . if I knew why you wanted it."

Eying him with doubt, she said, "For school." Then more enthusiastically, "There's this totally sweet school in New York. It's really hard to get into, but I've been accepted. I even have a partial scholarship, but my sister says we can't afford it this year. The room and board are too expensive."

New York, huh? It all fell into place. "Don't tell me—you want to be an actress."

Her eyes widened. "Yes, how did you know?"

Oh, maybe her over-the-top dramatics might have given him a clue? Ignoring her question, he asked, "What school?"

"Juilliard."

Now it was his turn to be surprised. She must be

better than he thought if she had made the cut there. "Don't you have to audition?"

"I did already. I used all the money I earned to get there, and I really wowed them."

She must have, to earn a partial scholarship. "It has an excellent reputation . . ."

"I know," she said in eager tones. "But if I don't pay my tuition by next week, my slot will go to someone else." She pounded a fist on the couch. "If I can't go, I'll die. I'll just die."

Stifling a grin at her dramatics, he said, "How about if I fund it?"

She frowned at him, saying hesitantly, "My sister says we shouldn't accept charity."

"But she doesn't mind if you steal?"

"Oh, she doesn't know I went through with it," the girl said in an artless tone. "Besides, I wanted to hurt you as much as you hurt us."

"I see." But stealing his mother's ugly, well-insured jewels wouldn't hurt him at all. Feeling guilty for what his father had done to her family, Scott stood up and said, "All right then, I'll help you steal the jewels."

She gaped at him. "What?"

"You've convinced me. You deserve it. Here, I'll help you." He grabbed the bracelet case she had dropped and shoved it into the tote bag. "Was that the last of the jewels?"

"Yes, but—"

"But you want more, I'm sure." He looked around. "Here, take these," he said, putting a pair of ugly, silver candlesticks in the bag. "I've always hated them. And Mother has way too many tchotchkes."

"What's a tchotchke?"

"This," he said, picking up a hideous antique snuffbox, "is a tchotchke. And this." A frilly porcelain Dresden figurine followed the snuffbox into the bag, as did a gaudy gold and crystal ashtray.

He went around the room, filling up the bag with knickknacks as the girl watched in disbelief. But he was careful to leave the really good stuff, taking only the things he wouldn't miss. When the bag was full, he said, "There, that should do it. Looks better with the clutter cleared out a bit, doesn't it?" More than enough remained.

She looked at him as if she suspected he had a screw loose somewhere, and maybe a whole lot of bolts and nuts loose as well. "Yeah, sure. Whatever you say."

He handed the bag to her. "Okay, that's it then. Good luck at Juilliard."

She just stood there, holding the tote bag with a disbelieving expression. "Uh, how am I going to get out?"

"Oh, that's right. The door's locked, isn't it? Here, I'll open it for you." He unlocked it and gestured her through with a smile.

She edged past him as if she wasn't quite sure what he was up to. He hid his amusement as he helped her out the kitchen door, from where she had obviously come in, and watched her speed off into the night.

Shaking his head with a chuckle, he closed the safe then reset the house alarm and wondered just how long it would take her to realize it might be a tad difficult to find a fence for those stolen goods.

Scott headed back up the stairs toward his office and his computer. Now that he knew who her father was, it shouldn't be difficult to use the Internet and his connections to track her down. He'd show up at her place first thing tomorrow to offer her cash to take the loot off her hands. It was the least he could do.

He shook his head. He had managed to make things right by all the other people his father had fired, but Dreyfuss had died by the time Scott was able to make restitution. Scott had offered the money that the valet should have received to his family, but someone had turned it down. Probably the sister. Tomorrow, he'd—

The doorbell rang, stopping his progress up the stairs once more. Who the hell could it be at this time of night? Had the Dreyfuss girl forgotten something?

Curious, he turned off the alarm, turned on the light, and opened the front door. A woman stood there, with sleek honey-blond hair tumbling to her shoulders, beautiful skin, and her slender body hidden under what appeared to be a hastily donned sweat suit. And, surprisingly, she bore a striking resemblance to the young thief who had just left.

Scott grinned to himself. So big sister had found out what little sis was up to, huh? *This is getting interesting.*

Nicole Dreyfuss stared, aghast, at the good-looking man who opened the door. His pleated shirt and cummerbund, the fresh-faced boy-next-door look, and his wicked grin let her know that Scott Richmond had answered his own door.

What was she going to do now? Chrissie had told her of her idiotic scheme to steal the Richmonds' jewels and Nicole had thought she had talked her out of it, but when she had woken in the middle of the night, she'd found Chrissie gone, along with the plans to the Richmond house. Worse, her little sister had left a pamphlet for a charity ball that showed Scott Richmond was one of the organizers and would be there tonight.

Putting the clues together, Nicole had rushed right over to stop Chrissie, but had probably scared her sister off by ringing the doorbell. Nicole hadn't thought through what she was going to do if anyone actually answered the door. "You weren't supposed to be here," she blurted out.

"So I understand," he said, his eyes laughing at her as he lounged against the door jamb, his arms folded across his chest. "How can I help you?"

What could she say? *Hi, I've come here to stop my sister from robbing your house. Oh, and has she been here yet?*

"I, uh, thought I heard a noise." *Good grief, how lame.*

He continued to smile at her. "What kind of noise?"

"I don't know . . . like breaking glass?" Just how had Chrissie planned to get in, anyway?

"I see." He continued to regard her with polite expectancy.

He was no help. She'd sort of expected him to volunteer that he'd been robbed after he heard her tale of broken glass, but he didn't say anything. Relief filled her as she realized that meant Chrissie wasn't here. Either she hadn't done it yet, or she'd been scared off by his presence and left.

But the relief evaporated as Nicole realized it

could also mean Chrissie was stuck hiding in the house . . . or he just hadn't discovered the theft yet.

Damn. When he did, he might remember Nicole had been here with her lame story and try to track her down as a witness. She'd better leave now and hope Chrissie was somewhere else. "Never mind. It must have been across the street."

She turned to go, but Scott said lazily, "Don't worry, Miss Dreyfuss, she didn't break any windows."

Nicole froze, then turned with a slow motion to meet his eyes, trying not to let the dread show in hers. "I beg your pardon?" How did he know her name?

"Your sister. She didn't break anything."

Nicole swallowed hard, then decided to try and brazen it out. "What do you mean?"

He raised an eyebrow. "Let's see if I can jog your memory. Your sister, a black bag, an open safe, my mother's jewels . . . and a wish to go to Juilliard. Ring any bells?"

Nicole closed her eyes in disbelief. *Damn. Chrissie has been caught.* Opening her eyes, she decided to throw herself on the mercy of this man. What other choice did she have? "Mr. Richmond, I—"

"Scott."

"What?"

"My name's Scott. And yours?"

There was no reason not to tell him. He already knew her last name. "Nicole."

"And your sister's name?"

"Chrissie."

He grinned. "It fits her." He made a sweeping gesture toward the door. "Won't you come in?"

She wasn't sure she wanted to go into that house. "Where is Chrissie?"

"Come inside and I'll tell you."

It didn't look as though she'd get any answers until she did as he asked. True, he didn't *look* dangerous, but just in case, she groped in her purse for her pepper spray. It made her feel better, just knowing it was there.

She followed him across the foyer to what had to be the living room. Though how anyone could live in such a fussy, ornate room was beyond her. They both seated themselves, and she realized he looked even more devastatingly handsome in full light. And even more like a good-for-nothing charmer, she reminded herself. She had to remember Chrissie. "Okay, I'm in. Where's my sister?"

"I don't know."

If he had caught her breaking and entering, how could he not know? "Why not?"

"I let her go."

"I—I don't understand."

"It's simple, really. I came home early and caught her with her hand in the safe, she told me her story, and I let her go."

Relief flooded through Nicole once more and she let go of the pepper spray. "Oh, thank you, Mr.— Scott. She's just a kid. She's a little spoiled, not really a thief. But she wanted to go to Juilliard so badly."

His eyes laughed at her again. "So I understand. Now she'll be able to."

"What?" How was that possible?

"She'll have more than enough money as soon as she sells my mother's jewels."

Feeling distinctly as if she had entered the twilight zone, Nicole said in confusion, "I thought you caught her."

"I did."

Nicole tried to sort through her confusion. "And you let her go . . . *with* the jewels?"

"Yes." And the man smiled at her as if it were a perfectly reasonable thing to do.

"But . . . *why*?"

"She put up a good case for them belonging to her."

Nicole gaped at him. "You must be joking." That's all this man seemed to do—joke.

"Not at all. Look, I'll show you." He opened the safe above the fireplace and invited her to look inside. "See? As I told you, it's empty. There are quite a few tchotchkes missing, too."

Nicole sat back down in disbelief. "You let her take all that . . . and you didn't stop her?"

"Now you're getting it," he said in an encouraging tone.

His twisted sense of humor was beginning to annoy her. "How incredibly irresponsible of you."

He raised both eyebrows this time. "Excuse me?"

Getting warmed up now, Nicole said, "You let a seventeen-year-old girl steal and get away with it?"

Looking puzzled now, he asked, "Would you rather I turned her over to the police?"

"No, of course not." And just in case he decided to change his mind, she moderated her tone. "But it's a bad lesson to teach a teenager."

Scott shrugged. "That's me. I've always been a bad influence."

That might be what he wanted people to believe, but she knew better.

Before she could answer, he added, "Don't worry. I actually did plan for this to be a lesson. Any moment now, she's going to realize how difficult it will be to find a fence for those stolen goods. I figured I'd find her first thing tomorrow and offer to buy them back."

"Why on earth would you do that?"

"I told you. She convinced me she was right. She deserves the money because of what my father did to your father."

"So you're going to *reward* her for stealing?"

"No," he said patiently. "I just plan to give her what's owed her. And you."

"You don't owe *me* anything. Or Chrissie, either."

He cocked his head to regard her with an appraising look. "Don't go all self-righteous on me, Nicole. That's Chrissie's shtick. Besides, this is all your fault, you know."

"Mine? How do you figure that?" She defied him or anyone else to control Chrissie when she was on one of her wild kicks. Ever since their mother had died eight years ago, Chrissie had been impossible.

"I distinctly remember sending a check to your family a few years ago, a check that represented what your father should have received in the way of a pension. It was returned to me with a snippy little note refusing my 'charity.' I assume you sent that note."

"Yes, I did. Obviously, I couldn't accept the money."

"Why not? Your father deserved it."

"Yes, he did. And your father should have given it to him when he let him go. But I don't want your guilt money."

"You'd rather I continue to feel guilty?"

If he put it that way, it sounded rather rude, but she had to admit he was right. "Yes, I suppose I do."

Surprisingly, he smiled again. "That's fair enough, I guess. Now it's your turn to feel guilty. If you had taken the money when I offered it, Chrissie would have gone to school and we wouldn't be in this mess."

There was some truth in what he said, but she wouldn't admit it. She just glared at him.

"Let me redeem the jewels from Chrissie for what my father owed yours," Scott said softly. "If Chrissie is as talented as she thinks she is, she deserves to go to Juilliard."

The thought of taking money from the family that had fired her father galled Nicole. "No thanks. She can attend next year. I'll have enough saved up by then." Somehow.

"But she assured me that if she doesn't go, she'll die. She'll just die."

Frowning at his levity, Nicole said, "She'll live. Besides, she shouldn't be rewarded for breaking the law."

Scott nodded thoughtfully. "Well, technically, she didn't, since I helped her."

"But she intended to rob you," Nicole shot back. "And at the very least, she could be charged with breaking and entering."

Scott looked puzzled again. "It sounds like you're angling to have your sister thrown in jail."

"It *would* teach her a lesson, but no. I wouldn't do that to her."

"Then take the money. It should be yours, anyway."

"No, and don't bother hunting us down. I'll catch her as soon as I get home and let her know exactly what I think of her. Then first thing tomorrow morning I'll bring the . . . the, uh . . ."

"The loot?" he said helpfully. "The booty, the swag?"

Someone obviously watched too many old gangster movies. "I'll bring the *jewels* back to you then. And anything else she took. No ransom needed or wanted." Then, because she knew it was the right thing to do, she added, "And thank you for not calling the police."

He shrugged. "No problem. I've done some dumb things in my time, too." He paused, then added, "But if you're not going to let me pay you what I owe you, you'll have to answer a question for me."

"What's that?" she asked warily.

"What exactly did you plan to do when you came to my door tonight?"

Nicole felt her face warm. "I—I'm not sure. I just wanted to stop her. Somehow."

He grinned. "That's what I thought. Until tomorrow, then."

She nodded, but wasn't sure she liked the idea of seeing him again. Nicole had always been the sensible one, the one in control of all situations. But the longer she was around Scott Richmond, the more she felt flustered, confused, and a little off-kilter. She didn't like the sensation at all, and she resolved to stay as far away from him as possible.

Chapter Two

Scott woke earlier than he normally did on a Sunday morning. He hadn't had such a keen sense of anticipation since his sister's husband had shown up unexpectedly at his own funeral last year.

This situation promised to be just as fascinating. But was it the circumstances or the very attractive Nicole Dreyfuss who had caused it? It didn't matter. Either way, the day proved to be very interesting.

He'd expected Nicole to arrive bright and early, but she didn't ring the doorbell until about ten o'clock. He met her in the area his mother called the drawing room and regarded Nicole in appreciation. The jeans and soft powder-blue sweater she wore showed more of her curves than the sweat suit had, and Scott wholeheartedly approved. The woman was a knockout and intelligent as well. Yes, he definitely wanted to get to know her better. But first, how was he going to convince her to take the money for Chrissie?

He glanced at the familiar black tote bag beside her and lowered his voice to a conspiratorial whisper. "I see ya brought the loot. Did the coppers spot ya?"

Nicole slanted him an exasperated look. "You can cut the act. It won't work with me."

"Excuse me?"

"I'm not buying the act. We both know you're more than a witless charmer."

"Oh, no. A *witty* charmer, surely."

But despite himself, Scott was taken aback. True, he did tend to take on the persona of a carefree good-for-nothing, but no one had questioned the role before.

Ignoring his comment, she added sternly, "I'm a reference librarian. So when your check arrived so many years after my father was fired, I did a little research on your family. It appears your father ran the jewelry business into the ground and was desperate for cash, so that's why he sold so much stock and laid off so many people. Right?"

True, but his mother had made Scott promise he would never admit how inept his father had been. Typical—Grace would rather his father be thought cruel for laying off employees than incompetent for losing his business. "What makes you say that?" Scott hedged.

"I can read between the lines, and from everything I've been able to gather, your family was dead broke, yet all of a sudden you're sending out pension or severance checks to your father's former employees . . . years *after* he died. I'm curious, how did you manage to do that despite bankruptcy?"

"Maybe because we weren't bankrupt?"

"I know you didn't *file* for it, but you sure sold the business in a hurry once your father died. You have an MBA—you could've tried to run the business yourself, but you didn't. The only reason that makes sense is that you needed a ready source of cash. Why? To pay for this monster of a house and your mother's gewgaws?"

Nicole was dead-on. How had she guessed so much about his family? But he just grinned and drawled, "Well, must keep up appearances, y'know." Or so his mother insisted.

Nicole gave him another exasperated look. "And it's quite obvious you took over the management of the family finances. A few years later, you're handing out money right and left. How'd you do it? Investments?"

He shrugged. "I was lucky." And he'd given Grace a strict allowance so she wouldn't put them right back in the hole they'd managed to crawl out of.

"No, you were shrewd. Don't deny it—the evidence is clear for anyone who cares to look." She shook her head in disbelief. "Why do you let people believe you're a frivolous fool?"

For a moment, he just stared at her, not knowing how to answer. She was the first person, other than his sister and her husband, who had penetrated his facade, and he wasn't quite sure how to react. "It's what they all expect of me," he said with a rueful smile. Then, letting his grin widen, he added, "Besides, it's not *all* a sham."

She nodded. "Yes, I can see that you are quite the charmer. Well, it won't work on me."

Wouldn't it? Now there was a challenge. If Nicole wouldn't be easily charmed, he might find it very worthwhile to get to know her better. Besides, her perceptiveness intrigued him. And she didn't seem to be impressed by the trappings of wealth, either.

But one thing confused him . . . . "So that's why you turned down the money I sent? Because you think you caught me in the act of pretending to be something else?"

"I know I did."

"I don't get it," he said without admitting a thing. "Why did you send it back?"

"Because your father and mother are the ones who owed us—not you. Taking money from you under false pretences would be like accepting charity."

Odd, no one else had any problems taking his money. "I didn't consider it charity or false pretences. I took on my father's debts and obligations when he died. He owed you, so I paid his debt." Scott paused, regarding her with curiosity. There had to be more to it than that. "What's the real reason you turned it down?"

"That *is* the real reason." When Scott just stared at her with one eyebrow raised, she added lamely, "That and the fact that it was too late to do my father any good."

Unfortunately, Scott hadn't had the money earlier than that, or he would have paid it. But her reason was one he could understand—her pride was involved.

Well, so was his, dammit. "But it's not too late to do Chrissie some good. Unless you want to keep refusing just to make me feel guilty?"

She looked a little chagrined at that. "No, of course not." Then she froze. "Oh, shoot. Chrissie—the jewels. I meant to tell you, but I got sidetracked." Then she had the nerve to glare at him as if it were his fault.

"What about the jewels? Aren't they in the bag?"

"No. I tried to get the jewels from her, but by the time I found her, they were already gone. The only things still there were the knickknacks you heaped on her." And Nicole slanted him another accusing look at that.

"Are you sure they're gone? Maybe she hid them."

"I'm sure. I checked all her hiding places—that's how I found the other things. But the jewels were gone, already sold."

"She *sold* the jewels already?" Scott repeated in disbelief. "How did she find a fence so fast?"

"I don't know. She must have had someone lined up ahead of time."

Could Chrissie really think that far ahead? "So she has the cash already for Juilliard?"

"Yes. Well, she did, but I took it away from her."

He eyed her with more respect. "What are you planning to do with it?"

Nicole threw up her hands in exasperation. "I don't know, but I can't let her keep it, now can I?"

"No, of course not," Scott said in soothing tones. If Nicole was too proud to keep the money he'd sent for her father's pension, she surely wouldn't accept money from stolen loot.

"Maybe you should take it?" Nicole asked. "I guess it really belongs to your mother, since it came from the sale of her jewels."

"No, thanks. I don't want it, either." How could he accept it, knowing where it came from?

"This is all your fault," Nicole said. "If you hadn't let her get away with the jewels, she couldn't have sold them."

Scott countered, "And if you had accepted my money, she wouldn't have had to resort to stealing." As stubbornness fired in her eyes, he added, "But we've chewed that bone already. Care to gnaw on a new one?"

"Like what?"

"Like what you're going to do about it."

"Me? What about you?" she asked indignantly. "You're involved in this too, you know."

He grinned to himself—just the reaction he'd been hoping for. "True. And it seems to me that the best thing to do is to buy back the jewels before anyone notices they're missing. Did she tell you where she sold them?"

"No," Nicole admitted with a sigh. "I tried to get it out of her, but she wouldn't talk. Maybe you'd have more luck."

"Maybe I would . . . ." Especially if he could offer her a college education as inducement if she revealed all . . . and threaten her with jail if she didn't.

"But how are you going to keep the fact that they were stolen a secret?" Nicole asked, looking worried. "Won't your mother notice?"

"Probably not for a while. She rarely wears this jewelry—it's mostly ugly family heirlooms. She keeps the stuff she wears all the time in her bedroom."

"Okay, then—" Nicole began, only to be interrupted by the door opening.

Grace Richmond breezed in, looking elegant and perfectly coiffed, followed by her portly attorney-boyfriend, Gerald Wainwright. She came to a halt when she saw Scott and Nicole. "Oh, hello, dear. I didn't know you were entertaining a guest."

Scott stood. "Yes, Mother. This is . . . Nicole Drey-fuss." For a moment, he had toyed with the idea of giving a false name, but Mother would never make the connection between her husband's former valet and this woman. She didn't even remember their housekeeper's name half the time.

He introduced Nicole to Gerald as well, and they all exchanged pleasantries. Nicole looked a little uncomfortable, but they didn't seem to notice.

"I didn't know you'd be back so early," Scott said. Or he would've taken Nicole to another room.

Grace waved an airy hand in dismissal. "The weather turned nasty in Aspen, so we decided to come back early. Don't worry. I won't bother you long. I just need to get my sapphire bracelet from the safe."

Uh-oh. Scott didn't need Nicole's panicked look to know they were in deep doo-doo.

He scooted over to stand between her and the fireplace, his mind working frantically as he leaned, oh-so-casually, against the mantel. "Your bracelet? Why?"

She raised an eyebrow in surprise. "When I wore it last week, I noticed the clasp was loose. I men-tioned it to Gerald, and he's going to have it fixed for me."

Scott smiled. "Very nice of him, but I can han-dle that for you. No need to bother Gerald."

"It's no bother," Gerald said with his lawyer face—the one that didn't reveal any emotions. "I'm happy to do these little things for Grace."

Scott was sure Gerald would be happy to do a lot more than that, but Mother had turned down at least two of his marriage proposals that Scott knew of. Gerald was always courteous and accommodating enough to escort Grace to all her social functions, so she probably figured she didn't need a husband.

"I like doing these things for Mother, too," Scott declared. "And I haven't done anything in a long time. Why don't you let me do this?" Okay, he sounded like an idiot, but if it kept her from opening that safe, it was worth it.

"Have you been drinking?" his mother asked.

Why was everyone accusing him of being drunk all of a sudden? "Only coffee." He threw Nicole a pleading glance, hoping for inspiration, but she just looked shell-shocked. No help there. He'd have to wing it on his own. "But—"

"What's that doing there?" his mother asked, her eyes narrowing as she swerved around Scott.

Uh-oh. He'd forgotten to move the chair back to its customary spot after Chrissie used it as a step-stool. "I was just, uh, showing it to Nicole. She has a passion for Louis XIV furniture."

Grace beamed at her. "Do you, my dear? I do so love antiques. Styles these days are so plain and stark, don't you think?"

Nicole murmured something appropriate, though from what little he knew of her, Scott was sure she would appreciate something a heck of a lot more modern and sleek. Moving the chair back to where it belonged, Scott said, "Why don't you show her the rest of the collection in your bedroom, Mother?"

Anything to get her out of here, even if he had to sacrifice Nicole's taste to do it.

"Perhaps later. For now, I need my bracelet. Open the safe, please."

Now what? He couldn't refuse without looking suspicious. Slowly, he swung the painting away from the wall and fiddled with the dial. "I'm sorry. I don't seem to remember the combination."

Giving him an exasperated look, Grace said, "Let me do it then."

"But don't you think—"

"Move," she said in a tone that implied she would brook no more nonsense from him.

Scott had no choice but to obey, especially since Gerald was giving him such an odd look. And poor Nicole cringed as if she expected the house to fall down around her ears at any moment. He retreated to Nicole's side and steeled himself, waiting for the inevitable.

Grace pulled a piece of paper out of her purse, consulted it, then opened the safe and peered inside. She froze for an instant, then said, "The jewels aren't here. Scott, did you move them—" She broke off suddenly and took a step back. "My silver candlesticks are gone, too," she said in indignation. She glanced around the room as if inventorying it. "And my snuffbox, and all my lovely things. We've been robbed!"

Simultaneously, he and Nicole used their toes to surreptitiously slide the stuffed tote bag out of sight beneath the ottoman in front of them. "It's all right, Mother. I'm, uh, having some of your knick-knacks cleaned—the metal looked so tarnished. They should be back tomorrow."

Grace relaxed visibly. "You should have told me."

"Yes, I should have. Sorry about that."

"But what about my jewels?"

He hesitated, really wanting to tell her that they'd been sent out for cleaning, too, but how could he possibly explain if he wasn't able to retrieve them?

He shrugged. "Oh, them. I helped a burglar steal those last night." Then he winced as Nicole's toe connected with his shin. Damn, he should have moved that concealing ottoman.

Grace scowled. "Very funny. But there's no doubt we've been robbed. We need to call the police at once."

"No," Scott blurted out. "Don't do that."

"Why not?"

He floundered around, looking for an answer. "Be—because it'll cause a scandal." His mother hated to be involved in anything that even hinted at disgrace.

She looked uncertain. "You think so? How?"

Hell, I don't know. "It just will," he said lamely.

Nicole rescued him. "He's right. You know how people like to gossip and snicker when something like this happens to someone else. They'll say your security wasn't good enough, or you deserved it. You don't want that to happen."

"Thanks," Scott whispered, but Nicole just gave him a wry look.

Grace still appeared unsure, but help came from an unexpected direction. "Quite right," Gerald said. "Perhaps we can hire a private detective to investigate the theft. Discreetly, of course."

"But what about the insurance company?" Grace asked. "I'll need to file a claim so I can be reimbursed for my loss. Won't they need a police report?"

"They might," Gerald conceded. "Then again, they might want to keep this quiet so they have an opportunity to find the jewels themselves. They'll probably want to use their own investigator." He took her arm gently. "Come, let's go to your study and call them, see what they have to say."

Grace allowed herself to be persuaded and they both left the room. As Gerald steered her out the door, Grace asked anxiously, "Do you think they'll pay right away?"

"I'm sure they will," Gerald said soothingly. "Let me handle it."

But Scott didn't hear any more as they passed out of earshot.

Nicole leaned close and whispered, "Do you think he'll be able to talk the insurance company out of informing the police?"

"If anyone can persuade them, it's Gerald." Despite his ordinary appearance, the attorney was a whiz at persuading people to do things they didn't intend to, as Scott had discovered when Gerald had smoothly extricated his sister from some legal troubles last year.

Nicole shook her head. "I almost died when you told her you helped a burglar steal them. Why would you say such a thing?"

"Because it was true?"

But Nicole's disapproving expression showed she didn't approve of his levity.

He shrugged. "Why not? I knew they wouldn't believe me anyway . . . and I thought it would be fun to see your reaction." He rubbed his shin ruefully. "I can't be right all the time."

She rolled her eyes. "Your sense of humor will be the death of you someday. Now what do we do?"

"First, let's go to my office where we won't be interrupted."

After he stashed the knickknacks in a better hiding place, they walked upstairs. Nicole seemed to relax when they entered his private sanctum. Sleek Ikea furniture with blond wood and clean lines filled the room, covered with a state-of-the-art computer system and the latest office tech toys. Electronics were Scott's one true indulgence.

Nicole glanced around, smiling. "I like this room."

"Even though your taste runs to Louis XIV?"

She grimaced. "That was your invention. I hate that frilly stuff. But this . . . this is nice."

He bowed. "Thank you."

At his inviting gesture, she sank into a side chair and asked, "Now what?"

Scott leaned back against the desk and folded his arms. "I'm not quite sure. There's something strange going on here . . . ." He paused, thinking, then said, "How did Chrissie get past my security system? And how did she know when everyone was going to be gone? Or that my mother's jewels would be in that safe?" He lifted an eyebrow. "Has she shown this sort of talent for planning a heist before?"

"No," Nicole said slowly. "Chrissie's good at anything that puts her center stage, but details are not her strong point. What are you saying? Do you think she had help from someone to get inside?"

"I'm afraid it looks that way, doesn't it?"

"Who do you suspect?"

"No one," he said frankly. He couldn't imagine

any of the help doing something like this. He'd always considered himself a good judge of character, but if something like this could happen, maybe he was wrong. "Maybe Chrissie can enlighten us. Is she at home?"

"She'd better be," Nicole muttered. "I told her I'd call the police if she left the house."

"Okay, good. Let's call her."

Nicole dialed the number, and Scott hit the speaker button so they could both hear.

"Hello?" Chrissie said, managing to sound sullen even through the phone lines.

"Hi, Chrissie, this is Scott Richmond. Remember me?"

"Oh, yeah. Hi."

Undaunted by the lack of enthusiasm in her voice, Scott said, "Remember that little adventure we had last night?"

"Yeah." Now her tone was apprehensive.

"Well, I know you had help from someone in the house. Care to tell me who?"

Silence. Then, "I didn't need any help." But she sounded a little *too* indignant.

"Then how did you know how to get in and where to find the jewels?"

"I'm not stupid," Chrissie protested. "I figured it out."

"Yeah, right, and Nicole moonlights by lap dancing."

"She *does?*"

Ignoring Nicole's exasperated expression, Scott said, "It was a joke. You know, sarcasm?"

"Oh."

But since he wasn't getting anywhere, he tried a

different tack. "So, who did you sell them to?" he asked casually.

Chrissie hesitated. "Why do you want to know?"

"I thought I might buy them back." Before the insurance company shelled out money needlessly or the heirlooms were broken up into small pieces and sold on the black market.

"Uh, I don't remember."

"Chrissie," Nicole said warningly, "tell the truth now. Mr. Richmond is trying to help you, not hurt you."

"Oops, sorry. Someone's at the door. Gotta go. Bye." And Chrissie hung up before they could get another word in.

As Nicole frowned at the phone, Scott asked, "Is it any use to call back?"

"No, she'll just ignore the phone. It would be better to ask her in person."

Scott nodded. "If we can keep Mother from calling the police until we figure out what's going on, we have a chance of fixing this so Chrissie won't end up in jail."

Nicole sighed in relief. "It looks like a good bet since your mother didn't seem too upset about it."

Wait a minute—she was right. "Hmm. Did my mother's reaction seem weird to you?"

"Not really," Nicole said in puzzlement. "Why?"

"I don't know . . . she seemed far more upset about the theft of her tchotchkes than her jewels, didn't she?"

"I guess so, but you did say she didn't care for the jewels."

"And she seemed more interested in notifying the insurance company than the police."

"What are you saying?" Nicole asked.

"I have a suspicion," he said grimly. "But I hope I'm wrong. Follow me."

He led the way to his mother's overdecorated bedroom and opened her personal safe. A bunch of jewelry boxes lay there, and he pulled one out.

"What are you doing?" Nicole asked.

"My father was afraid the jewels would be stolen, so he had some copies made for Mother to wear in public." Scott opened the box and pulled out the ruby necklace inside to take a look at it, then quickly inspected the contents of two other boxes. "Damn."

"What is it?"

"These are the real jewels. Mother must have moved them sometime in the last few months. Chrissie stole the fakes."

"That's good, isn't it?" Nicole asked, but looked uncertain as Scott continued to frown.

"It would be, if Chrissie hadn't already sold them."

"I don't understand."

"Well, how do you think the buyer will react when he finds out those priceless heirlooms are fake? The only one he knows to come after is Chrissie."

"Oh, no. What can we do?"

"First, we need to stop my mother from committing insurance fraud."

Nicole gasped. "Fraud? You think she knows the fake ones were stolen and she's going to report the real ones missing?"

"Yes, unfortunately, I do. She had to realize it was the fakes that were missing when she opened the safe. I think she decided to take advantage of that fact on the spur of the moment." *Damn it. How could she do this?*

"But that's . . . that's illegal," Nicole protested.

His mother wasn't perfect, but Nicole had no right to sound so shocked. "Yeah, well, so is stealing."

Nicole covered her face with her hands. "Don't remind me." Then she raised her head and asked, "But why would your mother do such a thing?"

"She's been pestering me for months for money to buy a villa in Italy, but I won't give it to her." How could he approve such a frivolous expenditure? "I'm afraid she sees this as a way of getting around me." It was the way Gracie's mind worked.

"You'd better stop her, then."

"I intend to. Come on."

Nicole followed Scott as he hurried downstairs to the study. Unfortunately, he got there just in time to find Grace and Gerald exiting it. Damn. It looked like he was too late.

"So, how'd it go?" he asked casually.

"Wonderfully," his mother assured him. "Gerald handled it all for me. The company is going to send a discreet investigator right away to try to locate the jewels first."

Great. Wouldn't you know this was the one time they were efficient? Hiding his anger at her deceit, Scott asked, "You filed a claim then?"

"Of course," Grace said. "Why wouldn't I?"

Oh, because she knew it was a lie? But he doubted that would sway his mother—not when she could see imminent cash within her grasp. Especially cash that Scott had no control over. "No reason," he said in as casual a tone as he could manage. "Let me know if I can help."

Then he steered Nicole back into the drawing room, out of earshot.

"You're not going to confront her?" she asked with a worried expression.

"No, I don't think it would do any good. Her morals and Chrissie's seem to be about on a par."

"So what are we going to do?"

"We'll just have to save my mother and your sister from themselves."

"How?"

Scott shrugged. "The only way to keep the buyer from coming after Chrissie and prevent my mother from committing fraud is to buy the jewels back." A sudden thought occurred to him. "Wait. The buyer still might be angry if he thinks Chrissie conned him. It will be better to replace the fake jewels with the real ones."

Dismay showed on Nicole's face. "You make it sound so easy. And just how are you going to do this?"

Yes, that was the question, wasn't it? He grinned at her. "Not *me*, sweetheart. *We*."

Shaking her head slowly, Nicole backed away with a wary expression. "Oh, no, you're not getting me mixed up in this crazy scheme."

Scott's smile widened. "You already are. You want to save your sister, don't you?"

"Yes, but—"

"Then you have to help me. I can't do it alone." Well, he probably could, but it would be so much more fun watching Nicole do something so alien to her character.

"But I can't steal," she protested.

"Don't worry, it's not stealing; it's replacing. I've never heard of anyone going to jail for replacing, have you?"

"I don't know . . ." she said in a hesitant tone, but he knew he had her now. Her principles wouldn't let her stand by and watch while her little sister went to the pokey.

"Good," he said as if the issue were settled. "Now, let's figure out how we're going to pull off this caper."

He couldn't help but grin. *This is gonna be fun. . . .*

Chapter Three

Nicole wasn't sure she approved of this idea of Scott's. In fact, she wasn't sure she approved of *Scott*. He was entirely too charming, too persuasive, and too good-looking for her peace of mind. In her experience, nothing good ever came of hanging around the wealthy. They had such a different outlook on life—totally foreign to the working class Nicole belonged to.

Yet here she was, sitting in his classic green Jaguar convertible, after getting a bite to eat, on their way to question Chrissie. How had Nicole let him talk her into this? And why was she secretly enjoying the ride?

It couldn't be the fact that she was sitting next to a gorgeous guy who had the most incredible smile she'd ever seen in her life. No, it was the car, she assured herself. Nothing more.

Too practical to own anything other than a low-maintenance compact, Nicole nevertheless enjoyed the feel of the wind in her hair on this balmy August day. In fact, riding in this expensive automobile made her feel decadent . . . even a little wild. Okay, so she had a few shallow moments.

So what? She was entitled to enjoy herself a little, wasn't she?

Chrissie had needed so much attention after their mother died that Nicole had put her own life on the back burner. And, knowing she had to be sensible and set a good example for her sister, Nicole had curbed all of her whimsical impulses. But one of these days, she promised herself, she'd put herself first. There were so many things she wanted to see, so many things she wanted to do . . . .

The only thing that had kept her going these past few years was keeping a mental wish list of all of these things, things like riding in a car like this.

But the ride came to an end all too soon as she directed Scott to her modest three-bedroom home in Aurora. It couldn't compare to the Richmond mansion, of course, but it was all hers, and she was proud of it.

Though their father's death had left them almost penniless, Nicole had been able to get by on what she made as a reference librarian at the Front Range branch of the Denver Public Library. And, by taking a few extra research jobs on the side, she'd even managed to qualify on a mortgage for this house.

But as they got out of the car, she looked at it anew, trying to see it through his eyes. The lawn was freshly mowed, though not as green as she would've liked due to the watering restrictions. Nothing to complain about there. And she'd just cleaned the house yesterday.

She led him inside where her living room was filled with the clean lines of mission style furniture, uncluttered by knickknacks. Her only extravagance was collecting antique cobalt blue glass, and she had a few pieces sitting here and there, the vibrant color shown off with splashes of bright yellow accents.

Scott glanced around, one eyebrow raised in surprise. "I think I'm in love."

"I like it, too," she said, pleased by his reaction.

"I didn't mean with the room," he said cryptically. Then, before she could react, he added, "Now who has hidden depths?"

"What?"

"Talk about the pot calling the kettle blue and yellow . . . ."

Sure, she liked color. Who didn't? "What do you mean by that?"

"Oh, nothing." But his amused expression belied his words.

Frowning, she wondered if he could really get an insight into her personality just from looking at her living room. She didn't care for that idea at all. And as for being in love . . . well, that was just ridiculous.

But before she could call him on it, he asked, "So where's our Robin Hood?"

Oh, yeah. Chrissie. "She's probably hiding in her room. I'll go get her."

Nicole found her sister lying on the bed in her room, sulking as expected. "Will you come into the living room, please?"

"Why? You've got that Scott guy here, don't you?"

"Yes, he's here to help you, Chrissie, so I suggest you meet him at least halfway."

"Yeah, right."

"I mean it. You're lucky he's not pressing charges."

Chrissie sat up on the bed, her expression full of indignation. "Who'd believe him? The guy is a certified wacko."

"No," Nicole said with a sigh. "He just pretends to be."

"Uh huh," Chrissie said in a tone that showed she didn't believe a word her sister said.

"No, really." But why Nicole was defending him, she had no idea. "Think of him as an actor playing a role."

That was all he was doing. He wasn't really interested in her. His flattering attention was just an act he put on for any female from nine to ninety.

"Oh, all right," Chrissie said with a pout.

She followed Nicole into the living room and crossed her arms, scowling at Scott. "What do *you* want?"

Scott raised an eyebrow. "So I'm to be the Sheriff of Nottingham, eh, Robin?"

"Huh?"

Nicole hid a smile. For someone who claimed to be well-versed in drama, Chrissie was lacking in some of the basics.

"Too bad," Scott said facetiously. "I'd rather be Little John. Or maybe Friar Tuck."

Chrissie rolled her eyes at Nicole as if to say, "See, I told you this guy is a nut."

Tired of watching Scott's jokes go over Chrissie's head, Nicole said, "He's referring to Robin Hood. You know . . . rob from the rich, give to the poor?"

"Oh." Chrissie looked enlightened. "I see." She even looked pleased at the comparison.

With an exasperated sigh, Nicole said, "Can we dispense with the jokes now?"

"If we must," Scott said with a sigh. Then he spoiled it by waggling his eyebrows. "But I have high hopes for the future."

Ignoring him, Nicole told Chrissie, "The situation is worse than we thought. The jewels you stole were fake."

"So?"

"So the person you sold them to thinks they're real."

Chrissie shrugged. "Not my fault. I thought they were real when I sold them."

"What do you think he'll do when he finds out?"

"Who cares? I got full price."

Nicole winced, then wanted to strangle Chrissie. How could she be so nonchalant about it?

"Besides," Chrissie said with a voice full of sarcasm, "what are they gonna do? Go to the police and complain that their stolen jewels are fakes?"

They? There were more than one? Nicole turned to Scott with a grimace, giving him a silent plea for help.

"She has a point," he said with a grin.

"You're not helping. This was all your idea—you explain it."

"All right," he said, and even seemed serious for a moment as he turned to Chrissie. "You weren't wearing a disguise when you stole the jewels. Did you wear one when you sold them?"

She looked uncertain. "No . . . ."

"So they know what you look like? They'll recognize you?"

"I guess so," Chrissie admitted.

"And who do you think they'll come gunning for when they realize you conned them?"

"But I didn't— I thought they were real," she protested.

Nicole could almost feel sorry for her as realization of her predicament dawned on Chrissie's expressive face. *Almost.*

Scott nodded. "That's what I thought. So, what are you going to do when these five people come after you?"

"Five?" she repeated in horror. "No, it was only three." Then she scowled as she evidently realized Scott had tricked her. "I bet you think you're really smart."

Scott shrugged, which only seemed to make Chrissie more angry.

Nicole decided to step back into the conversation. "Chrissie, for your own good, you have to tell us who these people are."

"Why?"

"So we can get the fake jewels back," Nicole explained, trying to keep her patience.

Chrissie gave her a thoughtful look. "But won't they still be mad at me when they find the jewels are gone?"

"They won't *be* gone," Scott explained. "We'll replace the fake jewels with the real ones. But we need to do it right away. If we can manage it before they discover the fakes, they'll never know the difference."

Chrissie scowled. "I don't get it. Why would you give away your mother's real jewels?"

"To save your ungrateful hide," Nicole snapped.

No sense in telling her about Grace Richmond's little dalliance in insurance fraud. Nicole didn't want Chrissie turning into a blackmailer as well.

Then, seeing that her sister wasn't buying it, Nicole added, "And because he doesn't want a scandal."

Evidently, that was a reason Chrissie could understand. "Okay. But how are you gonna do the switch?"

"That's where you come in," Scott said. "Tell me the names of your buyers, and I'll see to it that the jewels are replaced."

He'd see to it? Did that mean he planned to leave Nicole out of it? She almost breathed a sigh of relief. That is, until he quirked an eyebrow at her as if to tell her not to feel too secure.

"You don't need to know," Chrissie said with confidence. "Just give me the real jewels and I'll replace them. I know where the fakes are."

For a moment, Nicole could do nothing but gape at her. "Are you insane?"

"No, I stole them once. I can do it again."

"Oh, yes," Scott murmured. "And that turned out so well . . . ."

"Well, it did," Chrissie pointed out. "Besides, who's gonna stop me?"

"I am," Nicole and Scott declared in unison.

Nicole added, "There's no way in hell you're going to put yourself in danger like that again."

"But what about the money?"

"I told you before—we're not keeping it."

"Then I'm not going to tell you the names," Chrissie said in childish defiance. In fact, Nicole wouldn't have been surprised if she'd stuck out her tongue and chanted *na na-na na na*.

Evidently sensing her sister wasn't going to budge, Scott asked Chrissie, "Can I have a moment alone with Nicole?"

"Sure, why not?" Chrissie said with her trademark sarcasm. "Take all day. *I'm* not going anywhere."

She couldn't—Nicole had hidden her car keys and threatened her within an inch of her life if she left the house.

After Chrissie stomped off to her bedroom, Nicole turned to Scott. "You have an idea on how to get this out of her?"

"Uh, sort of. But I don't think you're gonna like it."

Nicole refrained from rolling her eyes á là Chrissie, but sarcasm still crept into her voice. "Why am I not surprised?"

"Because you're a very wise woman," Scott said with a grin.

"Okay, forget the phony compliments. What am I not going to like?"

"I think we're going to have to give her what she wants."

No way. "I am *not* going to let her take that chance—"

"No," he said, interrupting her. "I mean we're going to have to let her go to Juilliard."

"Are you kidding? Why should I let her go? Especially after what she's done?"

"Because it's the only way to get the information we need."

"You mean we should bribe her," Nicole stated baldly.

"Yes, I do. Unless you have a better idea of how to make her talk?"

Unfortunately, she didn't. Chrissie could be very stubborn when she set her mind to it. "No, but it really galls me to let her have her way."

"Don't think of it as letting her have her way," Scott said with a grin. "Think of it as getting her *out* of the way so she doesn't make a bad situation worse."

He had a point. And Chrissie was so talented, she really did deserve to go to New York . . . not to mention the fact that Nicole was looking forward to finally having the house all to herself. Maybe then she could start her new life. "But I can't afford it— and I'm *not* going to use the money from the stolen jewels."

"Don't worry—I'll fund it. I owe you, remember?"

"No, you don't. *Remember?*" They'd been through this before.

Scott sighed as if *she* were the difficult one. "All right, then. Consider it a loan. But I think you'll agree that the best way to keep your little sister from doing anything worse is to send her off to school."

True, but heaven help New York City . . . .

"Oh, all right. But I don't have to like it."

He patted her hand. "Of course you don't. And you can actively hate it all you want. Just let me handle it, okay?"

"Okay." She just hoped she wasn't making a huge mistake.

Scott sighed in relief. Finally, he was getting somewhere. Now, if only Chrissie would cooperate . . . .

Nicole called her sister back into the room. Naturally, Chrissie folded her arms and scowled.

Scott sighed. Being around a teenager was so

wearing. Didn't anyone warn her about the dangers of overacting? "All right, let's forego the pouting preliminaries and cut to the chase, shall we? Chrissie, we have a deal to offer you."

"Oh, yeah? What?"

"You tell us what we want to know and you can go to Juilliard."

Her face brightened. "Really?"

"Yes, really."

She jumped up and pumped an arm in victory. "All right!" Then she bounced all over the room like a demented human pogo stick, chanting, "I'm going to Juilliard, I'm going to Juilliard."

"Not yet," Nicole said sternly.

Chrissie stopped boinging. "But he said—"

"*Only* if you tell us what we want to know," Nicole reminded her. "And I want to make it very clear— this is *not* a reward. Your behavior was unforgivable. The only reason I agreed to this is because I don't want to see you get into any further trouble."

"I wouldn't do that," Chrissie protested.

"See that you don't. If I hear the slightest whiff of trouble at Juilliard, or you get anything less than a B, I'll cut off your funds immediately. Is that understood?"

Chrissie looked suitably impressed by her sister's threat, and so was Scott. Nicole had certainly learned how to manage her sister.

"Yes, of course," Chrissie said earnestly. "I won't get into any trouble. I'll be good—very good. You'll see."

"I think she means it," Scott said. "Besides, it's a tough school. I doubt she'll have time to get into trouble."

Nicole looked doubtful, but Chrissie said eagerly, "What do you want to know?"

"First," Scott said, "who let you into my house last night?"

Chrissie scowled. "I told you. No one. I let myself in."

"Then who told you how to get past the security?"

"I figured that out on my own, too."

It was an obvious lie, and even Nicole said warningly, "Chrissie . . . "

Why would Chrissie lie about this when she had so much to gain by telling the truth? "Are you afraid to tell us who helped you?"

"No."

He didn't quite buy it. There was a little fear there, and maybe something else. "Okay, let's use a hypothetical situation then. If someone *had* helped you, would you tell me?"

"I'm not a snitch," Chrissie said defensively.

Honor among thieves, huh? She was still playing Robin Hood. Well, at least she *had* some honor.

"You're not going to make it to New York with that attitude," Nicole warned her.

"It's okay," Scott said. He even admired Chrissie for her stand. "Chrissie, I'm not going to report your accomplice to the police. If I did, you would be implicated and I don't want that to happen." He liked these Dreyfuss girls and didn't want to hurt them. "I just need to know who I can no longer trust."

"I'm sorry," Chrissie said. "I can't help you."

But she looked so miserable as she said it that Scott figured she really meant it.

Nicole made a noise that sounded like pure exasperation, then turned to Scott. "Who do you suspect?"

Good idea. Maybe if he listed the potential culprits, Chrissie would show some sign of recognition. "I don't know," he said slowly, and though he spoke to Nicole, he kept an eye on her sister. "Our housekeeper, Marta, has been with us for several years, so I don't think she's the one." He doubted the staunchly loyal German woman would even think about stealing so much as a candle from them.

No reaction.

"Sherry, the maid, has only been with us a little while . . . ."

No reaction there, either. He wasn't surprised. Sherry seemed to jump at every shadow and acted terrified every time he spoke to her. He couldn't imagine her having the courage to pull off a heist.

"Maybe the cook, Ethel?" But Ethel was so complacent and immobile, he couldn't imagine her stirring herself to the level of activity the plan would have required.

He glanced at Chrissie, but her expression held nothing but boredom.

"That's all the household staff," he said in hesitant tones.

"Do you have a chauffer or gardener?" Nicole asked.

"A gardener, yes—Jimmy." But he was such a surly curmudgeon that Scott couldn't imagine him holding a civil conversation with anyone long enough to plan anything. "But he doesn't know the security codes."

"Someone at the security company, then?"

"No, I don't think so." He'd hired his college

friend, Boyd Jackson, to do their security, and trusted him implicitly. But were Jackson's employees trustworthy? Then again, how much did Scott really know about any of *his* employees?

Damn, he hated this. Hated having to suspect good people of doing nefarious things, hated having to worry about the future security of his home. But someone had given Chrissie inside information, and he wanted to know who.

Unfortunately, none of these names had elicited a reaction. Either Chrissie didn't know any of them . . . or she really was Juilliard material.

"Are there any other suspects?" Nicole asked with an annoyed glance at her sister.

"Not that I can think of right now. But who gave her the information doesn't matter as much as who she sold the jewels to. So, tell me, Chrissie, how did you know who to sell them to?"

"I'm not dumb, you know. I know how to do these things."

"You didn't use a fence or a pawn shop?" He'd suspected as much when she said she had three buyers, but didn't know how she found them.

"No. Heck, it wasn't hard to figure out who to sell them to. It was obvious who wanted them."

"It was?" Only if she had inside help . . . .

"Yeah."

"Then who bought them?"

Chrissie turned cagey. "If I tell you, do I still get to go to Juilliard?"

"Yes." Substituting the jewels was most important. He could figure out who helped her later. "What are their names?"

This time, Chrissie spoke with no hesitation.

"Claire Wyndham, Sara Harding, and Joan Larson.
I have a list of who took what, and I have their addresses if you need them."

"That won't be necessary," Scott bit out.

Nicole looked at him in surprise. "What's wrong?
Do you know these people?"

"I'm afraid so. They run in my mother's circle."
But why on earth would they buy his mother's
stolen jewels?

Chapter Four

For a moment, Nicole was so shocked she couldn't speak. Then she blurted out, "Your mother's *friends* bought her jewelry? Why?"

Scott looked grim. "Another sixty-four thousand dollar question. Care to enlighten us, Robin?"

Chrissie shrugged. "What does it matter?"

Angry now, Nicole narrowed her eyes and said, "Tell him."

"Oh, all right." Chrissie paused, as if judging the mood of her audience. "I overheard them talking at the tennis club about how much they envied her heirloom jewelry, so I made a deal."

Scott quirked an eyebrow at her. "You hang out at the club?"

Chrissie rolled her eyes. "Yeah, right, like watching a bunch of rich people bat a little ball around is my thing. No, I work there—as a waitress in the restaurant." She smiled knowingly. "You'd be surprised at what I hear."

"I doubt it," Scott drawled. "So, what happened? You just sidled up to them, opened your raincoat, and offered to sell them stolen goods?"

Looking wary, Chrissie said, "Something like that, yeah. But I used a little more finesse."

"So, how'd it go down?" he asked.

"I don't share my secrets."

"Honor among thieves, huh?" Scott asked with a grin.

Chrissie shrugged but her story didn't ring true, and Nicole could tell Scott felt the same. Obviously, Chrissie was getting into her role as a cunning jewel thief, and no one would be able to get her out of character now.

Nicole murmured as much to Scott, who nodded with a grimace. "I guess I'd better go," he said. "This is getting us nowhere."

As he stood, Chrissie frowned. "Do I still get to go to Juilliard?"

Nicole clenched her jaw to keep from speaking. It galled her to let Chrissie have her way.

Scott answered for her. "Yes. In fact, when are you supposed to be there?"

"In a couple of weeks."

"How would you like to go sooner?" he asked. "Say, in a couple of days?"

Chrissie perked up. "Really?" She turned to Nicole. "Can I?"

"I don't think so. Your room and board doesn't start for another two weeks," Nicole said. What was Scott thinking, for heaven's sake? "You don't have anywhere to stay."

Scott shrugged. "We own a small place in the city. Mother goes there occasionally to shop, see a show, that sort of thing. Chrissie can use it for a couple of weeks."

"That's kind of you, but—"

"It's not being used," Scott said, interrupting Nicole's protest. "And it's a very secure building.

Plus, I have a cousin who works in the theater. He'd be happy to show Chrissie around." When Nicole continued to look doubtful, Scott added, "Trust me, he's totally safe. He's a *dancer.*"

"That sounds great," Chrissie enthused. "I'd love to see a little of New York before I have to start classes."

Scott entreated Nicole with his eyes. "And it's better to have her there than here right now . . . ."

He had a point. It would be better to have Chrissie out of the way just in case something went wrong with Scott's plan. "All right," Nicole said grudgingly. Just how indebted was she going to be to this man? "But you'd better behave yourself, Chrissie. And find a job. You can't expect us to foot the whole bill for your schooling. You need to take some responsibility yourself."

"I will," her sister assured her. Then her eyes widened. "I'd better start packing—and tell the people at work I'm leaving sooner than I thought."

She hurried out of the room, and Nicole sighed in resignation as she followed Scott to the door and said good-bye.

He glanced down at her quizzically. "Aren't you coming with me?"

Puzzled, Nicole asked, "Why?"

"Because your car is still at my place."

Nicole had become so wound up in what was going on that she had forgotten. "Oh, yeah. I guess I am."

"Besides, we need to talk."

True, though this was one conversation Nicole wouldn't mind having postponed. "I'll just get my purse."

She retrieved her purse and told Chrissie where she was going, then followed Scott outside.

"Yoo-hoo," came a voice from next door.

Her neighbor, Missy Johnson, came hurrying over, all ninety pounds of her shrink-wrapped in tight-fitting jeans and a midriff-baring crop top with enough makeup on her face to clog a drain.

"Hello, Nicole," Missy said with a tinkling laugh. "I see you're coming up in the world."

Missy batted her mascara-laden eyelashes at Scott, though Nicole was hard-pressed to tell which Missy admired more—Scott or his Jaguar.

"Hi," Nicole said cautiously, wondering what Missy wanted. Her neighbor rarely gave her the time of day, so this performance had to be for Scott's benefit.

"I'm jealous," Missy proclaimed. "Won't you introduce me?" Missy held out her hand with a limp wrist, as if she expected Scott to kiss it.

Nicole made the introductions as Scott shook Missy's hand, though the devilry in his eyes made her wonder just what he was thinking.

"So nice to meet you," Missy said with a purr. "Nicole and I are very good friends, you know."

"Are you?" Scott asked with amusement.

Yeah, right. "So," Nicole said, her eyes narrowing. "Where's your *husband*, Missy?"

She waved in a dismissive gesture. "Oh, him. He's out of town. And I've been so lonely." Then her gaze turned bitchy. "So, is Scott your cousin? Or your boss?"

Her implication was clear—there was no way Nicole could attract such a man, so her relationship with Scott must be platonic. Unfortunately, Missy was right, and Nicole had no idea how to answer such rudeness.

Scott, on the other hand, had no such problem. "Sorry to disappoint you," he said with a laugh as he slid a possessive arm around Nicole's waist. "But we're lovers."

Nicole was so surprised, she couldn't say a word. Even more, she was secretly pleased that he'd managed to put Missy in her place. Nicole smiled up at him, thanking him silently for his intervention.

He must have taken it for an invitation, for he leaned closer and captured his lips with hers.

All rational thought went out the window as Nicole succumbed to his kiss. His lips were warm, soft, and incredibly sensual. His first exploration was tentative, as if he wasn't sure of her reaction. Then, as she responded to that sensual invitation, he deepened the kiss and drew her even closer against his body. She clutched at his shoulders and her knees turned to rubber. *Umm. Heaven.*

But he ended it all too soon. Still holding Nicole in his arms, he turned to a wide-eyed Missy. "You'll excuse us, won't you?" He grinned that devastating smile of his. "We have a date with a hot tub and a cold bottle of champagne." He turned back to nuzzle Nicole's neck. "I just love all those bubbles, don't you?"

Nicole could do nothing but nod as the feel of Scott's arms around her waist and his lips on her neck made her quiver with need and turned her limbs into limp spaghetti, pure pasta *al dente.*

Scott's noodle, on the other hand, seemed to be firming up nicely . . . .

Nicole blushed at her own thought and pulled away. *Now I'm beginning to* think *like him.*

She wasn't sure she could move on her own, so she was glad when Scott led her to the car and seated her in it, then took the driver's seat. Missy followed him, looking annoyed.

Scott started the engine, then leaned out to tell Missy in a confiding tone, "No need to be jealous. Nicole doesn't swing that way, you know. Lucky for me she prefers men." And with a wink, he peeled out of the driveway, leaving Missy speechless.

Nicole couldn't help it—she let out a peal of laughter.

Scott stared at her in surprise. "I didn't know you could do that."

"What? Laugh?" Surely he didn't mean the kiss . . . . "Of course I can laugh." And she did it again, out of pure exuberance. "You have no idea how snotty that woman has been to me."

Scott slanted her a smile as he made the turn out of her neighborhood. "Oh, I think I have some idea. 'How's your husband, Missy?'" he mimicked her.

Nicole was unrepentant. "Oh, I know it was catty, but—"

"No need to explain. I know her type. That's why I pretended to misunderstand her."

Nicole chuckled again. "Thanks. The memory of her expression will keep me laughing for months."

"Happy to oblige, ma'am," he said with a quirky smile. "I knew you had a sense of humor, somewhere deep inside."

"Of course I do." In fact, she appreciated his touch of the absurd more than she cared to admit.

"So what brought it out? The joke . . . or the kiss?"

Suspecting the kiss hadn't meant as much to him as it had to her, Nicole ignored the question as she pretended to watch the road ahead. "It's just that this situation hasn't given us much to laugh about until now."

"Oh, I don't know. I can pretty much always find something to laugh about."

She raised an eyebrow. "I know. You probably spend most of your time chortling at all those people who think you're a fool."

He winced. "Ouch. Okay, I get the hint. Back to business." He waggled his eyebrows at her again. "So, you ready to put on a catsuit and hit the rooftops?"

"You must be joking." *Again.*

"Must I?" he said in regretful tones. "Yes, I suppose I must. Though I would like to see you in a catsuit . . . ."

"Fat chance," Nicole blurted out.

"Oh, no, not fat at all." And he took his eyes off the road long enough to give her figure a searing glance, one that left her feeling as if her skin had warmed everywhere his gaze had touched. "Curvy in all the right places, from what I saw . . . and felt."

Nicole felt her face heat, then suppressed a sudden urge to find a catsuit and model it for him—just to see the look on his face. She might not be as fashionably thin as Missy, but Nicole had no reason to be embarrassed by her body.

"So, are you thinking about it?" Scott asked.

"No, of course not," Nicole said with just a touch of scorn. She didn't want him to think his charm

had won her over. Even if it had. *Especially* if it had.
"I'm sure you don't really plan on clambering over
the rooftops."

"I'm afraid not," he said, looking regretful.

"Then you do have a plan?"

"Oh, yes. It should be easy to get into their
houses."

"How?"

"They're always having parties for some reason
or another. I'm sure all three of them have something planned in the next few months at their
houses. I'll just make sure I'm invited."

"It's that easy?"

"Well, yes." He shrugged. "Unattached men are
always welcome at these functions, you know."

Nicole believed it—especially when they were as
good-looking and as good-natured as Scott. But relief filled her at his words. "You won't need me,
then."

"Oh, but I do need you, sweetheart."

Despite herself, Nicole felt herself melt. Then
she stiffened her spine as she reminded herself this
man was a charmer and, if that kiss was any indica-
tion, a master of seduction. She couldn't believe
anything he said. "You need me for what?"

"For many things," he said caressingly. But when
Nicole gave him a warning look, he said, "I'll need
a lookout of course, while I switch the jewels."

"Am I really necessary?"

"Yes, not only to help with the jewels, but to keep
the husband-hunters off my trail. I need a decoy,
ducky, and you're perfect for the job."

"But I can't," Nicole protested. "I don't know

these people and they don't know me. Why would they invite me to their parties?"

"Because I ask them to," Scott said. "You'll be my guest."

Nicole could only stare at him. She wasn't convinced, but what exactly was he planning to do? "You still think the best thing to do is replace the jewels?"

He thought about it for a moment. "Yeah. Until I can figure out their motives, I don't want them confronting my mother about her fake jewels at some fancy do."

"I thought they were her friends."

"More like acquaintances. They run in the same circles, but those three aren't her best buds."

"But if they discover the jewels are fake, they won't come after Chrissie, right? Not with guns and knives, anyway."

"Hmm. More like capped teeth and acrylic claws. You don't mess with a society dame and her jewelry."

He shivered dramatically, which didn't help Nicole's apprehension at all, and she said so.

"Don't worry," he said. "Everything will be fine. You'll see."

They pulled up to the house then and she followed him as he entered and greeted the housekeeper. "Marta, is my mother at home?"

"No, Mrs. Richmond has gone out, but she should be back soon."

Scott nodded, then motioned at Nicole to follow him.

"Where are we going?" she whispered.

"To her study," he whispered back, looking amused. "I want to look at her calendar."

He led her into a study that was obviously designed with his mother's taste in mind and flipped through the calendar on her desk. "Good, the Hardings are having a cocktail party Friday night. The timing is perfect, and I'm sure I can get us invited to that."

"How? They don't know me—"

"What are you doing in here?" a voice asked behind them.

Nicole whirled around to see Scott's mother in the door, looking curious. Nicole felt rather like a kid with her hand caught in the cookie jar, but Scott, of course, had an answer for everything.

He glanced down at his hand, still on his mother's calendar. "I was just, uh, checking to see if you had any . . . open dates."

"For what?"

Nicole cringed, expecting him to blurt out the truth again, but he surprised her.

"For an engagement party." He slung an arm around Nicole. "Congratulate us—we're getting married."

Scott didn't know who looked more stunned—his mother or Nicole.

His mother recovered first. Years of society training came in handy that way. "How wonderful for you, dear. I'm sure you and . . ."

"Nicole," Scott supplied.

"Yes, of course. I'm sure you and Nicole will be very happy." Then she wandered away, saying in vague tones, "I need a drink."

When his mother left the room, Nicole elbowed

Scott sharply in the side. "Why did you say that?" she whispered fiercely.

"Think about it," he said persuasively. "It solves the problem of people not knowing you. They'll be more than happy to invite you as my fiancée—just to get a look at the woman who finally put a ring through my nose."

She rolled her eyes, looking a lot like her little sister. "Then they'll know it's a hoax. Who would believe a guy like you would want to marry a woman like me?"

Scott affected a hurt expression. "What's wrong with me?"

"Nothing," she said with a quelling glance. "You know perfectly well I meant me. Just look at your mother's reaction. She was stunned—and not in a good way."

"Don't worry, she'll be fine with it." Once she got used to the idea. After all, she'd finally warmed up to his sister's husband.

"Oh, sure. That's why she needs a drink—to celebrate."

Scott grinned. "I just caught her off guard, is all. Mother doesn't deal well with change. She probably thought I'd never marry. Besides, her friends will believe anything of me." His reputation came in handy that way.

"I don't doubt that," Nicole said dryly.

"Come on," Scott coaxed. "I promise I won't make you actually marry me. And it solves our problem, doesn't it?"

"I guess so, but . . ."

"But what? The thought of being engaged to me

isn't totally abhorrent, is it?" He seemed to recall Nicole melting in his arms just a short time ago.

"No, it's not that."

"Then what is it?"

She hesitated for a moment as if weighing and discarding several answers, then blurted out, "I have nothing to wear."

He couldn't help it—he chuckled. Not that he believed for a moment that was her real reason, but he let it go. "No problem. As your fiancé, it's my responsibility to ensure you are dressed correctly for any event I drag you to."

"It is?"

She sounded doubtful, and he rushed to put her mind at ease. "Absolutely. I can't have you embarrassing me, now can I?"

She slanted him a worried glance, and he realized this really did bother her. "I'm kidding," he assured her. "I'm sure you would never embarrass anyone. Don't worry—I can afford it. Just consider it compensation for having to put up with me. Or, in Chrissie's terms, just think of it as providing you with the costume you need for this performance." He let his tone turn plaintive . . . and lecherous. "Unless you'd rather wear the catsuit?"

She laughed, in surprise and delight. "I don't think so."

He pretended disappointment. "All right, then. We'll go shopping tomorrow to find you something to wear."

"I have to work tomorrow," she protested, but it was a weak one.

"Tomorrow night, then," he insisted, not willing to take no for an answer. "After work. I'll pick you up at the library." When she hesitated, he added, "Come on, it'll be fun."

"Yeah," Nicole muttered. "Sure. Fun."

Scott suppressed a smile. Teasing Nicole out of her shell was fast becoming a hobby with him. With any luck, it would turn into a vocation.

Nicole shook her head in disbelief. Scott sure had a strange idea of fun. But she couldn't let him know the truth. How could she tell him that she hated being put in this position, hated the thought of what people would say?

No doubt the word would be out all over town in a matter of hours, with people staring at her and wondering what the hell suave, debonair Scott Richmond saw in a sober, boring librarian. Then, when the engagement inevitably came to an end, there would be snickers and I-told-you-so's. And would they believe for a moment that Nicole had called off the engagement? No, Nicole Dreyfuss would go down in history as the woman Scott Richmond dumped.

Won't that *be fun?*

Grace wandered back in then, looking a little more coherent with a drink in her hand. "I'm sorry for being so rude earlier," she said with a smile. "But you caught me by surprise. It was so unexpected. I didn't even know you two were seeing each other."

Scott threw Nicole a triumphant look. "That's all right, Mother."

Grace glanced at Nicole. "You will stay for dinner, won't you?"

She should have realized this was coming. "I—I'm not sure I can," Nicole protested, looking at Scott for help.

"But you must stay," Grace said. "I want to know all about my future daughter-in-law."

Scott gave her a reassuring look. "Maybe now isn't the right time—"

"Nonsense," Grace declared. "What better time is there? I need to be prepared when my friends ask questions . . . and I know nothing about her." That last sounded like an accusation. "Except that she likes Louis XIV furniture."

And that was a lie.

Scott hesitated. "Why don't you stay?" he asked Nicole. Under his breath, he added, "I won't let her eat you, I promise. But she has a point."

Damn it, he was right. Grace Richmond did have a right to get to know her future daughter-in-law, even if that daughter-in-law was as bogus as Grace's stolen jewels. "All right, I'll stay," Nicole said. But she feared the smile she turned toward Grace was a little sickly.

"Good," Grace declared. "We're having dinner a little early tonight since Gerald and I are going out afterward. I'll see you in half an hour." She swept out of the room, saying over her shoulder, "I hope you like veal . . . ."

Scott turned to Nicole with a polite expression. "*Do* you like veal?"

"What does that matter?" she asked, exasperated. "More to the point, what am I going to tell your mother when she asks about my family?"

"The truth?" Scott ventured.

Oh, yeah. That would work. *Not.*

"You want me to tell her I'm the daughter of her husband's valet and the sister of the person who stole her jewels?" Nicole rolled her eyes. "I'm sure that will go over *real* well."

"No, you don't have to tell her the *whole* truth. Good Lord, who tells their parents that? Just tell her enough so she doesn't get suspicious." When Nicole glared at him, Scott said, "Don't worry. If you're not sure how to answer, let me. I'll come up with something."

"Good. You're glib enough to answer for both of us. And you should—this is all your fault."

"How do you figure that?" He had the nerve to look surprised.

"Maybe because you're the one who so casually announced that we were *engaged*? Without consulting me?" What kind of trouble would his smooth tongue get her into next?

He cocked his head and regarded her with a faint smile. "You're right. I'm sorry, I should've talked to you first. But I acted on impulse."

"That's the problem—you always act impulsively." It made Nicole a little nervous, not knowing what he would say or do.

"True," Scott acknowledged. "But it makes life so much more interesting . . . don't you think?"

"Maybe," she muttered. The past twenty-four hours had certainly not been dull. "But it can also be confusing, foolhardy, dangerous—"

"Exciting?"

Okay, that, too. But she wasn't about to admit it. Instead, she cast about in her mind for a change of subject and recalled her appearance. Her jeans and sweater were fine for a Sunday afternoon doing errands, but not the sort of thing she would have chosen to be grilled by Scott's mother. "Uh, you don't dress for dinner, do you?"

"Do you think we eat in the nude?" He shook his head with a sigh. "Not that I would mind, but Mother might have some objections."

Did he never stop with the jokes? "I mean dress *up.*" And he knew that perfectly well.

"Sometimes. But Mother knows you won't have time to change, so don't worry about it. But if you'd like to freshen up, I could show you to the guest room . . . ."

"That sounds good," Nicole said with relief. A little time to herself to think things over would be a good thing right now.

He showed her upstairs to a lovely room decorated in soft periwinkle and cream—a soothing place with an attached bathroom that was just what she needed. She repaired her makeup and brushed her hair into something resembling order, then sat down in a comfortable chair to relax for a few moments.

Her eyes closed, Nicole wondered how the devil she had gotten herself into this predicament. Just yesterday morning, she had been living a normal, boring existence. Now, suddenly, she was the sister of a felon, an accessory to grand theft, and had somehow become engaged to a financial wizard who pretended to be a frivolous fool. True, she'd wanted her life to change, but not this way . . . .

What did I do to deserve this?

And what could she do to get out of it? Unfortunately, the only one with a viable plan to rescue them all was Scott. She'd just have to follow his lead—as quirky and strange as it was—in order to get out of this with her family's reputation intact.

A knock sounded on the door and Scott poked his head in. "Ready to face the lioness in her den?"

Nicole sighed. "Ready as I'll ever be, I guess."

She stood and allowed Scott to lead her downstairs. She had expected dinner to be only the three of them, but Gerald joined them as well.

The older man came forward as they entered the dining room, holding his hand out to Nicole. "Very happy to see you again, my dear," he said in a kind tone. "But I didn't catch your full name last time . . . ?"

"This is Nicole Dreyfuss," Scott said as he slipped an arm around her waist. "My fiancée."

He sure seemed to do that a lot. Nicole had no idea Scott was so touchy-feely. But for some reason, it seemed entirely natural.

Gerald looked puzzled. "Dreyfuss? That name sounds familiar."

Nicole felt panic seize her. Had he known her father? Her mother? Her *sister*?

Scott grinned. "You're probably thinking of Richard Dreyfuss, the actor. *Jaws*?"

Gerald's face cleared. "That's it. Thank you, Scott. Are you related to the actor, Nicole?"

She relaxed. "Not that I know of."

Evidently sensing her tension, Scott changed the subject. "How's the investigation coming?"

"I haven't heard anything yet," Gerald said.

Frowning, Scott said, "That's odd, don't you think?"

And so was Scott's question. Did he *want* the insurance company to find out the truth, for heaven's sake?

Gerald shrugged. "I hadn't thought about it."

"Come, let's be seated," Grace said, making a graceful gesture toward the table, and they all sat down to dinner.

As the cook served the salad, Grace said, "So tell me, dear. Who are your people? Do I know them?"

Nicole almost choked on a bit of lettuce. But luckily, it gave her an excuse to think as she continued to chew.

"I doubt it," Scott said. "Her father worked in the clothing business."

Nicole raised an eyebrow at him. True, her father had worked with clothing, but as a valet. Scott made it sound like he owned a haberdashery. "We don't come from money," Nicole clarified, before Scott could utter a fib she couldn't live with.

"I see," Grace said, and her expression was nothing but polite. "Is your mother still living?"

"I'm afraid not," Nicole said. "She's been gone for over eight years now. And my father died a few years ago."

"I'm so sorry," Grace murmured, and Nicole had the feeling she meant it. "I'm sure it's difficult for you not to have your family with you at this joyous time. Do you have any siblings?"

"One. A sister. She—"

"She's in school in New York," Scott said, interrupting her.

Nicole slanted him an annoyed glance. Didn't he trust her not to reveal anything?

As the main course was served, Grace asked, "So, what do you do, dear?"

Nicole gave Scott a quelling glance before he could make something up. "I'm a librarian."

Grace perked up. "Oh? Whose library do you manage?"

Realizing Grace thought she worked for a private residence or library, Nicole clarified, "I work for a branch of the public library. In the reference section."

"An excellent calling," Gerald declared. "I make use of the library quite often."

In his profession, he probably did. But Grace didn't look like the type who read . . . .

"Quite respectable," Grace said.

With relief, Nicole realized the woman was actually trying to be nice to her. Scott grinned at her. *See?* his expression seemed to say, *she's not an ogre.*

They conversed on several other innocuous topics for a while, then Grace said, "So, where did you meet?"

Quickly, Nicole shoved a bite of veal in her mouth and gave Scott an imploring look. There was no way she was going to tell Scott's mother the truth. Let him make something up.

"We met at the library, actually," Scott said. "Between the stacks. She dropped a book, I picked it up, our eyes met . . . and that was it. I knew she was the girl for me."

Nicole was impressed—he even managed to make the library sound a little romantic. She smiled and nodded, hoping Grace would take her silence as meaning Nicole was besotted with her son.

Grace smiled. "That's very sweet. How long have

you been seeing each other . . . and why didn't I know you two were dating?"

"Nicole is very shy," Scott said. "Especially of the press. And you know how they make a big deal out of any little meeting."

True—even Nicole had seen Scott's picture gracing the society page with one or another beautiful woman on his arm. As far as she knew, he'd rarely been seen twice with the same woman. Except one—a gorgeous brunette.

Scott continued, "So we wanted to keep it quiet and keep her out of the limelight."

"Commendable," Gerald murmured, and Grace nodded in agreement. The lawyer gave Nicole a sympathetic look. "But you know that won't last once your engagement is announced."

"Announced?" Nicole repeated, and hated the way her voice squeaked on the word.

"Yes, of course," Grace said as if it were a foregone conclusion. She paused in the act of cutting her veal. "I plan to send an announcement to the papers first thing tomorrow morning. And we'll have an engagement party, of course."

"Is that absolutely necessary?" Couldn't they keep this sham engagement as quiet as possible . . . for as long as possible? Her frantic look at Scott elicited only a shrug.

"Of course," Grace said in surprise. "It is the proper thing to do. And everyone will want to meet you. Why? Is there some reason we shouldn't announce it?"

"No, of course not," Scott interjected smoothly. "Nicole's just a little nervous about being in the public eye."

The lies just kept mounting . . . .

Grace nodded. "Well, it is a cross we must all bear. You'll do fine, dear. You'll see. Just be your lovely, gracious self, and they won't have anything to complain about."

Nicole's mouth almost dropped open at the unexpected compliment. Scott grinned at her.

Grace's tone turned diffident. "Would you like some help in planning the party? I have a little expertise in that area . . . ."

Unsure how to answer, Nicole shot a pleading look at Scott.

"Mother's parties are the best," he confirmed. "And since you don't have the time to do it, honey, why don't you let Mother do it for us?"

"I'd like that," Nicole said and felt guilty when Grace beamed at her.

"Wonderful. Just give me a list of who you want invited, and I'll take care of the rest. Have you set a wedding date yet?"

Before Scott could make something up, Nicole said hurriedly, "No, not yet."

"We want her sister to be able to attend," Scott added smoothly. "We're just waiting to hear when her school breaks are."

Chrissie at the wedding? That would be a disaster. Grace's friends were bound to attend and recognize Chrissie as the thief who had sold them the stolen jewels.

What am I thinking? Nicole admonished herself. She wasn't really getting married. This was all a lie.

"We'll let you know as soon as we decide," Scott said.

Grace set her napkin down on the table. "Of

course, there will be quite a few parties in the next few months, and people will be anxious to meet you. Do you . . ." she paused delicately, "need assistance in acquiring a trousseau?"

A trousseau? At first, Nicole had no idea what she was getting at. Then the light dawned. Grace was asking if Nicole had the proper clothes to move in society.

In a word, no.

Scott rescued her. "I'm taking care of that, Mother. We're going shopping tomorrow night."

"Good," Grace said and seemed to sigh in relief.

"Though Nicole is a little reluctant to let me spend money on her," Scott added, then grinned when Nicole scowled at him.

"Nonsense, dear," Grace said. "There's nothing that makes a person feel so confident about moving in society as having the right attire. Let Scott do this for you. He put you in this situation so it's only right that he does everything to ensure you feel comfortable in it."

That was true enough, and, even better, it was a reason Nicole could live with. "All right," Nicole said, though she felt guilty for deceiving Grace. Maybe, if she was very careful, she could return the clothes later.

Gerald nodded. "Well, if that's settled, perhaps we should go."

"Yes," Grace said and rose. "I only ask that you keep me informed when you do set the date, dear. And if you like, I'd be happy to stand in for your mother and help you with the details."

Nicole felt tears prick at her eyelids. Grace was

being so nice to her, and she was doing nothing but lying to the woman.

"We will," Scott assured her as he rose to see his mother to the door. Feeling odd being the only one still seated, Nicole joined them in the doorway.

Grace patted her son's arm. "You've done very well for yourself, Scott. I never imagined you would be so . . . sensible. Nicole is a lovely girl. I approve."

Scott grinned and gave her a little bow. "Thank you."

Grace handed him a small jeweler's box. "And here's something your father had set aside for this occasion."

Scott opened it, displaying a beautiful, emerald-cut solitaire ring.

"It's a champagne-colored diamond," he murmured.

"Yes, and of the highest quality." Grace smiled. "I didn't think you had the time yet to get a ring, and your father saved this from his stock so you would have it at this time."

Scott looked as stunned as Nicole felt. "B—but he didn't leave anything for Kelly . . . ."

"Of course not. It was your sister's husband's duty to provide her with a ring."

"I see." Scott took the ring from the box and gave Nicole a warning look his mother couldn't see as he grasped her left hand to place the ring on her finger. Feeling like a horrible fraud, Nicole let him place it there, though she could react with nothing but numbness when he gave her the obligatory kiss.

"Wonderful," Grace said. "It fits perfectly."

"Yes, it does," Nicole murmured, fascinated by the way the large stone caught the light. "Thank you so much, Mrs. Richmond. I—I've never had anything so beautiful."

Grace patted her on the arm. "No need to thank me, Nicole. It's what you deserve for putting up with my son."

And Gerald escorted Grace out of the room, leaving Nicole stunned.

Scott turned toward her with a grin. "She must really like you. She remembered your name."

"I can't do this," Nicole wailed. "She's so nice. I can't lie to her like this."

"Sure you can," Scott said. "You just did. Besides, don't forget that this is the same woman who has no compunction about defrauding the insurance company."

"I know but . . ." Maybe Grace had a good reason.

"It's settled," Scott said firmly. "Don't worry. Everything will be just fine, you'll see."

Oh, yeah? Then why did Nicole have this feeling of impending doom?

As soon as Gerald got home, he picked up the phone and called his associate. "We can't stall the investigation any longer. And we may have a problem."

"Why? Does Mrs. Richmond suspect something?"

"No, but I think her son Scott does . . . and possibly his fiancée. We need to lull them into believing everything is aboveboard."

"How do we do that?"

"I'm not sure, but I'll think of something. We can't afford to let them learn the truth."

Chapter Five

The next day, Nicole had second, third, fourth, and even fifth thoughts. But each time, she came to the same conclusion: she had to continue with this deception, for Chrissie's sake.

Nicole had thought about trying to keep her engagement a secret at work, but the word would be out soon enough in the newspaper, and her coworkers would never forgive her if they learned it there instead of from her. So, when she arrived at the reference desk, she casually waved her left hand under her best friend's nose.

Alyx Hannigan, an energetic dynamo with short spiky blond hair and an irrepressible attitude, grabbed her hand to gawk at the ring. "Wow, are you *engaged*?"

"It looks that way, doesn't it?" Nicole said.

"But how? Who?" Alyx demanded. "I didn't know you were even *seeing* anyone. Why didn't you tell me?"

Concerned by the hurt lurking in her friend's eyes, Nicole said truthfully, "I barely knew about it myself. It was a whirlwind courtship and proposal. In fact, I'm still reeling a bit."

Alyx seemed a little mollified. Then another librarian caught sight of the diamond and soon Nicole had a whole gaggle of women standing around and babbling at her.

"Who's the lucky man?" Alyx asked.

"His name is Scott Richmond."

"*The* Scott Richmond?" one girl asked. "From the Richmond mansion on Capitol Hill . . . and the society pages?"

Nicole nodded, and the girl placed a hand over her heart. "Wow, he's gorgeous. And rich. How'd you meet him?"

Not knowing how to answer that, Nicole was glad when their supervisor came by to see what was going on and sent them back to work. But Alyx wasn't satisfied. "You'll have to tell me everything later," she whispered fiercely as she went back to her desk.

Her mind churning, Nicole wondered if she should tell her friend the truth, then immediately decided against it. If she did, she'd have to explain about Chrissie and that would probably make Alyx an accessory as well. Instead, Nicole made something up that sounded plausible, and at the break, she spun a tale of meeting at the library and a series of increasingly romantic dates over the course of a couple of weeks.

Luckily, they bought it and even seemed satisfied when Nicole told them she hadn't set the date yet. Thank heavens. These people were true friends. When the day came that she would have to announce the engagement was off, they'd be there for her.

But the day seemed to stretch out forever as she fielded questions she didn't know how to answer and waited for the library to close. Then, about ten minutes before closing time, Alyx hurried to Nicole's desk, her eyes brimming with amusement. "There's a man waiting for you over in the first aisle of the reference section," she said.

"What does he need help with?"

"I'm not sure," Alyx said with a grin. "But he said he's just waiting for you to drop a book so he can pick it up."

Nicole laughed, remembering Scott's account of their first meeting. "That must be Scott."

"I thought so," Alyx gushed. "He is gorgeous. So tell me, does he kiss as good as he looks?"

Nicole felt herself flush. Then, on impulse, she whispered, "Better," as she breezed past Alyx.

Scott looked just as yummy as Alyx said. He glanced expectantly at her and, feeling a bubble of irrepressible amusement, Nicole decided to play along. Smiling to herself, she pulled a small volume from the shelf and let it fall to the floor. "Oops."

He picked it up and handed it to her with a delighted grin. "I think you dropped this."

"Why, so I did. Thank you so much." She fluttered her eyelashes at him. "However can I repay you, kind sir?"

"You already have," he said, moving closer to stare down into her face. "I love this side of you. Can I keep it?"

Suddenly feeling silly, Nicole said, "I'm afraid it doesn't last very long. Enjoy it while you can."

"I will." Then he added in a casual tone, "Don't look now, but there are half a dozen women behind you pretending not to stare at us . . . ."

Nicole didn't bother looking over her shoulder.

"My friends and coworkers," she explained. "They saw the ring, but I think some of them don't really believe me about the engagement. They just want to get a look at you."

"Well, let's give them a really good look then, shall we?" And Scott bent his head and kissed her.

Nicole knew he was only doing it to entertain her friends, but her body reacted as if it were real. His mouth was so soft, so persuasive, so seductive . . . . She melted into his embrace with dizzy anticipation and felt all her nerve endings stand up and cheer as he slid one arm around her waist and cupped her head with the other.

He kissed her slowly, thoroughly, until she felt completely cherished. When he finally released her, he looked almost as stunned as she felt.

Applause sounded behind Nicole, and she whipped around in embarrassment to see practically half the library staff giving them an ovation. Cursing herself for forgetting where she was, Nicole wanted to crawl away somewhere and hide, but Scott gave them a grin and bowed as if accepting the accolades as his due.

"Thank you very much," he declared. "Our next performance will be at—" He broke off and gave Nicole a considering look. "On second thought, our next performance will be private. Totally private."

Everyone laughed, and Nicole took the opportunity to mutter, "I need to clock out. If you would wait for me outside?"

"But of course," he said with an extravagant flourish. "Your chariot awaits." Then, with a brief, promissory kiss, he left.

Her face burning, Nicole moved back to her desk to clean up.

Alyx sidled up to the desk. "Holy moley, you weren't kidding about that kiss." She fanned herself, miming intense heat. "I need a cold shower now."

Me, too. But a mental reminder that this was all a charade acted like an icy splash and was just as effective. Scott had only been playing to the crowd, to give more verisimilitude to their act. Well, he was damned good at it, she had to give him that.

Nicole clocked out and met Scott, then reprimanded herself for enjoying the envious looks she garnered as they sped off in his convertible. *This isn't real.* She had to keep her distance, had to keep reminding herself that he was only playing a part . . . before her heart succumbed to his charm and she got hurt.

They grabbed a fast bite to eat, then Scott took her to Cherry Creek Mall. Nicole rarely shopped there because she couldn't afford the upscale stores, but she was glad at least that they were at a mall. She had been afraid he'd take her to some exclusive haute couture place where the dresses cost a fortune and she'd feel extremely guilty.

Instead, they cost half a fortune and only made her feel half as guilty.

But Scott made it into a game, holding up index cards with the numbers one through ten as she modeled outfits for him. The last dress she'd modeled had received a seven, but as Nicole shrugged into a simple black cocktail dress in the Saks dressing room, she had a feeling this one would get a ten.

Deceptively simple, the slinky black material hugged her curves with a silken caress, and the slit up the front of the short skirt gave tantalizing glimpses of her thigh. And if it looked this good now, imagine how it would appear when paired with some killer high heels . . . .

Smiling with satisfaction, Nicole slipped out of the dressing room to see a tall, young, dark-haired woman approach Scott and throw her arms around him.

"Scott," the brunette declared, then gave him a kiss. "It's been so long. How *are* you?"

Seeing Nicole over the woman's shoulder, Scott smiled and said, "Engaged," then turned her around gently to look at Nicole.

"What?" the woman said in surprise.

Damn, she was beautiful . . . and vaguely familiar. This was the brunette Scott had been seen with most often on the society pages. Was there something still going on with them? Would the woman figure out their deception?

"Hello," Nicole said in cool tones. She knew what Grace meant now. Having the right clothes and knowing she looked her best was worth the outrageous cost of the dress. "I'm Nicole Dreyfuss, Scott's fiancée."

She held out her hand, and the other woman shook it.

"Uh, Melinda Harris." She turned to look at Scott. "Your fiancée? Is this one of your jokes?"

"No," Scott said with a smile. "It's the plain truth."

He moved to Nicole's side where he slid his arm

around her waist and held her left hand out to Melinda. "And here's the ring to prove it."

Melinda still looked stunned. "But I haven't heard anything about it . . . ."

She must still think this was one of Scott's jokes, and from the pole-axed expression on her face, she must be *hoping* it was.

"We just became engaged yesterday," Scott explained. "The announcement should be in the papers any day now, and we're planning an engagement party soon."

"Party . . ." Melinda looked down at the ring again and Nicole could almost feel sorry for her. No doubt the woman had expected to wear Scott's ring herself. But his uncharacteristic seriousness must have convinced her he was telling the truth, for she gave him a false smile. "I wish you every happiness then. You and . . ."

"Nicole," Scott supplied.

"Yes, of course." Melinda turned to Nicole. "Tell me, how did you do it?"

"Do what?" Nicole asked warily.

"Snare Scott Richmond, the town's most eligible—and elusive—bachelor. We had all decided to give up on him, since it seemed obvious he never planned to marry."

Nicole didn't know how to answer that, but Scott did it for her. Squeezing her a little tighter, he said soberly, "She did it by being herself. Beauty, intelligence, principles, passion . . . what's not to love?"

And as he gazed down at her with a loving expression, Nicole's heart gave a little leap. She could almost believe he meant it . . . .

Worse, she had begun to hope he did.

* * *

Seeing Nicole's expression, Scott wished for a brief moment that the situation were real. When Nicole was in his arms, she was responsive, sultry, and very, very desirable. In fact, her response was so genuine that, at times, he even forgot they were playing a part.

Melinda broke into his reverie, saying, "I don't believe it."

"Don't believe what?" Scott asked warily.

"I don't believe Scott Richmond has actually grown up." She patted him on the cheek in a condescending manner. "Too bad—I kind of liked the other Scott." And with that, she walked off.

Scott frowned. Melinda always had been fond of pithy exit lines. Though he rather liked the old Scott, too. Did association with Nicole really make him seem that changed?

With one arm still around Nicole, he felt her relax when Melinda disappeared from sight. "Did that bother you?" he asked in surprise.

She cast him an annoyed glance and slipped out of his embrace. "Don't be ridiculous."

"But ridiculous is what I'm good at . . . ."

Ignoring him, she headed back toward the dressing room.

"By the way," he called after her, "that dress is definitely a ten." Then, as he caught the way the back dipped low and sexy to her waist, he revised his estimate. Maybe even an eleven or twelve.

"I know," she said, and threw him a flirtatious glance over her shoulder as she swung her hips in a move that ought to be illegal.

Scott's eyebrows raised. Nicole might have a buttoned-up exterior, but every once in a while, he caught glimpses of an unbuttoned personality hidden deep inside. How could he entice that Nicole to come out and play permanently?

When Nicole had changed and returned with the clothes she'd tried on, Scott said to the saleswoman, "We'll take the black dress."

"That makes three outfits," Nicole said. "I think that's enough, don't you?"

For the moment. But Scott had found that he really enjoyed shopping for Nicole. She looked good in anything, and she had excellent taste. The only reason she didn't have the proper clothes was because she hadn't had the money to indulge herself. But Scott was more than willing to do that for her.

"Shoes now?" he asked. "Or shall we visit Cartier or Tiffany's?"

She gave him a quelling look. "Jewelry would be going too far—I feel bad enough wearing this engagement ring. Don't worry, I have a few simple pieces that will do just fine. And I can supply my own shoes."

With her pride, he had expected that answer. "Okay. Victoria's Secret, then?"

"No."

Too bad. The blush that came with that vehement reply was intriguing. "Then can I tempt you with a chocolate shake at Johnny Rockets?"

"Now that sounds more like it," she said with a grin, and they walked down the mall to the retro diner. With a chrome counter, red bar stools, jukeboxes on the tables, and the soda jerk uniforms, the diner made him feel as if they had gone back in time to the fifties.

They were seated in a secluded corner, and after the waitress took their order for two chocolate shakes, Nicole looked around. "I feel like I should be wearing a poodle skirt and saddle shoes."

Scott grinned. "I can arrange that."

"I'm sure you can, but it's not necessary. Really, Scott, you've done too much already."

He shrugged. "I bought a few dresses, is all. Consider it payment—or armor—for what you are about to face."

"Will it be that bad?"

He immediately regretted his words, but couldn't lie to her. He waited until the waitress delivered their order, then said, "I don't know. Getting into the parties will be the easy part. Replacing the jewels will be harder."

She frowned. "I hadn't thought about that."

If she wasn't worried about replacing the jewels, what was she worried about?

"But now that you mention it," she continued, "how *are* we going to do it? Won't they all have safes like your mother's? How will we get the combination? And how are we even going to know where the jewels are? It's not like we can come out and ask."

"I've been thinking about that," Scott said. "The insurance investigator showed up this morning—"

"He did?" she asked, almost spitting out her shake in her haste to get the words out. "Why didn't you tell me? What did he say? Do you think he'll find out who did it?"

Scott frowned. "I doubt it. He didn't seem very

competent. All he did was take the basic information and say he'd look into it."

"Maybe he's new."

"Maybe." And maybe Gerald had pulled some strings to get the claim processed as fast as possible.

"You think Chrissie's safe then?" Nicole asked in a lowered voice.

Scott took a gulp of his shake, thinking. "If this guy is all we have to worry about, yeah. But we still need to replace the jewels. Luckily, the investigator's presence gave me the opportunity to casually ask Mother about Sara Harding and where she kept her jewelry."

"And?"

"And she brags about not needing to keep them in a safe because the security on her house is so tight."

Nicole's shoulders slumped. "That's not good."

"On the contrary. The security alarm won't be in effect while the party is in full swing. Too many people."

Nicole stared at him. "How are we going to replace the jewels while the party is going on?"

Scott hid a smile. *We, huh? At least she's finally accepted the fact that she has to help.* "Chrissie gave me a list of who bought what. Sara Harding has the fake rubies, so I'll wait until Mother's gone, then take the real ones out of her safe. She'll be less likely to notice they're gone if I take them out of the boxes."

"And they won't be so conspicuous in your pockets that way, either."

"True, but . . . they'd make too big a bulge in my pockets. We'll have to use your purse. That's why I bought you that large one."

Nicole closed her eyes. "Oh, great. And what happens if they spill out into the punch or something?"

"Don't worry, they won't. We'll just slip away at the party, make a quick switch, and return so fast no one will know we're gone."

"Do you really think it will be that easy?"

"I hope so." And he saw no reason why it wouldn't. But she seemed overly concerned about the whole thing. "What's really wrong?"

She dropped her eyes and took a sip of her shake. "I don't know what you mean."

Now he knew he was on to something. "It's not the switch that's bothering you—what is it?"

She shrugged. "I just don't want to embarrass you."

"Hey, I was kidding," he protested. Surely she knew that; when did anyone take him seriously? "Appearances aren't that important."

"Really? Then why are you spending so much money to make me look presentable?"

"Not to make you *look* presentable—you look great in anything. The purpose of the clothing is to make you *feel* presentable—to give you confidence." His mother was right about that.

"Oh."

But he still sensed there was more. "Does Melinda bother you? Because I can assure you there is nothing between us."

She gave him an annoyed glance as she pushed her empty glass away. "What? You think I'm jealous?"

Well, he *had* thought that, but . . . "No," he lied. "But I thought you might be upset if you thought our engagement was breaking up a relationship. Believe me, Melinda and I are friends, nothing more."

"She didn't seem to think so." Nicole's tone was thoughtful rather than accusing. "And you have spent a great deal of time with her. I've seen you pictured together a lot in the paper."

Scott waved his hand in a dismissive gesture. "We just found it convenient to have someone to go to all the parties with, with no pressure on either of us to find a date." At least, that's how he'd viewed it and thought Melinda had, too. But lately she had seemed more possessive. Maybe this engagement was a good thing. "So, she doesn't bother you, then?"

"Not in the way you mean."

From the way she kept her gaze on the table and wouldn't meet his eyes, he sensed this was important. "In what way, then?"

"Everyone you know will have the same reaction when they hear about your engagement—disbelief."

"So?"

"So what do you think will happen when we eventually have to call it off?"

"Nothing. It's not like they're going to throw rotten vegetables at you or anything. They'll just write it off as another thing I didn't follow through on."

"They'll say you dumped me," Nicole said, spearing him with a glance.

Oh, so that's her problem. "Then you do the dumping."

"Yeah, sure. Like they'll believe that."

"Why do you care what they believe?"

"Having people laugh at you is humiliating no

matter who does it. I know—I've seen how people of your set treat people like me."

He raised his eyebrows. "Don't you think you're being a little too judgmental?" Not to mention snobbish. "They're not like that."

"If you say so." But her tone indicated she didn't believe a word he said.

"Why don't you give them a chance? You might find you like some of them. And you might even find they like you."

Nicole shrugged, but he could tell this really bothered her. He didn't know which was worse— her reverse snobbery, or her belief that she wouldn't be accepted for who she was. In either case, he vowed to prove her wrong.

Chapter Six

Over the next few days, Nicole was a bundle of nerves. Not in the spine-tingling, ohmigod-I-want-him kind of way, but in the stomach-dropping, ohmigod-I'm-going-to-make-a-fool-of-myself sort of way.

Her only comfort was that Scott had helped her get Chrissie safely off to New York. He had even arranged for Nicole to talk to his cousin, whose sensible attitude and knowledge of the city put Nicole's mind at ease. Chrissie was in good hands . . . in New York, anyway. Here in Denver, Nicole and Scott had yet to prove themselves. And they were going to start this very night.

As she waited in her living room, she didn't know which she was more nervous about: being seen as Scott's fiancée for the first time in public or switching the jewels. But she didn't have any more time to worry about it because Scott had arrived at her front door.

She opened the door and just stared for a moment. Though he was great-looking in casual slacks and a shirt, in a suit he was devastating. That *GQ* look combined with his open expression made him look like the well-dressed boy next door. That was, until he grinned at her. Then his devilish smile made him look wicked, more like the bad boy from across the tracks.

"You look beautiful," he said admiringly.

Her tailored navy blue evening suit made her feel good, which was its primary asset. But the snug double-breasted jacket flattered her bustline, making her feel . . . bigger than normal. And as Scott's gaze lingered in the V shadow of her neckline, Nicole felt her breasts swell in response, as if yearning toward him with minds of their own.

She felt herself flush again. Where the heck were all these thoughts coming from? Scott was stimulating her imagination far too much . . . not to mention other parts of her body.

Now cut that out.

"You look good, too," she said hurriedly. "I'm ready. Shall we go?"

He looked surprised by her haste. "Sure."

She gave him an apologetic glance as she locked the front door. "It's just that Missy has been lurking outside the past few nights in very feminine dresses, apparently just waiting for you to show up again."

He laughed. "She feels she has something to prove?"

"I guess. But, I don't want to stick around long enough to find out how she plans to prove it. Do you?"

"Good point," he exclaimed and hustled her to the car.

Thank goodness the top was up this time. She didn't want to arrive at the cocktail party looking windblown. Scott barely gave her time to buckle up before he sped off.

When Nicole looked up in surprise, Scott said merely, "Missy alert."

She glanced back and saw her neighbor stumbling after them in ridiculously high heels and a fluttery dress, waving frantically. Nicole chuckled. "I think you've injured her feminine pride."

Scott shrugged. "It'll be good for her." He reached into the backseat and pulled out a padded envelope, then dropped it in her lap. "Here."

"What's this?"

"The rubies. You need to put them in your purse."

Oh, yeah. A sinking feeling hit Nicole in the pit of her stomach. She glanced into the envelope to see what she was risking her reputation for. There was a necklace, bracelet, earrings, and a pin, all covered in large stones. Gaudy and ugly. "Do the fakes really look this real?"

"Yes, they do. My father paid quite a bit to make sure they do, and the gold is only plated. They'll pass a casual inspection, but won't fool anyone who really knows gemstones."

Reluctantly, Nicole succumbed to the inevitable and placed the gems, envelope and all, in the large purse Scott had bought her for the purpose. She felt like a criminal, but kept reminding herself that she was doing this for Chrissie.

Scott kept up a light banter all the way to the party, but it didn't make Nicole feel any better. She knew she was going to screw up somehow and be unmasked as a fraud. And Scott's blithe reassurance was no help. By the time they reached the party, she was almost sick to her stomach.

"You'll be fine," Scott said, evidently sensing her unease. "Just be yourself."

As if that would help. "Just don't leave me alone in there," she muttered as he steered her through the front door.

Scott chuckled. "You make it sound like we're entering a war zone."

"Aren't we?"

"No—" He broke off to say in a low tone, "This is our hostess," as an elegant older woman came to greet them.

"Hello, Scott," the woman said. "Is this your fiancée?"

Nicole tensed for a moment, not knowing what odd thing might burst out of Scott's mouth.

He played it straight for a change. "Yes, this is my fiancée, Nicole Dreyfuss. Nicole, this is Sara Harding."

Nicole murmured something appropriate, and Mrs. Harding beamed at her. "We're so happy to see Scott settling down at last. I'm sure you'll be good for him."

"Oh, but he's good already," Nicole said without thinking, then felt herself blush. She hadn't meant to make it sound like an innuendo.

But Mrs. Harding just laughed. "Oh, we know he's a lot of fun, but he's never serious. Maybe now he'll grow up a little."

Nicole glanced uncertainly at Scott. Grow up? What did these people think he was? A little boy? Scott merely shrugged and looked unconcerned.

Wanting to set the record straight, Nicole said earnestly, "But he's quite grown up. He only pretends to be otherwise."

Mrs. Harding patted her on the arm. "You see? You've had a good influence on him already if he can convince you of that." Not waiting for Nicole's answer, she made a welcoming gesture toward the party. "Please enjoy yourself." Then she wandered off to greet another guest.

Scott gave Nicole a quizzical look as he led her into the party. "How chivalrous of you. But I assure you, I don't need a champion."

What was she thinking? She should have just made polite conversation and moved on. She really didn't want to draw attention to herself for any reason. "It just gets my goat when people underestimate you."

"Then I'm afraid you'll lose a lot of goats tonight." He shrugged. "Ignore it; I do."

It was good advice. She just hoped she could take it.

Nicole let herself relax a little. At least Mrs. Harding hadn't kicked her out immediately, even though Nicole had felt sure everyone could see the word "fraud" emblazoned on her forehead.

Grace and Gerald appeared then and Grace took them under her wing. As Grace introduced her around as Scott's fiancée, Nicole began to feel more comfortable. She was wearing the right clothes and she had the approval of Scott's mother, so everyone seemed to be accepting her at face value. Maybe she would be able to pull this off after all. If only they would stop treating Scott as if he were a silly nonentity.

As one more person made a remark about Scott's wild, carefree bachelor days being over, Nicole couldn't help but scowl.

Scott pulled her away, asking privately, "What's wrong? He didn't mean to insult you, you know."

"I know. He meant to insult you."

Scott blinked in surprise. "That's what bothered you? Don't worry about it. I don't."

"Well, maybe you should. Or do you want to go through the rest of your life with people thinking you're a fool?"

He gave her a half smile that showed no amusement and said softly, "Having everyone underestimate me isn't necessarily a bad thing."

"Is that the reason you let them laugh at you?" Nicole asked. "Or is it because you enjoy secretly laughing at them for misjudging you?"

He cocked his head to regard her thoughtfully. "Are you trying to pick a fight with me?"

Nicole opened her mouth to deny it, but in all honesty, she couldn't say he was wrong. "I guess I am," she admitted.

"Good Lord," Scott said, placing a hand over his heart and staggering back a little. "Honesty . . . here, of all places. I don't think I can stand it." Then, dropping the pose, he asked, "*Why* are you trying to argue with me?"

"I don't know." She lowered her voice so only he could hear. "Maybe because I'm nervous about meeting everyone. Maybe because I hate lying to all these people about why I'm here. Or maybe because I hate the way you let them make fun of you."

"And maybe there's another reason."

"Like what?"

"Like you're trying to find a reason for us to leave so you don't have to go through with the plan."

Subconsciously, perhaps. "But—"

"But there's one good thing about everyone see
ing our spat. It gives us a good excuse to go upstair
for a little privacy."

"Why would we want to do that?"

He grinned. "It's showtime."

Her heart lurched in her chest. Damn. She'
hoped he'd forgotten about that.

"Come on," he said, taking her hand. "Let's go.

He pulled her up the staircase, the full length o
their arms stretching between them. "Good," h
whispered. "Pretend you're reluctant."

"I *am* reluctant." Unlike Chrissie, she was no ac
tress.

But Scott just smiled and hauled her up to the
second floor. No one pointed or called attention t
them, which made Nicole feel a little better, but no
much. What she was about to do felt wrong, ever
if it wasn't. If nothing else, it was certainly an inva
sion of her hostess's privacy.

When they reached the top, Scott tugged her
little harder. "Come on, let's get out of sight."

She moved closer to whisper, "Do you knov
where you're going?"

"Not really, but her bedroom has to be up her
somewhere."

As he opened and closed a few doors, Nicole wa:
glad that they couldn't be seen from downstairs. Fi
nally, he said, "This must be it."

He led her into a lush bedroom that smelled ex
pensive, like the cosmetics counter at Neiman
Marcus. As he turned the lights on low, she said, "
thought I was supposed to be the lookout."

"You are. Just crack the door open a little and let me know if you see anyone coming."

She peeked out the door at the empty hallway, then couldn't resist turning back to see what Scott was doing. He headed immediately for the jewelry box on the dresser and rummaged through it.

When he put his hands on his hips and stared at it in exasperation, she asked, "Aren't they there?"

"No, just a few pieces of costume jewelry. I wonder where she keeps the good stuff?"

He opened all of the dresser drawers and searched them, but had no luck. From Nicole's vantage point, everything looked very neat and orderly, a testimony to Mrs. Harding's personality . . . or her maid's.

Moving faster now, Scott searched the other drawers in the room, to no avail. When he stood in the middle of the room looking frustrated, Nicole said, "I thought you said she kept them out in the open."

"That's what Mother said. But not out in the open, per se, just not locked up tight."

"Are you sure?" While Scott searched, Nicole glanced around the room. "Over there by the bed, that looks like it might be a safe." A square was clearly visible in the plaster panels.

He examined the wall where she pointed. "You're right, it is a safe," he said as he pulled back one of the moldings to reveal a combination dial.

Her heart sank. "That's it, then. We'd better go." They'd been here too long already, and the longer they stayed, the more nervous she got.

"I don't think so."

"But we don't know the combination."

"Look at the bedside tables," Scott urged. "This safe is on her husband's side, not hers."

Okay, she could see that the masculine accessories were on that side, but . . . "So?"

"So, I think this is his safe, not hers. I bet her jewelry is still someplace else in the room."

"But where?"

"I don't know. You're a woman. If you wanted to have your jewelry accessible but not obvious, where would you put it?"

Nicole glanced around wildly. "I don't know—the bathroom, maybe?" The door to the master bathroom was slightly ajar.

Nicole stayed at her post while Scott hurried into the bathroom. She could hear him rummaging around, but he came out looking more frustrated.

"Not there."

"Then let's go," she urged.

"No, they're here somewhere, and I'm going to find them. But where?"

Damn, he was as stubborn as Chrissie. "Try the closet then." But if they weren't there, she was going to leave without him.

He opened the door to the large walk-in closet. "Wow, this thing is almost as big as the bedroom. It's more like a dressing room."

"But is her jewelry in there?" Nicole asked, wishing Scott would develop some sense of urgency.

"Bingo. I found a jewelry armoire."

Relief filled her. "Good, now are your mother's jewels in it?"

"I don't know. It's locked."

Feeling ready to scream, Nicole said, "That's enough. Let's get out of here." His mother or someone was bound to miss the two of them and come looking for them soon.

"Wait, I remember seeing a key in the jewelry box." Quickly, Scott sorted through the box on the dresser and pulled out a key. He hurried back to the dressing room. "It fits!"

Thank heavens. "Are the jewels there?"

"I don't see them," Scott said, his voice sounding muffled.

"They have to be there." Nicole left the doorway to join Scott in the dressing room. Quickly, she sorted through the contents of the very neat armoire. No rubies in sight.

Damn. Where could they be? Then she spotted a navy and gold plastic bag next to the armoire. "What's in the bag?" she asked. "It looks like it came from the gift shop at the tennis club."

Scott opened it and out tumbled a set of velvet jewelry boxes. "That's it. Brilliant, Nicole."

Despite herself, Nicole felt a glow of satisfaction at his compliment. "She must not have had time yet to put them away."

"Right. Let me have your purse," he urged.

Quickly, she pulled out the padded envelope and handed it to him. But just as he was pouring the rubies into his hand, she heard something.

"Voices," she whispered urgently. "Someone's coming."

Scott shoved both sets of rubies in the bag, pushed the bag back where he had found it, and grabbed her hand. "Follow my lead," he whispered and tugged her to the bed where he placed a hand on her shoulder and pushed her down until she sat.

"What—"

"Pretend you're upset," he said.

Not knowing how to do that, Nicole covered her face with her hands and bent over. Maybe if she hid her face, no one would know who she was. *Yeah, right. The ostrich school of disguise.*

She felt more than saw Scott drop to his knee beside her just as the door opened and the light came on full force.

A woman said, "Thank you, Mrs. Harding. Maybe your husband could give me a legal opinion—" but broke off when Mrs. Harding gasped.

Nicole couldn't help it—she whimpered. How were they going to get out of this? They couldn't leave, not with both sets of jewels in the closet. How would they ever be able to explain the missing rubies to his mother?

"It's okay," Scott said as he rubbed her back, obviously playing more to the audience than trying to soothe Nicole's raw nerves.

He stopped massaging and said, "I'm sorry, Mrs. Harding. Nicole was a little upset, and we needed a private place . . . ."

"I see," she said, and Nicole could hear the disapproval in her voice.

"We had an argument," Scott confided. "And I didn't want to disturb your guests, so I thought it might be wise to give Nicole a few minutes to calm down."

"Quite right," Mrs. Harding said hurriedly. "I appreciate your thoughtfulness. Stay as long as you like. I can come back later."

Nicole heard the sound of the door closing, then Scott said, "It's okay. They've gone."

She raised her head. "I can't believe that worked."

"You were perfect."

No, I was petrified. But she didn't want to admit that to Scott. "I mean your story."

He shrugged. "Sara has a horror of scenes and scandal. I played on her fear, is all."

Too bad he had to make Nicole look like a blithering idiot in the process. She sighed. "Let's do what we came to do and get out of here."

Scott nodded, then quickly put the real jewels in the velvet boxes and the fake rubies in the envelope in her purse. He was right—they did look real.

"Can we go now?" Nicole asked. Any more of this and her nerves would be totally shot.

"Just as soon as I put the key back. Okay, let's go."

They headed back to the stairs, with Scott's arm around her. Nicole knew he was just doing it for show, but she was glad of the comfort. She had a feeling she was going to be facing some serious embarrassment very soon.

"What will they think of me?" she murmured as they slowly walked downstairs.

"Nothing bad."

Yeah, right. "They'll think I'm an idiot, getting all upset over nothing." Thanks to Scott.

He shrugged and nuzzled her ear, murmuring, "Well, would you rather be thought an idiot . . . or arrested as a thief?"

Thrills coursed through her at the touch of his lips on her neck, but she tried to ignore him. Damn it, he was right. But no matter how well-intended his actions or distracting his sexy ways, it didn't make it any easier to face the crowd below.

* * *

Scott felt a surge of satisfaction as he led Nicole back to the party. They had accomplished their objective, they hadn't gotten caught, and he had found more excuses to touch Nicole. It was the perfect night so far as he was concerned.

Unfortunately, Nicole didn't seem to feel the same way. She was still a bit shaky. He rubbed her shoulders with one hand, hoping to help her relax. But she tensed again when his mother and Gerald approached them.

Gerald frowned. "Why were you upstairs?"

"Is everything all right?" Grace added.

"Yes, Mother. We just had a little tiff, is all. Everything is fine now, isn't it, honey?" He hugged Nicole tighter, not only to convince his mother everything was okay, but also to give his partner in crime some support.

Nicole smiled weakly. "I'm sorry for being so silly. Just a case of nerves, I think."

Grace looked relieved. "Good. Don't let my son bully you."

"Hey, what did I do?" Scott said in protest.

Grace frowned. "I don't know, but you must have done something. Don't do it again."

Trying to look cowed, Scott said meekly, "Okay, I won't."

But as she left, he couldn't help but flash Nicole a triumphant glance. "See? They'll blame me, not you."

"Your mother is only one person," she said doubtfully.

Obviously, he wasn't going to convince her on this one. "Well, shall we go now? We got what we came for." And Nicole didn't look like she could stand any more excitement.

"Is it really okay to go now?" she asked as he steered her toward the door. "What will they think?"

He whispered back, "Don't worry. They'll think we're heading off to have makeup sex."

She stopped dead, a look of horror on her face.

"I'm just kidding," he assured her. "The party is winding down, anyway. See? Other people are leaving, too."

She relaxed then and allowed him to lead her out the door.

"There," he said, seating her in his car. "That wasn't so bad, was it?"

"It was horrible. I can't stop shaking."

"Nonsense. You were great. You did everything exactly right."

"I did?"

"You did," he reassured her, then was surprised when she seemed to glow with his simple compliment. Good grief, had no one ever praised this woman before? "I couldn't ask for a better accomplice."

She gave him a wry glance, and he added, "We just have one more thing to take care of before we can call it a night."

"What?" she asked, her tone apprehensive again.

"I want to replace Mother's rubies before she gets home. Who knows when I'll get a better chance?"

Apparently, Nicole couldn't find a good argument to that, so he sped off toward the mansion.

When they arrived, Nicole said, "I'll wait here."

"Nope, sorry, not going to happen," he said as he opened her door.

"Why not?"

"Because if Mother comes home soon, she might get suspicious if she sees you sitting alone in the car. What will you say if she asks you what you're doing?"

"Oh, all right."

He knew that would get her. Nicole had no confidence in her ability to think on her feet, though she had done very well this evening.

He led her upstairs where he quickly replaced the rubies in the velvet boxes in his mother's safe. But it somehow didn't feel right. It was too easy.

I know how to liven it up, he thought wickedly.

As they left his mother's room, Nicole still looked nervous despite the fact that the jewelry was no longer in her purse. Scott stopped abruptly in the hallway. "Wait, I heard something. Quick, in here."

He whisked her into a nearby guest room and shut the door, leaving the dark room lit only by moonlight.

"What—"

"Shh," he said, putting a finger to her soft, luscious lips. He backed her gently against the wall by the door, murmuring, "She might hear us."

"Who?" she whispered.

"Marta. She's making her rounds." He placed his hands on both sides of Nicole's shoulders in a protective gesture, then leaned into her, letting his senses fill with her enticing essence. She smelled clean, without the heavy perfume he hated. Baby powder combined with the light floral scent of her soap made an irresistible combination on her skin. Her smooth, touchable skin.

He ran his fingertips over her cheek and she inhaled sharply. Was she as aware of him as he was of her?

That suit she wore had driven him nuts all evening, the fitted bustline with its shadowed cleavage providing tantalizing glimpses of Nicole's generous assets. The slacks made her legs look long and lean, making him wonder how they would feel wrapped around his waist.

When she didn't protest his nearness, he pressed his body against hers, wanting to feel the curves hidden beneath that tailored exterior, wanting to rub the hardness between his legs against her softness.

Slowly, gently, he kissed the pulse beating at the base of her neck.

Her breathing quickened, but she didn't move.

"What are you thinking about?" he asked.

"Pasta," she blurted out.

He reared back. "What?" That wasn't exactly the reaction he'd been hoping for.

She shook her head even as she covered her face with her hands. "Never mind. It was . . . Never mind."

He pulled her hands gently away from her face. "Are you hungry?"

"No."

"Not even for me?" Her response certainly seemed to indicate so.

"Maybe. Oh, no," she moaned, shaking her head. "Forget I said that."

"How can I?" he asked in an unexpectedly husky tone, "when I feel the same way?"

And, linking her fingers with his, he leaned in to

capture those sinful lips of hers. She responded soulfully, giving him her all as her lips became as eager and demanding as his. He released her hands and drew her body tighter, closer. So soft, so compliant, so very desirable. He felt himself drowning in her sweetness as their mouths devoured each other, and he let go of her hands to roam her luscious backside.

When he came up for air, he backed her against the wall again. The muffled thump made him murmur, "Sorry."

"It's okay," she said breathlessly. "Don't stop."

Thank God. Her chest heaved, bringing his attention to the enticing mounds of flesh before him. With a couple of swift moves, he unbuttoned the jacket to see her wearing nothing but a lacy bra beneath it. *Perfect.*

When Nicole gasped and watched him with anticipation, Scott obliged them both by leaning down and kissing the swell of her breast above her bra. Nicole moaned, and he slowly licked her cleavage from one swell to the other.

"Oh, yes," she breathed.

Thus encouraged, he ran his tongue over the lace at the peak of her breast and sucked on the hard bud he found there. Nicole's iron grip on his head further proved that his advances weren't unwelcome, so he reached behind her to unclasp her bra. But before he could even find the hook, he heard the doorknob turn.

Quickly, he turned toward the door and shoved Nicole behind him. He might not care if anyone found them there, but he knew she would.

The door opened and Marta's face showed in the

doorway, looking suspicious. "What are you doing here?"

Feeling Nicole frantically fix her clothing behind him, Scott said casually, "I was just showing my fiancée the rest of the house." *And my mouth just happened to get caught on her nipple.*

He kept that latter thought to himself, though, doubting anyone else would appreciate him voicing it aloud.

Marta frowned. "In the dark?"

"Sure, it's the best way," he said. Then added with what he hoped was a disarming smile, "Actually, we were leaving and you caught me just as I turned off the light." He turned to Nicole, who had stopped making urgent movements behind him. "Isn't that right, honey?"

"Of course," she said, her voice sounding only a little breathless. "Maybe we should go now. I can see the rest of the house later."

"Good idea," he said. "I'll take you home." Damn it. But there was nothing else he could do. No doubt Marta would stand around and glare at him until Nicole left.

Glad that his suit jacket concealed his arousal, Scott led Nicole downstairs under the disapproving eye of the housekeeper who remained on the landing.

When they reached the bottom, Nicole said, "You didn't really hear anything before you dragged me into that room, did you?"

He shot her a grin. "Only the sound of the blood rushing from my head." Straight to his crotch.

"That's what I thought. You're very good at that, you know. Seducing a woman."

Uh-oh. He didn't care for the tone of her voice. "Is that what you thought was happening?"

"Of course. What else?"

"Oh, I don't know. I thought I was making love to you."

"It's the same thing."

"Not in my book."

"Yeah, right," she muttered, and headed off to the garage without a backward glance.

Scott followed, feeling frustrated in more ways than one. For once he regretted the fact that his reputation for jokes made someone misunderstand his motives.

Then again, what *were* his motives? Was Nicole right? Was he only trying to get into her pants?

Hell, why not? What was wrong with that?

Nothing . . . but he couldn't fool himself. The hell of it was, he wanted more than that from Nicole. Much, much more.

"It's worse than I thought," Gerald said into the phone.

"What is?"

"I saw Scott Richmond go upstairs at the Hardings' house last night."

Sounding alarmed, his associate asked, "Why would he do that?"

"I think he found out his mother's rubies were there."

"What did he do? Did he find them?"

"I don't know, but I don't think so. He didn't say anything, and I think he was interrupted before he could do anything."

"How did he find out? We were so careful . . ."

"I don't know, but we need to keep a close eye on him. If we're not careful, he could ruin everything."

Chapter Seven

The next morning, Nicole barely had time to wake up and wonder what she was going to do with her weekend when Scott called.

"Good morning," he said in a cheerful tone. "How's my partner in crime?"

"Don't say that," Nicole snapped. "Someone might hear you."

"Don't worry. Even if someone could hear me, they wouldn't think anything of it. It's me, remember?"

Nicole made a noncommittal sound. He hadn't fooled *her*, so what made him think no one else would catch on to him?

"I'll be over in an hour to pick you up."

"Why?" she asked warily.

"Because though Joan Larson is having a party in two weeks, Claire Wyndham doesn't have anything planned anytime soon."

For a moment, Nicole wondered what he was talking about, then realized these were the women who had the other two sets of jewels. "And . . . ?"

"And I have an idea how to get into her house."

"Please tell me it doesn't involve breaking and entering."

"Okay, it doesn't involve breaking and entering."

She sighed. "But is it the truth?"

"Yes. We're going to the tennis club. Can you be ready in an hour?"

"Of course, but why?"

"I'll explain when I get there."

He hung up, and Nicole was left staring at the phone. She had no plans for the day, so she might as well go along. She didn't want to spend it at home, anyway. The house felt so empty without Chrissie.

Yes, and wasn't it wonderful? Her mouth slowly widened into a grin. Might as well start checking some more items off on her get-Nicole-a-life list. And having some mysterious outing with Scott sounded like it definitely qualified.

Going to her closet, Nicole wondered what she should wear. She wasn't dumb enough to think they were actually going to play tennis, but she didn't think jeans and a T-shirt would be appropriate, either. She put on a pair of nice slacks and a conservative short-sleeved blouse. It would have to do.

As she brushed her hair, she wondered why she was doing this. With any other man, this excursion might feel a bit uncomfortable after last night, but Scott's teasing tone hadn't allowed it, hadn't even admitted any awkwardness might exist.

Nicole felt it, though. And she couldn't forget that she had made the mistake of succumbing to his charm the night before . . . something she had vowed not to do. She could see past the surface to the man underneath, so why had she given in to temptation?

Precisely because she could see through him. His undeniable charm made her feel all woman, but the man beneath the façade challenged her, made her want to know more. It was a devastating combination, especially when he took pains to keep the real Scott Richmond hidden.

Luckily, Nicole was very good at research, at uncovering hidden nuggets of information. He made her want to dig deeper, to get to know him until his soul was laid bare.

Instead, she was the one who had been laid bare the night before. Almost, anyway. If it hadn't been for Marta showing up when she had, Nicole might have found herself naked and spread-eagled beneath him. She still felt a little warm when she remembered the feel of his mouth on her breast.

No. She wouldn't allow it. She wouldn't let herself be seduced by this man, not when she had the feeling he treated it like a game. She hated feeling like a pawn—just another expendable playing piece. She would try to stay out of the game as much as possible, and once this farce of an engagement was over, she would make sure she never saw him again. It ought to be easy since they sure didn't play in the same sandboxes.

But, for now, they had to work together, for Chrissie's sake and his mother's. *So why not enjoy it while it lasts?* a little voice asked inside her.

Nicole tried to ignore it. Listening to little voices was what got people into trouble, what made people like Scott so impulsive and unpredictable. On the other hand, people like Nicole played it smart and suppressed those voices. It was safer that way. And often boring.

She heard a knock on the door and opened it. It was Scott, looking as delicious as ever in casual slacks and a shirt. Nicole's heart skipped a beat, and she sternly ordered it to stop. Skipping hearts should be firmly locked away, right next to little voices.

"Ready?" he asked with a grin.

"Yes, but . . . why are we going to the tennis club?"

"I'll tell you on the way," he said as he stepped aside and motioned her outside.

Scott cocked a significant glance in the direction of Missy's house, and Nicole dropped the subject. She didn't want to chance running into her neighbor. Once on the road, though, she asked him again.

"Mrs. Wyndham and her cronies like to spend Saturdays at the club," he explained.

"But I don't play tennis." Well, except for a little bit in high school, but that was so long ago as to be useless.

"Who does? People like Mrs. Wyndham mainly go there to eat, chat, and see their friends."

"So why are we going?"

"I figure we can have lunch and, with any luck, we'll run into Mrs. Wyndham."

"And what? Invite ourselves to her house?"

"You got it."

"That's it? That's the extent of your plan?" She should have known.

"What's wrong with that? I'll just play it by ear."

"That may work for you, but I'm not good at that sort of thing. I need more planning, more guidance, and more of an idea of what to expect."

Scott slanted her a wry glance before turning his attention back to the road. "You don't need as much as you think you do, but to make you feel better, how much do you know about gardening?"

"Not much, but if you give me a few hours, I could do some research and—"

"No time. Besides, you don't really need to know a whole lot. All you need to know is that Mrs. Wyndham is passionate about miniature roses. She has an entire room devoted to them in her house. See if you can get invited to see them."

Just like that, huh? He made it sound so easy. "Why don't you get yourself invited?"

"Because I doubt she'll suddenly believe I have a passion for flowers after all these years of indifference."

"Oh." But she wasn't as quick as Scott. How was she going to do as he asked? She spent the rest of the ride trying to come up with casual ways to drop the topic of miniature roses into the conversation. Unfortunately, she didn't have any inspiration. She'd just have to follow Scott's lead and play it by ear, hoping something came up. The whole situation made her nauseous.

They arrived at the club then, and Scott led her into the chichi restaurant, glancing around. "There she is, with Mrs. Harding and Mrs. Larson."

All three buyers. Nicole had thought Chrissie was exaggerating about making them the offer at the club, but if they often hung out together, maybe she was telling the truth this time.

"Let's head in that direction," Scott murmured.

With his hand at her waist, Nicole walked toward the three, not sure how to feel. She had embarrassed herself last night in Mrs. Harding's bedroom. Or rather, Scott had embarrassed her by pretending she was upset by their fight. Would Sara Harding be upset at Nicole?

Then again, these three women had bought stolen jewels. Maybe Nicole shouldn't be so concerned about what they thought.

That helped, and she was able to smile when Scott "accidentally" ran into them. Nicole had already met them at the party, so she was able to smile and nod without feeling out of place.

"Scott, dear," Mrs. Wyndham said. "Our waiter seems to have disappeared. Could you track him down for us? We'll take care of your fiancée while you're gone."

"Of course," Scott said, and gave Nicole a significant glance that indicated he expected her to take advantage of the opportunity.

Great, just great.

"Please have a seat," Mrs. Harding said.

"Yes," Mrs. Larson agreed, "please do. And tell us, do you have a date set for the wedding yet?"

Glad for a question she could answer honestly, Nicole said, "Not yet." Then, sensing they wanted more, she added Scott's story. "I'm waiting to find out when my sister can join us from New York." *Please don't ask me her name or to see a picture,* she begged silently. Then, with sudden inspiration, she added, "But I have started looking for dresses, flowers, and that sort of thing."

"Really?" Mrs. Harding asked. "Do you know what your colors will be?"

What colors did miniature roses come in? Nothing strange, she was sure. "Oh, nothing special," Nicole said with a deprecating smile. "I was thinking about something simple, like pink and ivory."

"A delightful combination," Mrs. Larson said. "Not outlandish like some of the weddings I've been to lately. Why, the Landover girl had her attendants wear purple of all things."

Sara Harding grimaced. "And a garish shade at that. It was horrible."

Trying to steer the conversation back to where she wanted it, Nicole said, "I don't want anything that unusual, though I thought I might do something a bit different with the flowers and decorations."

"Like what?" Mrs. Larson asked, a wary light in her eye.

"Oh, I don't know. Maybe use miniature pink roses. I think they would look so pretty in a bouquet with baby's breath, and they're just a little out of the ordinary."

"Why, that's a wonderful idea," Mrs. Wyndham said, her face brightening with enthusiasm. "Do you know much about miniature roses?"

"No," Nicole said, not wanting to be caught out in a big lie where she could so easily be tripped up. "I'm not a gardener. But I had a friend who had a couple of plants, and they were so adorable, I decided I wanted to have them in a bouquet someday." The little lies were a lot easier . . . .

"Well," Claire Wyndham said, "I raise the minis, you know."

"You do?" Nicole tried to look suitably astonished. "Maybe you could advise me, then, on what would be best?"

"I'd love to." The older woman thought for a moment. "I know, why don't you come over next Saturday? I could show you my minis, and we could talk about what would suit your bouquet."

"That sounds wonderful," Nicole said, feeling smug that she had managed to acquire the invitation without Scott's help.

Scott arrived then, saying, "The waiter will be shortly here with your lunches." Then he turned to Nicole with a quizzical look. "Did I hear you say Saturday?"

"Yes," Claire declared. "I want to show Nicole my roses."

Nicole added, "I'm thinking about using miniature roses for my bouquet, and Mrs. Wyndham was kind enough to offer to show me hers. We don't have anything planned next weekend, do we?"

"No," Scott said. "We'll be happy to come on Saturday."

Though the invitation had really been only for Nicole, he had accepted for both of them as she hoped.

"Wonderful," Claire said. "Is two o'clock all right?"

"Perfect." Scott paused, then gave a hesitant glance back the way he had come and lowered his voice. "You know, while I was looking for your waiter, I talked to a man at the bar. Someone stole his wife's jewelry last night."

"Really?" Mrs. Wyndham said.

Uh-oh. Where was Scott going with this? But when Nicole glanced apprehensively at the other two women, she realized they weren't even paying attention. When the conversation had switched to roses, they had withdrawn to talk about something else.

Scott nodded, keeping his attention focused on Claire Wyndham. "Right out of her bedroom." He gave her a concerned look. "I know you have some stunning jewelry. I hope yours is safe?"

"Oh, yes," she said with relief. "It's not in the bedroom. I keep it in a safe in my husband's study."

And though Nicole looked carefully, she couldn't see anything but faint alarm and concern in the older woman's expression. Didn't the mention of jewel theft give her even the smallest hint of remorse or guilt? Evidently not. Did moving in society make you an actress?

"Good," Scott declared. "And does it have a good lock on it?"

"The best," she declared. "With a combination lock that is very difficult to pick."

"I'm glad to hear that," Scott said. As the waiter arrived with a laden tray, he said, "We'll leave you to your lunch, then, and see you next Saturday."

Claire Wyndham nodded graciously. "I'm looking forward to it."

As Scott and Nicole seated themselves at a table on the far side of the room, she felt like kicking him. "Why did you ask about security?" she whispered fiercely.

He shrugged. "I wanted to know what we were up against. And I found out, didn't I?"

"Why didn't you just ask her for the combination while you were at it?" she asked, unable to stop the sarcasm.

He grinned. "You think she'd give it to me?"

"Of course not. You've probably already made her suspicious. What will she think now if she catches you in the same room with her safe?"

"Don't worry, she won't."

He was a bit overconfident. "And how do you

propose to get the combination? You won't be able to rely on luck for that."

"No, I plan to rely on you."

"What?" Though he was grinning, she had the distinct impression he wasn't kidding.

"I have a friend in the security business. He says most people don't use random numbers for combination locks. Instead, they use numbers they can remember, like birthdays or social security numbers. That's where you come in."

"Me?" she asked, though she had a sinking feeling she knew where he was headed with this.

"Sure. You're the one with the research skills. Just find out all the birthdays, anniversaries, and other numbers related to Claire and her family. I'll take it from there. While you're in one room sniffing flowers, I'll be exchanging emeralds and diamonds in another."

So much for leaving the dirty work to Scott. Somehow Nicole seemed to be getting sucked in deeper and deeper every day.

Scott had hoped to spend the whole day with Nicole, and he had gotten his wish but not quite in the way he wanted. Instead of a lazy day getting to know each other, they had spent most of the time talking about Chrissie's adventures in New York or him watching Nicole ferret information out on the computer.

Not exactly romantic. Then again, she had seemed a little spooked after their intimate interlude the night before, so he had tried to keep things cool. Maybe it had worked too well.

Now it was past ten o'clock on a Saturday night, he was alone with his fiancée, and what was he doing? Following her into the library, of all things. "Why are we doing this again?" he asked in plaintive tones.

"I told you," Nicole said as she unlocked the library door. "I couldn't find all those dates you wanted, but I have access to some databases here at work that I can't get to from home."

"Oh, yeah." More work. "But why am I here?" Surely this was something she could do on her own.

"So you can play lookout for me," she reminded him. "The library is closed, but they sometimes have a night watchman making the rounds or other people working late."

"Is it a problem for you to be here?"

"Not really." She lowered her voice to a whisper. "But I just want some warning so I'll have time to get rid of any incriminating evidence on the screen. Okay?"

"Okay," Scott said, but he resigned himself to living through another boring hour or two watching her coax information from the computer.

He followed her into the shadowy library. It was kind of eerie being here at night, in the silent darkness. He could almost feel the weight of all that knowledge measuring him, summing him up . . . finding him wanting. Creepy. He shivered.

"What's wrong?" Nicole asked.

"I don't know. The books seem to be . . . watching me," Scott said with a grin. "I can handle disapproving people, but inanimate objects with attitude are another story."

Nicole chuckled. "It's all right. It's probably because we just passed through the mystery section. Those books are naturally suspicious, you know."

He laughed in delight. "That explains it, then."

"But don't worry, the ones in the reference section are mostly old and stodgy, concerned only with their own self-importance. They won't care what you do."

Liking this whimsical side of her, Scott pulled her into the dark area between two sets of shelves. "Let's go in here, then," he said in a low, suggestive tone.

Stopping in the center of the aisle, he stood as close as he dared and lightly ran his fingers down her arms. Encouraged by the goosebumps he felt on her skin, he leaned down to whisper in her ear, "Can you feel it?"

"Feel what?"

"The ambiance. I sense . . . first kisses, exotic places, romantic evenings, steamy thoughts, and hot, lusty bodies. This must be the romance section."

"Wrong," she whispered back, pushing him away. "It's juvenile."

Ouch. Another mood ruined. With resignation, he followed her to the reference section.

Once there, she turned on a desk light and powered up the computer. "I don't want to turn on the overhead lights," she explained. "It might draw too much attention."

Soon she was seated at the desk, staring intently at the computer screen. He angled behind her to get a look at what she was doing.

She glanced over her shoulder at him. "I'm sorry,

but it makes me uncomfortable when someone hovers behind me."

"Shall I pull up a chair?"

"Well, no," she said frankly, though she looked a little embarrassed. "You're supposed to be the lookout, remember? Can you just sit somewhere else and look . . . out? It shouldn't take too long—I only need a few more dates."

"All right," he said grudgingly as he wandered over to look out the window. This wasn't at all what he had in mind for the evening. And the view outside was uninspiring. He glanced back at Nicole, seated in a small pool of light in the otherwise dark library.

Now there was an inspiring view. She looked focused, intelligent, and competent as her fingers flew over the keys. He found her absorption incredibly sexy.

Sometimes he wondered about himself. Tight clothing, revealing cleavage, long legs . . . those things were sexy. Not a bookworm staring at a computer screen, right?

He heard the printer start up as Nicole grinned. "I found it."

"Found what?" a woman asked from out of the shadows.

Nicole jumped in surprise and let out a little screech. Not sure if he'd been seen, Scott moved into the shadows as the woman he'd seen at the library the other day came into the light. Some lookout he was—he hadn't seen or heard her come in.

"Alyx, you scared me," Nicole said, with a hand over her heart. "What are you doing here?"

"I left my wallet in the back by mistake, then saw the light on from outside. I thought I'd check to see what's going on, especially since there have been a few thefts lately of personal property."

"I wouldn't steal anything," Nicole said.

"I know, so what *are* you doing here?"

Panic flashed momentarily across Nicole's face. "I, uh, had some research to do. With Chrissie gone, I couldn't sleep so I thought I'd do some work."

From the doubting expression on Alyx's face, Scott could tell she wasn't buying it. Stepping out of concealment, he said, "She's looking something up for me."

Now it was Alyx's turn to jump and screech. "You scared me," she accused, in almost the exact same tone Nicole had used to her.

"Sorry, I figured you knew I'd be wherever Nicole was."

Alyx glanced back and forth between them. Scott kept his expression bland, but Nicole's guilt-filled expression was a dead giveaway.

"What's going on here?" Alyx asked. "Are you doing something you shouldn't?" She crossed to the desk and pulled out the page Nicole had printed. "Names and dates . . . what is this?"

Scott shrugged. "I needed a few birthdays, and Nicole said she'd look them up for me."

"Uh huh." But Alyx didn't sound convinced.

"Come on, this is Nicole we're talking about. You know she's a straight arrow."

"I know," Alyx said. "But I don't know about you." Turning to Nicole, she asked, "Did he talk you into this?"

"Yes, but—"

"I knew it," Alyx declared. "What's he making you do?"

"Nothing," Nicole said.

"Yeah, right." Alyx flourished the paper at her. "What's this? A list of drug drops or something?"

It was so ridiculous, Scott couldn't help but laugh. "No, no, nothing like that."

Alyx glared at him. "Well, you'd better tell me what it is right now, or I'm calling the cops."

For a small thing, she sure was gutsy. And it appeared she wasn't buying his birthday story. He glanced at Nicole with a raised eyebrow.

"We'd better tell her the truth," Nicole said with a sigh.

Scott shrugged. It was Nicole's decision.

Quickly, Nicole explained about Chrissie's adventures in thievery and what they were trying to do.

"I don't get it," Alyx said. "You're trying to give these women the real jewels . . . in place of the stolen fakes they have?" When Nicole nodded, Alyx said, "Why?"

Nicole glanced uncertainly at Scott, evidently unwilling to expose his family skeletons as she had hers.

"That's where I come in," Scott said. If Nicole trusted Alyx, he could, too. "My mother has reported the real jewels stolen, but with an investigator nosing around, I'm afraid he'll find out she still has them and prosecute her for insurance fraud. Plus, if those three women find out they have fake jewels, I'm afraid of what they might do to my mother."

"What *could* they do?" Alyx asked.

He shrugged. "I wouldn't put it past them to have the jewels returned, then start a whispering campaign about how everything she has is fake. It would devastate her."

Alyx shook her head. "You two have quite the relatives, don't you?"

Nicole sighed. "You see why we need to replace the jewels? We hope these numbers will get us into the second safe."

"Why don't you just tell them the truth and give 'em the real gems?"

"Bad idea," Scott said. "What am I supposed to say? 'I know you bought my mother's stolen jewelry, but I promise I won't tell. And, by the way, those are fake. Here, let me give you the real ones.'"

Alyx still looked suspicious. "How do I know you're telling the truth?"

Nicole looked indignant. "Would I make up something that complicated?"

"No, but *he* might."

Scott hid a smile. All too true.

"It's true," Nicole assured her. "Chrissie admitted it to me. That's why I sent her off to school early."

"So . . . this is how you really met?" Alyx asked.

As Nicole nodded, Scott said, "Yes, Nicole showed up at my door hoping to stop Chrissie, but it was too late, so we cooked up this plan between us."

"Then you're not really engaged?"

"I'm afraid not," Nicole said. Then, in a rush, she added, "I wanted to tell you, but then I'd have to tell you everything else and I was afraid that if the police questioned you, you'd be in trouble for concealing evidence."

Alyx waved that away as if it were inconsequential. "I wondered why you hadn't asked me to be in your wedding," she murmured.

"Oh, Alyx," Nicole said, looking stricken. "If there was a wedding, you'd be my maid of honor—you know that. I didn't ask you because I knew there wasn't going to *be* one."

Looking rueful, Alyx said, "I realize that now. So, is there any way I can help?"

"No, you keep out of it," Nicole declared.

"I don't know," Scott said. "Maybe she can help. And it will convince her we're doing exactly what we said we were."

"What can I do?" Alyx asked, perking up.

Nicole glared at Scott. "Don't even think about involving her. She's my best friend, and I don't want her getting into trouble because of me."

Alyx's smile widened. "Hey, what are friends for?"

"My thoughts exactly," Scott said, smiling back at her. "Besides, if we don't convince her, she might still go to the police."

"I might at that," Alyx said with a grin.

Nicole looked upset with both of them. "What did you have in mind?"

"You said yourself she would be your maid of honor. Don't you think it's appropriate to have her along next weekend to look at flowers with you?" Quickly, he explained the plan to Alyx. "If the two of you can keep Mrs. Wyndham occupied with the flowers, I can slip away and exchange the jewels." When Nicole looked doubtful, he added, "You're always worried about thinking on your feet. I bet with two of you there, there won't be any problem."

"True," Alyx said. "And it sounds like fun. Let's do it."

Nicole shook her head. "You are two of a kind. What happens if we get caught? I'm already in this up to my neck, but you're squeaky clean, Alyx. Why don't you leave it that way?"

"Oh, no, you're not keeping me out of this one. You owe me for not telling me the truth. Besides, I bet Scott here could talk his way out of hell with the devil." Turning around, she tossed over her shoulder, "I'm coming along. Count on it." And with an airy wave, she left.

Scott laughed. Alyx wasn't allowing any more room for argument.

Nicole glared at him. "It's not funny."

"No, it's great. *She's* great. I like your friend."

"So do I, and I don't want to see her get hurt."

"She won't."

"She'd better not," Nicole warned him. "Or I'll know exactly who to blame."

Chapter Eight

It was Sunday afternoon, and somehow Scott had managed to convince Nicole to invite him and Alyx over to do some planning. Handing them each a glass of iced tea, Nicole joined them at the dining room table, prepared to do battle.

Coming right to the point, she said, "I still think this is a bad idea."

Alyx frowned. "We went over this last night—"

"Yes, and I didn't agree then. Not only is it dangerous, but wouldn't it be rather rude to show up on Mrs. Wyndham's doorstep with an extra guest?"

"It won't be a problem," Scott assured her. "I'll call her and explain that you want your maid of honor to help you select your flowers. Claire loves to show off her roses. I'm sure she'll be more than happy to have a bigger audience."

"Besides," Alyx added, "it doesn't sound dangerous at all."

Nicole shook her head impatiently. "I don't mean danger in the physical sense, though that's still a possibility. But . . . what if we get caught? What if they think we're stealing and call the police? What if you're arrested for burglary?" Alyx was as impulsive as Scott—couldn't she see the danger?

Alyx waved that away as inconsequential. "You worry too much. That's why we're here now, to make enough contingency plans so we *won't* get caught."

"And to come up with plausible stories in case we do," Scott added.

"Yeah," Alyx said. "And so what if they do catch us? What are they gonna do? Call the police to say that someone broke into their safe to replace their stolen fake jewelry with the real stuff?"

"What if they caught us with our hands in the safe?" Nicole asked. "You think the police would believe we were putting the real jewels in and taking the fake ones out?"

Scott shook his head. "It wouldn't get that far. Alyx is right. We definitely have leverage to talk them out of it."

"Better living through blackmail?" Nicole asked sarcastically. "That's illegal, too, you know."

"I know," Scott said with a raised eyebrow. "And I hope to avoid it altogether by making a foolproof plan."

"Come on," Alyx coaxed. "It'll be fine, you'll see. Besides, you wouldn't want to cheat me out of the most excitement I've had in years, would you?"

Nicole gave her friend an exasperated look. "If you want excitement, why on earth did you become a librarian?"

Alyx shrugged. "I like books, too. Can't I have both?"

Nicole understood the desire to want more out of life than a job, but Alyx's question left her a little bemused. "Why have I never seen this side of you before?"

"It never came up. But now that it has, I'm going for it."

Sighing, Nicole realized that she wasn't going to be able to convince them to see it her way. And Alyx would think her a horrible friend if Nicole deprived her of her fun. "All right. But we're going to be very careful and not take any chances, right?"

"Sure, sure," Alyx said, and Scott echoed her.

Unconvinced, Nicole tried not to feel resentful that she was the one doing the worrying for all of them.

Quickly, Scott sketched out a plan for the Wyndham house. "The roses are in an atrium at the back of the house on the right," he explained. "And the study with the safe in it is in the middle left. Both on the ground floor."

Nicole frowned. "So how are we going to make the switch if we're in one room and the safe is in another?"

"That's why I thought it would be nice to have Alyx along," Scott said. "As extra distraction."

"Distraction? I can do that," Alyx said eagerly.

Scott grinned. "Good. Once we're in the garden, I'll need to find an excuse to leave you for a while. While you keep Mrs. Wyndham occupied, I'll make the switch."

"Are the jewels going to fit in your pocket this time?" Nicole asked.

"No, the tiara is too big." He paused. "Oh, I see what you mean. We'll need to use your purse again."

"Oh, I know," Alyx said, flapping her hands in excitement. "Nicole can sort of casually leave her purse in the foyer when no one's looking, then she can send you back for it."

"That'll work," Scott said with an approving grin. "And I'll act bored, so Mrs. Wyndham won't be surprised if I take my time about it. You two can keep her so busy with questions that she won't even notice I'm gone."

"Perfect," Alyx exclaimed.

Nicole wasn't so sure, but these two were so busy congratulating each other that they didn't want to hear her objections.

They spent some more time ironing out the details, then Scott glanced at his watch. "Sorry, I have to go now. I promised Mother I'd meet her at home."

Nicole walked him to the door, and when they got there, he leaned down to say, "See you later, honey."

Without thinking, Nicole raised her face to his and he planted a brief, hot kiss on her lips that left her nerve endings tingling and begging for more.

Embarrassed by her instinctive reaction, she said, "Wait a minute. That wasn't necessary—Alyx knows our engagement isn't real."

"Oh, that's right," Scott said with a wink at Alyx. "But you have to admit it was fun." Grinning, he opened the door.

He didn't get very far, though. There stood Missy with her hand upraised to knock, wearing a low-cut sequined evening gown, three-inch heels, two pounds of makeup, and a cloud of cloying scent. "Well, hello," she said in a low, throaty voice, gazing up at Scott. "I didn't know you had company, Nicole."

Yeah, right. Like the two cars out front weren't a dead giveaway. Nicole raised an eyebrow. "So you thought you'd just drop by in your evening gown? On a Sunday afternoon?"

Missy wriggled, trying to show off her meager assets. "I just wanted to get your opinion on the dress. Do you think it'll be okay for the nightclub?"

Nicole considered. "Well, it's a little over the top—"

"I think men will just love it," Missy said, not even listening to Nicole's response. She lowered her voice even more and gave Scott a smoky glance. "Especially when they think about taking it off me . . . ." And she ran a finger suggestively down her barely visible cleavage.

She was so obvious, Nicole tried to suppress a smile.

Scott didn't even try. "You know," he said with a grin as he squeezed past Missy in the doorway and headed for his car, "I was wrong about you."

"You were?" Missy almost purred, and Nicole could see the smug satisfaction in her eyes as she teetered after him on her high heels.

"Yes," Scott said as he pulled out his keys. Opening the car door, he looked back at her and gave her an appreciative once-over. "Remind me to introduce you to my cousin—you look great in drag."

Missy's mouth dropped open, and she seemed frozen in disbelief as Scott drove away from the curb with a jaunty wave.

Nicole couldn't help it—she chuckled. But when Missy clenched her fists and made a strangled sound of frustration, Nicole decided that retreat was advisable and closed the door.

Behind her, Alyx laughed. "So that was the infamous Missy, huh? She's even worse than you described."

"Well, this was a bit much, even for her."

"I wonder what she'll do next to convince Scott she's all woman?"

Nicole shuddered as she led the way to the living room. "I don't want to know. Maybe I should take pity on him and tell him to stay away."

Alyx dropped onto the love seat in the living room as Nicole took a seat opposite her on the couch. Giving her a sly smile, Alyx asked, "You think you can do that?"

"Do what?"

"Tell him to stay away."

"Sure. Once we fix this mess, there will be no more reason for the engagement—and no reason to see each other anymore." The thought gave her an unaccustomed pang of regret.

"And how do you feel about that?"

When Nicole hesitated, Alyx added, "No need to lie—I can see it in your face. You're gone on the guy."

That was a bit of an exaggeration. "Well, he is attractive, in a boyish sort of way—"

"Attractive, hell. I've seen him kiss you twice now. Both times I thought you were going to melt into a puddle of pure goo at his feet."

Nicole made a face. "Ick, what an image." But it did rather describe how she felt in Scott's arms. When Alyx gave her a warning look, Nicole added, "Okay, so his kisses are to die for. That doesn't mean I'm in love with him."

"Aren't you?"

Nicole didn't even want to think about the possibility. "It would be stupid to fall in love with him. Once this is over, I'll probably never see him again."

"I doubt that," Alyx said with a laugh.

"What do you mean?"

"Well, it's obvious the guy can't keep his hands—or his lips—off you. If you ask me, he's not gonna let you dissolve the relationship that easily."

Nicole's heart skipped a beat at the thought, but she sternly told it to behave. It was wishful thinking, that was all. "It wouldn't work," she said aloud as she twisted the engagement ring on her finger. "We're from two different worlds, with two totally different personalities."

"Ever hear the saying 'opposites attract'?" Alyx drawled.

"Yes, but attraction isn't enough. There's no foundation for a relationship. We have nothing in common, really."

Alyx chuckled. "Nothing but the hots for each other. Wonderful marriages have been built on less, you know." She rose and slung her purse onto her shoulder. "I guess I'd better go, too."

Nicole felt her cheeks burn as she let herself consider the possibilities for a moment. A life with Scott would be . . . fun. Laughter-filled days and love-filled nights. What more could she want?

Oh, maybe . . . reality?

Rising to walk Alyx to the door, Nicole said, "I appreciate what you're trying to do, but really, it wouldn't work. I told him I wouldn't fall for his charm and he sees me as a challenge. That's all." One she'd already lost, though she hadn't admitted it to him yet.

At the door, Alyx patted her on the arm. "You go on believing that, sweetie." Just as Nicole was shutting the door behind her friend, Alyx couldn't resist tossing out an exit line. "But don't forget I'm your maid of honor when you two get married."

As Scott drove to the library where he had arranged to meet Nicole and Alyx, he was surprised at his level of anticipation. He hadn't seen Nicole since last weekend, primarily because he hadn't been able to find a good reason to be with her—one she'd buy, anyway. She seemed apprehensive about being with him for *any* reason, except when they had to talk about the jewels or play his fiancée when his mother thought appropriate.

He had talked with Nicole a few times, but that wasn't nearly as satisfying as seeing her smile, hearing her laugh, feeling her body snuggled tight against his . . .

Get a hold of yourself, man, Scott told himself. *She doesn't see you in that way. At least, not yet.* But he was working on it . . . .

He arrived at the library where Nicole and Alyx were already waiting for him. Nicole glanced in surprise at the Mercedes he was driving. "Where's your Jag?"

"Three people wouldn't fit in it, so I borrowed my mother's car."

Alyx grinned. "Good thing you didn't pick us up at Nicole's house. Imagine how Missy would drool if she got a load of this."

That's exactly why they had arranged to meet at

the library. Scott opened the back door for Alyx then helped Nicole into the front seat.

"Wow," Alyx said, running her hands along the leather seat. "I could get used to this."

Seeing Nicole's tight smile, Scott figured she was still nervous. He'd just have to find a way to lighten her up or she'd give away the whole thing with her attitude.

He waved a padded envelope at her and lowered his voice to a conspiratorial whisper. "Hey, doll, I got the swag. You got the bag?"

Nicole gave him a small smile. "I couldn't use the purse you bought me—it's an evening bag. But I found a tote bag at the back of my closet that should do—it has a zipper, too, so you can't see inside."

"Perfect."

He started to slip the envelope inside, but Alyx said, "Wait, can I see them? I doubt I'll ever be this close to real gems again."

"Sure," Scott said. He passed the envelope to Alyx who poured the emeralds and diamonds into her lap.

"Wow, just think, Nicole. If you did marry him, all these would be yours someday."

Nicole rolled her eyes. "You mean the fakes would be mine. We're replacing them, remember? Besides, we're not getting married. And even if we did, could you see me wearing them at the library?"

Scott was tempted to suggest it might liven the place up, but kept his mouth shut.

"You know what I mean. Imagine actually being invited to a party where a diamond tiara wouldn't look ridiculous."

She lifted the tiara as if to try it on, but Nicole snatched it out of her hand. "Are you crazy? We don't want anyone to know we have these things here, in public."

Alyx regarded her friend with a puzzled expression. "Are you afraid someone might steal them?"

"No, I'm afraid someone who knows you will see you wearing diamonds you can't afford and start asking questions," Nicole said with a frown.

Alyx shrugged and put the jewels back in the envelope. "You're just afraid, period."

"Yes, I am," Nicole said in a tight voice. "And if you had any sense, you would be, too."

Whoa. Before Nicole could start a fight she didn't really mean, Scott said, "Better buckle up. It's time to head over to the Wyndhams'."

He kept up a light banter on the way over, and managed to relax Nicole a little. When they arrived at the Wyndham house and he helped her out of the car, Scott leaned down and pressed his lips to hers. Nothing suggestive, just a sweet kiss that claimed her as his to the world. Well, to anyone who was watching, anyway.

Looking a little flustered, Nicole said, "You didn't have to do that, not for Alyx's sake."

No, it was for my sake. "I did it in case anyone is watching from the house," he lied. And to give her something to think about besides the role she was about to play. She hadn't fought him, either, so Scott had hopes that if he kept kissing her at every opportunity, she might get used to it.

As he led her up the walk to the front door, Alyx gave him a surreptitious wink. She wasn't fooled, but it appeared she wasn't going to call him on it, either. At least he had Nicole's friend on his side.

"Don't forget to leave your bag in the foyer," Scott murmured. Nicole nodded in reply, though her grip seemed to tighten on the bag.

A short, portly butler with a ring of gray hair around his scalp opened the door, with Mrs. Wyndham and her maid right behind him.

As Claire Wyndham gave them a warm welcome, Scott watched out of the corner of his eye as Nicole casually let her purse slip from her shoulder to rest against the hallway table on the floor. He suppressed a smile. She had done it so smoothly, he never would have guessed that she hadn't practiced it.

"Come this way," Claire urged them. "I can't wait to show you my minis. Charlotte, get us some refreshments, won't you?"

As the maid left, presumably toward the kitchen, Mrs. Wyndham led them out the door to the right, but they were stopped by the butler who said, "Excuse me?"

"What is it, Weatherwax?" Mrs. Wyndham asked.

Weatherwax held up Nicole's bag and addressed her. "Is this yours, Miss?"

A look of dismay crossed her face, but was just as swiftly gone. "Oh, yes it is," she said with a shaky laugh. "How silly of me." She took the bag and followed Mrs. Wyndham and Alyx out the door once again. Dropping back, Nicole gave Scott an inquiring look as if to say, "What now?"

Scott shrugged and whispered, "Wait until we're out of sight of old eagle eye."

Nicole nodded, and when they stepped into the atrium, he gave her a nudge. Casually, she dropped the bag by the door, a little out of sight. Good. He had the list of potential combinations in his pocket. Now all he needed was an excuse to leave for a little while.

Mrs. Wyndham led them into the glass-walled atrium attached to the back of the house, and he was immediately hit with the lush scents of roses in bloom, rich soil, and moisture-laden air—a rarity in dry Denver. Small bushes, most no higher than a foot tall, bordered the atrium, and several tables were filled with potted plants. It seemed as if every one was in bloom, with rose colors running the gamut from white to deep red, lavender, pink, dark gold, and every shade in between.

Nicole stopped and smiled. "Oh, my. How beautiful."

She couldn't have said anything more calculated to please their hostess, though Scott could tell it wasn't calculated at all.

Alyx echoed her, and Mrs. Wyndham beamed. "Now, dear, what do you plan to use the roses for? Just your bouquet? Or throughout the entire wedding?"

"I hadn't really thought," Nicole said. "I guess throughout the whole wedding."

"Of course," Alyx exclaimed. "They would look great in your hair, in the bouquet, as a boutonniere, maybe even a little potted plant on each table as a centerpiece. You could have a whole miniature rose theme."

Nicole nodded, "Good idea."

Mrs. Wyndham smiled. "Yes, a wonderful idea. But what type of rose were you looking for, exactly? One of the larger miniature varieties, or one of the micro-minis? A fragrant rose, or one with less scent? An exhibition form or a modified tea hybrid?"

"I—I don't know," Nicole said in confusion. "I had no idea there were so many types."

Charlotte, the maid, entered and set down a tray containing a pitcher of iced tea and some glasses, along with some dainty cookies. "Excuse me, Miss," Charlotte said, "but I think you left your bag by the door."

She returned the bag to Nicole who gave her a weak smile of thanks. Scott could do nothing but shrug. Who knew the servants would be so conscientious?

As Scott and Alyx helped themselves to a glass of iced tea, Nicole took the opportunity once more to drop the bag—this time under one of the tables. As she did so, Nicole spoke, evidently to distract Mrs. Wyndham from noticing. "Why don't you show me some of each type so I can make a decision?"

"All right," Mrs. Wyndham said, pride clear in her expression. "Let's start with the micro-minis then, over in the far corner. They're the smallest of the miniatures roses and—" She broke off as she started to lead them away and glanced down beneath the table. "Dear, I think you've forgotten your purse again."

"Oh, so I have," Nicole said. Then with a glint in her eye, she picked it up and thrust it at Scott. "I don't seem to be able to hold onto it today. Would you watch it for me, honey?"

What an excellent idea—why hadn't he thought of that? "I'd be glad to," Scott said. Now that he had the jewels, all he needed was a good excuse to get away. He grinned to himself. Even better, what if he were sent away? Time to be obnoxious. "What's this one called?" he asked, pointing at an orange rose.

"That's Bambino," their hostess said.

Scott hid a grin. *Perfect.* "Hmm, better not choose that one," he advised. "Stick a bunch of Bambinos on the tables and wedding guests might be checking out Nicole's waistline."

When Claire did nothing but gape at him, he asked, "And what are those two called?"

"The white one with the pink edge is called Child's Play."

Scott shook his head. "Again, not a good idea. What about the white one with the red edge?" It looked a little racy.

Mrs. Wyndham opened her mouth as if to answer, then closed it again. "I don't remember," she said, not meeting his eyes.

With a spark of humor in her eyes, Alyx stepped forward to pull a little stick out of the plant. "It says here that the name is Whoopi."

"Whoopee?" Scott repeated in glee. "Oh, I like it. We can tell people there's whoopee on every table." He grinned at Nicole. "You'll have whoopee in your hair, whooppe in your bouquet, whoopee all over the place. They'll never forget this wedding."

"No, no, no," Mrs. Wyndham said, looking frantic. "It doesn't have that . . . that meaning. It's named for Whoopi Goldberg, the actress."

"We can keep that part to ourselves," Scott assured her. "Won't it be fun?"

"But Nicole said she wanted pink for her wedding, not red," the older woman said in desperation. "It wouldn't be suitable."

Nicole patted Mrs. Wyndham's hand and threw

Scott an annoyed glance that had humor hidden beneath it. "Scott is just joking," she assured Claire. "But you know, this decision is probably best left to us girls. Scott, why don't you go find a book to read or something? We'll let you know when we're done."

Oh, well done. But Scott pretended to be reluctant. "I don't know. You said you wanted me to be involved in all the decisions for the wedding . . . ." Then he smiled when Nicole frowned at him.

"Yes, of course," Alyx said briskly. "But there's really no room in here for this many people. Go away, Scott, and let Nicole surprise you."

"Oh, all right." But he hid a smile at the palpable relief on their hostess's face. Leaning down to kiss Nicole, he murmured, "Keep her busy until I get back."

Nicole nodded, and Scott made his way back to the foyer. Damn. The butler was there, talking to someone at the door. He shut the door and turned around just as Scott reached the study.

"May I help you, sir?" Weatherwax asked.

"Oh, no, thanks. The women kicked me out and told me to find a book to read. Is this the study?"

"Yes, sir. There are a few books here, on the far wall." Weatherwax opened the door, and Scott went in, glancing around.

As the stone-faced servant continued to watch from the door, Scott made a show of perusing the shelves, though he surreptitiously scanned the room, trying to figure out where the devil the safe could be. It wasn't in view, that was for sure.

He glanced back at the door and, seeing the man was gone, he grabbed a book at random then quickly tested paintings and panels on the wall. Not there. One wall was covered with draperies, and he pulled them aside impatiently. Ah, there it was, hidden behind a set of curtains that made it look like a false window.

"May I help you, sir?" Weatherwax asked once more.

Damn. Couldn't the man go away? "I was just . . . trying to open the windows to get some more light. It's too dark in here to read."

"I see," the man said, though his tone showed he didn't quite believe Scott. "Perhaps you would care to use the front parlor? The light is very good there."

"No, that's all right." Scott sat down in a leather chair by the window. "Wouldn't want to put you out."

"It's no bother," Weatherwax assured him.

"That's okay, I'll stay here." And if Weatherwax would just leave, he could get on with his business.

But the butler didn't seem to be in an accommodating mood. "I'm sorry, sir, but Charlotte is due to clean this room. I wouldn't want you to be disturbed."

Oh, wouldn't you? Scott toyed with the idea of insisting he send Charlotte back at another time, but it would look too suspicious. In this battle of wills, the butler won. "All right," Scott said, rising. "Show me to the parlor."

After Weatherwax deposited him there like an unwanted salesman, Scott sighed. He'd give the man a few minutes to go about his duties, then Scott would try again. He glanced down at the book in his hand, wondering if it would provide distraction. *Interim Report on Judicial Capacity Regarding Intellectual Property: Enforcement and Dispute Settlement.*

Now there was some scintillating reading. Discarding the book on a nearby table, Scott hauled Nicole's bag out to the hallway once again. But just as he left the room, Weatherwax appeared again in the hallway with a forbidding expression on his face. What? Did he have radar or something?

"Bathroom?" Scott inquired with a false smile.

Weatherwax pointed the way, and Scott went in to lean against the counter and brood. He could try getting in to the study all day, but he doubted the suspicious Weatherwax would let him near the room again. And though Scott had faith in Nicole and Alyx's ingenuity, he doubted they could keep Mrs. Wyndham busy much longer. He'd just have to give up for now.

With a sigh, he flushed the toilet, let the water run in the sink, then left the bathroom and nodded at Weatherwax as he breezed past. Scott could still feel the butler's suspicious gaze on the back of his neck, but since he was heading in the opposite direction from the study, the man didn't stop him.

When he entered the atrium again, Nicole was saying, "I just can't decide . . ." Her expression brightened when she saw Scott, showing more than a little relief. "Which one do you like?" She held out two plants to Scott, both with shell-pink roses.

"What are their names?"

"The bigger one is Baby Boomer," Claire told him. "It's fairly new. And the smaller one is Spice Drop."

He feigned disappointment. "Can't do anything with those names," he lied. "The color is good on both of them, but won't the bigger one be easier to . . . do things with?"

"Just what I said," Alyx exclaimed. "The micro-mini is cute, but the bigger boomers will make a nicer bouquet, and look fabulous in her hair. Plus they'll make a perfect size boutonniere."

Nicole sighed. "The Baby Boomer it is, then." Turning to their hostess, she said, "Thank you so much, Mrs. Wyndham, for letting us look at your roses and providing your expertise. I really appreciate it."

"I was happy to do it," the woman said, patting Nicole on the arm. "Just let me know when you set the date, and I can help you order them from my supplier."

"I will, thanks."

They said their good-byes and left the house.

Halfway to the car, Scott said, "Good job. You looked like you actually enjoyed that."

"We did," Nicole said. "It was fascinating, and those little roses are so cute. I just feel bad about deceiving Mrs. Wyndham."

"Did you do it?" Alyx asked Scott eagerly. "Did you make the switch?"

"Afraid not."

Nicole stopped dead and looked up at him in dismay. "You didn't? Why not?"

"The butler spied on me like he thought I was a thief or something," Scott said indignantly. "I didn't have a chance."

"What do we do now?"

"Isn't it obvious? We'll have to try this again." Then he grinned at the look of horror on her face.

* * *

Once again, Gerald found it necessary to make a phone call. Without preamble, he announced, "Scott Richmond went to the Wyndhams' yesterday."

"Damn," his associate said. "I don't suppose it's a coincidence?"

"I doubt it. I think he suspects something, but hasn't been able to prove it yet."

"You think he knows about me?"

"Not yet, and I hope he won't find out. You're our ace in the hole, and we need to keep it that way. You know what to do."

"Yes, I think the insurance investigator needs to know a little more about the origins of the jewels . . . ."

Chapter Nine

Four days later, Nicole was still wondering how on earth they were going to get back into the Wyndham house. Luckily, Scott and Alyx had seen the wisdom of not trying the same thing again, but since Scott had made Weatherwax suspicious of him, finding a way to switch the jewels was going to be difficult.

That evening Scott had persuaded Nicole to come for a family dinner so they could discuss the matter afterward. Nicole was wary of being alone with Scott, fearing she would succumb all too easily to his charm, but he had convinced her that having the occasional dinner with Grace and Gerald was necessary to continue the pretence of their engagement.

So, after work, Nicole drove over to the Richmond mansion where she was welcomed by Marta. Nicole felt a little embarrassed, considering the situation in which Marta had seen her last, but the housekeeper's stoic demeanor made the situation a lot less awkward than it could have been. She showed Nicole into the overdecorated drawing room where Scott, Grace, and Gerald were seated.

After they had all greeted each other, Grace asked, "Would you like something to drink?"

Why not? Everyone else seemed to have a drink in their hand, and she could use something to relax her. No matter how gracious Grace was, Nicole just didn't feel comfortable here. "A glass of white wine would be nice," Nicole said.

Scott poured her a glass of wine from the bar at the far end and brought it to her, seating himself next to her on the love seat. Nicole was glad of his presence—it gave her more self-confidence in dealing with his mother.

Grace moved to a chair closer to them. "I hear from Claire Wyndham that you visited her home the other day."

"Yes, I mentioned that miniature roses might be nice for the wedding so she invited us to see hers."

"That sounds lovely. Did you decide on colors, then?"

The doorbell rang, but since everyone else ignored it, so did Nicole. "Yes, I'm thinking of using pink and ivory." Actually, she would prefer something a lot bolder, but she had already mentioned these colors to Grace's friends, so she needed to be consistent.

Grace nodded approvingly. "That would look marvelous with your complexion." Marta arrived at the door then and Grace turned to her with a questioning look.

"Excuse me, ma'am, but there's a Mr. Digby here to see you. Says he has an appointment."

"An appointment?" Grace said in surprise. "Who is he? And why would he have an appointment at this hour?"

"I'm afraid I'm to blame for that," Gerald said. "Remember, Digby is the insurance investigator. You talked to him the other day."

"Oh, that's right," Grace said. "But why is he here now?"

Gerald patted her hand. "He had a few more questions for us, and I knew this was the only time we'd all be together. I hope you don't mind."

Us? What us? Did the man suspect Nicole? Why did he want to question her?

Nicole felt herself grow rigid, and Scott stroked her back soothingly. "Don't worry," he murmured. "It's just routine."

Maybe . . . and maybe not. She took a gulp of her wine.

"This will only help expedite your claim," Gerald added shrewdly.

"I suppose it's all right," Grace said. "Show him in, Marta."

Mr. Digby was a slight young man with thinning blond hair and an earnest expression. "Thank you for seeing me at this hour," he said. "I'll try not to keep you long."

He refused the offer of a drink but took a seat. Checking his notes, he said, "Now, Mr. Richmond, where were you on the night of the burglary?"

"Are you assuming the burglary was done the night before we found the jewels missing?" Scott asked.

Oh, good point. Nicole threw him an admiring glance. She wouldn't have thought of that.

"Yes. In our last meeting, Mrs. Richmond said she had opened the safe only a day or two before, and nothing was missing."

Scott nodded. "That night I was at a benefit dinner, and I didn't get home until midnight."

"Did you see or hear anything unusual when you got home?"

Nicole's heart raced. What would Scott say? She clutched at his hand, silently begging him not to be too flippant.

"Not really, no."

Digby jumped on that. "Not really? So you did see something unusual?"

"I meant only that it was very quiet, since all the servants were gone."

"And why was that?"

Scott nodded toward his mother. "Mother gave them the time off because she was out of town for the weekend."

Digby nodded. "How do you think the burglar got in?"

"It's hard to say. I would have thought it impossible with our security system, but obviously I was wrong."

"Does the system arm itself or does a person have to arm it?"

"It requires a person," Scott said.

"So, is it possible you forgot to arm it?"

"It's possible, I suppose." Scott paused. "I can't remember for sure if I did or not that night."

"Surely you did," Grace protested. "You always remember."

She sounded a little *too* eager to assure Digby of the fact. Grace was obviously worried that Digby might not pay on the claim if there was any hint that they hadn't done as they should.

"But the thief got in somehow," Digby said. "If

you didn't forget to arm it, then how did the thief know the code to get inside?"

Good question. They still hadn't figured out how Chrissie had managed it—she must have had inside help. Trying to find a plausible explanation Digby would accept, Nicole ventured, "Maybe the code was an easy one the thief could guess? Like Mrs. Richmond's birthday or something?"

"Was it?" Digby asked Scott.

Scott shook his head. "No, it's composed of random numbers."

"Then maybe someone wrote the code down where someone else found it?" Nicole said. *Come on, Scott. Work with me here.*

"That's possible," Scott said. "Mother, did you write it down somewhere?"

"Yes, you know how bad I am with numbers. But I have it well hidden. No one would know where to look for it."

"Who else knew the code?" Digby asked.

"Just the household staff," Scott said.

"And me," Gerald said.

Scott raised his eyebrows at that, but Grace said, "Oh, we can trust Gerald. He sometimes runs little errands for me, so he had to have access to the house. But he doesn't have the combinations to the safes."

Digby nodded. "Then it was probably an inside job."

"Nonsense," Grace exclaimed. "It couldn't be. I trust my staff implicitly."

"Then who could have done it?" Digby asked, no emotion showing on his face as he stared straight at Nicole.

Dear Lord, why was he looking at her? She shrugged helplessly. What could she say without sounding totally unbelievable? She wasn't good at lying. "I—I don't know."

"Some master criminal I suppose," Grace said with a dismissive wave of her hand.

Nicole almost choked at the thought of Chrissie being a master anything. To cover, she took another sip of wine.

Digby questioned them a little more on the background of the staff and the security system, then abruptly changed tactics. "I understand all of you were present when the jewels were discovered missing. Miss Dreyfuss, would you give your version of what happened?"

"M—me?" she stuttered.

"Yes. I've heard from the others; I wanted to get your account as well."

She took a fortifying sip before saying, "Well, I had come to see Scott, and we were talking when Mrs. Richmond and Mr. Wainwright came in."

"Talking where?"

"Here, in this room."

"Then what happened?"

"Mrs. Richmond said she needed to get something from the safe."

"What, exactly?"

"I'm not sure. I think she said it was a bracelet—a piece of jewelry, anyway. She said the clasp was loose, and Mr. Wainwright was going to get it fixed for her. So she opened the safe, then said her jewels were gone. She thought some of her knickknacks were missing, too, but Scott told her he had just sent them out for cleaning." There, she had managed to tell the truth without implicating anyone.

Digby nodded. "That tracks with what the others said."

Nicole relaxed a little. Okay, maybe she was home safe.

Then Digby asked, "Were the gemstones genuine?"

When she realized he was looking at *her* with a piercing gaze, Nicole almost gasped aloud, but turned it into a cough instead. What would make him ask that question?

Luckily, Grace answered for her. "Of course," she said in indignation. "My husband owned a jewelry store, and he was very particular and very knowledgeable about stones. Believe me, they were quite genuine."

Nicole watched, impressed. How did Grace manage to lie so easily?

Scott added, "I believe you have the appraisal— from an independent jeweler—in your files."

"Yes, of course," Digby said. He checked his notes again. "That's all I have for now, but if you think of anything, give me a call."

"We will," Scott assured him. But Nicole noticed that no one volunteered the information that Scott's father had also had imitations made of those same jewels.

Scott showed him out the door, but Nicole could only gulp down the rest of her wine. She had no head for alcohol, so it made her slightly tipsy, but it helped her to deal with the alarming nature of the insurance investigator's questions. Was he on to them? Is that why he'd asked those questions about security and fakes? And when could she get Scott alone to talk about this?

Unfortunately, she had to survive dinner first. She made it through somehow, fielding questions about their nonexistent wedding, and fending off inquiries about setting a date. It was difficult walking this fine line. She didn't want to raise suspicions by appearing as if she didn't care about her wedding, but she didn't want to set anything in stone, either, knowing everything would just have to be cancelled later.

Luckily, Scott helped as much as he could, steering the conversation in other directions and telling funny stories when it seemed Grace was about to grill her again.

The food had helped dull some of the effects of the several glasses of wine she had imbibed, but Nicole was still feeling rather mellow when Scott excused them both after dinner to talk in private.

He led her to his office where the clean lines of his furniture and lack of clutter immediately made her feel more relaxed. As she sank into a comfortable chair by his desk, she let out a sigh, though it came out louder than she intended.

Scott grinned. "It wasn't that bad, was it?"

"It was a bit of a strain," Nicole admitted. "Especially when that guy Digby started asking me questions."

"He wasn't singling you out for any nefarious reason. He had already talked to the rest of us."

"I don't think so," Nicole said, the wine making her tongue freer than normal. "Don't you think it's odd that he wanted my version of events when he already had yours? And why did he ask me about fakes? Do you think he suspects something?"

He grinned at her. "You worry more than anyone else I know."

"I do not," she said indignantly. *Do I?* Well, maybe she did, but someone had to do it. Scott certainly never did, nor did Chrissie or Alyx.

But how did this fit with her desire to be someone new and different? To cast off the old reliable Nicole and reinvent herself?

It didn't. Instead, she sounded like someone's mother, whining and worrying about what might happen instead of taking each day as it came.

"You're right," she said finally. "I do worry too much. But you don't seem to worry at all. How is that?"

He shrugged. "What good does it do? Whatever is going to happen will happen anyway. It doesn't help to worry about it."

"So, you believe everything is fated and can't be changed?"

"No, I didn't say that. I still try to influence the outcome. The difference is, I don't *worry* about it."

She wished she could do the same, especially where this insurance investigator was concerned. Then she realized Scott had never answered her question. "Do you think Digby suspects something?"

"It did seem that way," Scott conceded. "But his questions might have just been routine."

"Or they might have been very pointed—specifically to us. I got the feeling he was trying to scare me."

Scott cocked his head and regarded her with a curious look. "Why would he do that?"

"To make me say something I shouldn't?"

"You're assuming he knows there's something wrong about this burglary?"

"Yes, don't you?"

"Maybe. Maybe not."

His seeming lack of concern irritated her. "Well, if you're not going to worry about it, can you at least think what we could do to convince him everything is okay?"

"I have thought about it," Scott assured her. "But take a minute and think it through yourself. What could we do?"

All right, she'd play it his way. Thinking aloud, she said, "The main problem is that some of the real jewels are still in your mother's safe. If he thinks to check the other safe and finds that out, she's in real trouble."

Scott nodded. "And if he finds only fakes?"

"We never mentioned them so he still might suspect, but he can't prove anything. Your mother couldn't be prosecuted for fraud."

"Exactly."

"Then," she continued slowly, "we should continue doing exactly what we were doing—replace the fake gems with the real ones. We have to keep on with the original plan, and do it as soon as possible." No matter how wrong it felt.

"Give the lady a prize," Scott said with a smile.

"Okay, you're right. I'll even do it without complaint," Nicole said with a sigh. "And I'll try to stop worrying."

Scott looked taken aback. "Really? Why?"

She shrugged. "Now that Chrissie's gone and I don't have to be the responsible one, I feel as if I can finally emerge from my chrysalis." The only question was what would emerge when her transformation was complete—a moth or a butterfly? "I just want to find out who I'm going to be. Right now, I'm a work in progress, trying new things to see if they fit."

"Ah, I've seen flashes of that work in progress. And I must say, I like the Nicole I see."

"You do?" That was the riskiest part—trying out her new wings without leaving the cocoon.

"Yes. So, tell me," he said with a confiding grin, "what other new things have you always wanted to try?"

"Oh, I don't know." She let her imagination roam wild, her mind and tongue freed by the wine. "The list is in flux all the time, but I'd like to do lots of things, like fly in a hot air balloon, take singing lessons, hike through Europe, shoot the rapids, learn how to paint, have a mad, passionate fling with a total stranger—"

She broke off, and tension abruptly filled the space between them, as if all the air molecules had suddenly started vibrating as fast as a hummingbird's wing.

Sparks lit in Scott's eyes. He left his perch on the desk to lean on the arms of her chair and gaze into her eyes. "Will I do?" he asked with a smoldering look.

She swallowed hard, wanting to say yes but holding back as the old, sensible Nicole warred with the new, adventurous one. Both of them wanted him, but one argued it would be folly while the other wanted to drown in his caresses. "You're no stranger," she whispered.

"Perhaps not." He nuzzled her cheek with his nose, letting his lips come to rest under her ear as he murmured, "But mad, passionate love I can do. Just say the word."

Indecision kept her motionless. His suggestive tone left her quivering with need, but she had never let herself be ruled by her emotions. Should she let go now? Could she afford to fall for him and risk being hurt?

Apparently taking her silence as assent, Scott kissed her. Only their lips touched as he explored her mouth thoroughly, hungrily. Her resistance dissolved, and she wrapped her arms around his shoulders. He pulled her to her feet, and they fused together as they devoured each other with kisses.

Finally, Scott pulled back for a moment. "You taste like wine," he said softly. "Tell me, is this the new Nicole responding . . . or is it the wine?"

"A little of both," Nicole admitted breathlessly. The wine helped her break through that shell, but she suspected it was Scott himself who made her feel giddy.

"Ah," Scott said, sounding disappointed as he pulled away. "I was afraid of that."

She reached for him. "Why?"

"I don't want to take advantage of you in a vulnerable state." He kissed her on the nose. "But if you feel the same way when you're sober, give me a call."

Damn. That was the problem. Sober, she'd never have the courage to make the first move.

Zebra Contemporary

To start your membership, simply complete and return the Free Book Certificate. You'll receive your Introductory Shipment of FREE Zebra Contemporary Romances, you only pay $1.99 for shipping and handling. Then, each month you will receive the 4 newest Zebra Contemporary Romances. Each shipment will be yours to examine FREE for 10 days. If you decide to keep the books, you'll pay the preferred subscriber price (a savings of up to 30% off the cover price), plus shipping and handling. If you want us to stop sending books, just say the word… it's that simple.

FREE BOOK CERTIFICATE

Yes, Please send me FREE Zebra Contemporary romance novels. I only pay $1.99 for shipping and handling. I understand that each month thereafter I will be able to preview 4 brand-new Contemporary Romances FREE for 10 days. Then, if I should decide to keep them, I will pay the money-saving preferred subscriber's price (that's a savings of up to 30% off the retail price), plus shipping and handling. I understand I am under no obligation to purchase any books, as explained on this card.

Name _____

Address _____ Apt.___

City _____ State _____ Zip _____

Telephone (___) _____

Signature _____

(If under 18, parent or guardian must sign)

Offer limited to one per household and not to current subscribers. Terms, offer and prices subject to change. Orders subject to acceptance by Zebra Contemporary Book Club. Offer Valid in the U.S. only.

Thank You!

CN035A

llı.ılı.....lll.ıılllı.lıl.ıllı.lıl.ılllı.ıllı.ll

Zebra Contemporary Romance Book Club
Zebra Home Subscription Service, Inc.

P.O. Box 5214
Clifton , NJ 07015-5214

PLACE
STAMP
HERE

Chapter Ten

Scott met with Nicole and Alyx on Friday night at his home. The two women had arrived together, and Alyx was glancing around as if trying to memorize everything in the overdecorated drawing room. Scott closed the door so they wouldn't be inadvertently overheard by the staff and motioned for Nicole and Alyx to take a seat.

"So this is the scene of the crime," Alyx murmured as she eased down into a chair. "Where's the safe?"

"Why?" Scott asked with a grin. "You casing the joint, too?"

Alyx laughed. "No, I was just trying to picture what happened."

Nicole gave her an admonishing look. "That's not necessary. Instead, we should be worried about how to replace the second set of jewels."

Seeming surprised, Alyx said, "You're not arguing with the fact that we need to do this?"

"No."

Alyx turned to stare at Scott in surprise. "What got into her?"

"Digby."

"What's a Digby?"

"He's an insurance investigator. I think he put a scare into Nicole the other night." But more than that, she seemed to have come to some sort of realization or decision, and he wondered what it was.

"Hel-lo?" Nicole said sarcastically. "I'm still here, remember?"

How could he forget? Whenever Nicole was anywhere in the same building, his internal radar seemed to click on and home in on her exact location. He was constantly aware of her, no matter where she was or what she was doing.

"I'm sorry," Alyx crooned. "Did the Digby dude scare you?"

Nicole slanted her an annoyed glance. "A little. He asked some very pertinent questions about the alarm system and whether or not the jewels were real. But that's not important. What *is* important is that we get these things replaced as soon as possible. Scott, did you research the Wyndhams' schedule?"

He nodded. "So far as I can tell, they don't have anything scheduled at their home for the next couple of months. Nothing that Mother is invited to, anyway."

"Do you have to do it before then?" Alyx asked. "I mean, can you go on to the third buyer and come back to this one later?"

"We would," Scott said, "but I'm having some trouble figuring out where the jewels might be in the Larson house. Until I can locate them, it's useless to go there."

Nicole nodded, all business. "And I still have those jewels in my purse at home. We need to exchange them soon, before Digby demands to see them, or Scott's mother figures out they're gone. Either that or we'll have to put them back temporarily."

"Okay," Alyx said. "So what do we do?"

Good question. Scott thought for a minute. "We can't just call on Claire again. We don't have a good reason, and it would look suspicious. We'll just have to get the Wyndhams out of the house."

Nicole gave him a doubtful glance. "Like how?"

"Fake a fire?" Alyx suggested.

Nicole shook her head. "Too dangerous, plus it would draw too many people. We want to be able to get in and out unseen."

"I know," Alyx said. "We'll stage a big commotion outside, a diversion so they'll run outside to see what's going on."

"No," Scott said slowly. "They may peek out of the windows, but I doubt they'd come out to gawk and stare." He grinned. "Wouldn't be proper, doncha know?"

Looking frustrated, Alyx said, "Why can't we just knock on the door and invite ourselves in?"

"It's rude, for one thing," Nicole said. "And it would look very suspect."

Alyx frowned. "Well then, maybe we can show up and pretend to have an appointment with Mrs. Wyndham . . . at a time when we know she isn't there."

"Now there's a good idea," Nicole said, then turned to Scott. "Did you check on the servants to see when they get a day off?"

"Yes, they have Sunday off, when the Wyndhams spend most of the day at church and the club. They all leave for the day . . . all but Weatherwax, that is.

I don't think he's ever taken a day off in his life."
And that might prove to be a problem for them.

"Probably doesn't trust anyone not to mess up
the house," Alyx said with a sniff. "Well, that's out
then. Weatherwax is already suspicious of Scott, so
we won't be able to slip by him."

"Unless you can distract him," Scott suggested.
"If you two can keep him occupied long enough, I
can replace the jewels."

Nicole shook her head. "I don't think that would
work. I wouldn't know how to keep him with us if
he was bound and determined to check up on
you."

"Maybe you could take lessons from Scott," Alyx
said. "I bet he could come up with a line for anything."

"Good point." A slow smile spread across Nicole's
face. "Maybe we can make that work for us."

"How?" Scott asked.

"If we give Weatherwax something to focus on—
you—I can replace the jewels."

Scott frowned. "I'm not sure you should take the
risk." He didn't want her getting hurt.

Nicole's answering glance was annoyed. "So it's
okay to risk myself by helping you, but not by taking the lead?"

"That's not what I meant," he protested.

"Then what did you mean?"

He meant that he felt protective, that he wanted
to keep her safe. But he wasn't dumb enough to
voice that thought aloud—not with the challenging
expression on Nicole's face. "Er, never mind. Mo-
mentary madness. What's your plan?"

Nicole didn't look convinced, but she must have

decided to drop it because she said, "I figure if you tell him you're waiting for Claire, then ask to wait in the study, he'll make sure you wait anywhere but there. Then all you have to do is act suspicious, and he'll stick around to keep an eye on you."

"Okay, I can do that. But what about you? He probably won't approve of you wandering off, either."

"But I won't be coming in with you."

Confused, Scott said, "Explain, please."

"While you keep the butler occupied, I'll just sneak in."

"Sneak? You?" Alyx said with a grin.

It did sound rather out of character for up-front Nicole, but she looked so offended at Alyx's humor that Scott kept his mouth shut.

"Yes, me." Nicole tossed her hair back, looking miffed. "You two aren't the only ones who can do this sort of thing, you know."

Still amused, Alyx asked, "So how are you going to sneak in without eagle-eye catching you?"

Nicole shrugged. "When we were in the atrium, I saw where the back entrances were. It should be easy enough to let myself in while Weatherwax is keeping his eye on Scott. He won't even know I'm in the house."

Scott nodded slowly. "That might work."

"It should work," Nicole said in a touchy tone. "If you can keep the butler occupied."

"Oh, I think I can do that," Scott said. "But I'd appreciate it if you don't dawdle. I don't know how long I'll be able to keep him from suspecting something."

"No problem."

"But what about me?" Alyx said, sounding annoyed. "What's my job?"

"Your job is to be the lookout and stay in the car," Nicole said firmly. "When you see me come out, honk twice or something so Scott will know the coast is clear."

Alyx pouted. "That sounds boring. Trade with me. I'm sure you'd prefer my job, and I know I'd prefer yours."

"I need to do this," Nicole said with an enigmatic look. "Besides, it's my sister who screwed up, not yours. I'm doing it and that's final."

Alyx didn't look happy about it, so Scott added, "It's an important job driving the getaway car."

Alyx perked up. "I can drive the Mercedes?"

That wasn't exactly what he had in mind, but what could it hurt? "Okay."

"All right," Alyx said with more enthusiasm.

Nicole gave Scott a questioning look. "It's a plan, then?"

It was the best idea they'd come up with yet, so Scott nodded. But the thought of how many things could go wrong skimmed through his head. What if Nicole couldn't get the safe open? What if she was caught? What if she was arrested?

Damn, this kind of worrying must be what Nicole went through all the time . . . .

Sunday arrived all too soon for Nicole, and waiting for the servants to leave the Wyndham house was nerve-wracking. Though this plan was her idea, the thought of going through with it made her nauseous. What if—

She cut the thought off abruptly. No. She was not going to worry about what might happen. All that did was make her stomach even more upset. Instead she was going to act more like Scott or Alyx and pretend this was going to be one big adventure.

"There she goes," Scott said. "That's the last of them . . . except for Weatherwax, of course." He glanced at Nicole. "You ready for this?"

"I guess," Nicole said. Ready as she'd ever be anyway. "Let me get to the side of the house before you ring the bell, okay? Once I'm sure you're inside, I'll go around to the back." Turning to glance at Alyx, still in the backseat, Nicole added, "Remember, honk twice when I come out so Scott knows the coast is clear."

"I know," Alyx said, rolling her eyes. "You've reminded us at least a dozen times now."

Feeling a little defensive, Nicole said, "I just want to make sure nothing goes wrong." But maybe she was trying to compensate for her apprehension by overcontrolling everything.

"It won't," Alyx assured her.

Nicole didn't share her friend's confidence. She just hoped she could make it through without being sick. As she and Scott got out of the car, Alyx went eagerly to the front.

Scott handed her the keys. "No joyriding, now."

"Don't worry," Alyx assured him as she slid behind the wheel. "I won't let you down."

As nonchalantly as she could, Nicole strolled to the side of the Wyndham house, trying to look as if she belonged there. Once there, she paused and bent over, pretending to tie her shoe, as she listened for Scott's progress.

She heard a doorbell ring, then the door opened and the butler said, "Good afternoon. I'm sorry, but the Wyndhams are not at home."

Scott's reply was characteristically breezy. "Oh, they will be soon. We have an appointment."

"They didn't mention it to me," Weatherwax said, sounding uncertain.

"Really? That's odd," Scott said. "Mrs. Wyndham probably just forgot to tell you. I've noticed she's been a bit forgetful lately. I'll just come in and wait."

He must have put action to words, for his voice seemed a bit muffled as he said, "If you don't mind, I'll just wait in the study—"

The door closed then, muffling Scott's voice completely. Good, the first part of the plan had worked. Now for her part. Nicole made it swiftly past the unlocked gate and into the immaculately kept backyard, then hurried across the grass to try the door she'd spotted next to the atrium. Locked.

Locked? How could it be locked? She hadn't planned for this. Feeling nausea roil in her stomach, Nicole glanced around frantically. Aha, another entrance. She tried the door, and it was locked as well. Damn, who locked their back doors in the middle of the day?

Weatherwax, evidently. Now what? Was her plan over before it had barely begun?

No, Nicole wouldn't let it be. She wouldn't let a little setback jeopardize her first attempt at doing something a bit dangerous. But how could she get in? The window maybe?

She hurried back to the gate and yanked it open, then ran smack dab into Alyx. She almost let out a screech until she realized who it was.

"What are you doing here?" Nicole whispered fiercely. "You're supposed to be in the car."

"There's nothing for me to do there," Alyx whispered back. "And I thought you might need some help. What are *you* doing here?"

Nicole tugged her over behind a bush so they couldn't be seen from the street. "The doors are locked in back. I can't get in."

"Damn," Alyx said. "Now what? Are you just going to give up?"

"No, I thought I'd try the window." She pointed to the one just above them. "Based on the plans Scott showed us, that must be the one to the study." At least she thought it was; she had never actually seen the inside of it. Only Scott had.

"What if it's locked?" Alyx whispered, looking anxious.

"Now who's the worrywart?" Nicole couldn't help but feel a bit smug. "Let's try it first."

She edged upward and peeked in the window, then dropped back down.

"What did you see?" Alyx asked.

"Shh, he might hear you. The window's already open." Not many homes in Colorado had air-conditioning since there were so few really hot days. Luckily, today was one of them, and providing cross breezes through open windows was a time-honored tradition.

"I should be able to pop the screen out." Slinging the bag with the jewels more securely across her chest, Nicole said, "Here, help me up." With a boost from Alyx, she was able to remove the screen and climb in the window. She even managed to do it quietly.

Alyx peered up at her. "What are you going to do about the screen?"

Nicole glanced at it. There was no way she could fasten it again from the outside. "I'll have to put it back into place now," she said in a low tone, conscious of Weatherwax and Scott's voices in the other room.

"Then how are you going to get out?"

"I'll just walk out the front," Nicole said with more confidence than she felt. If Scott kept up his end of the bargain, it should be easy to exit unnoticed.

Alyx looked worried. "Okay, but be careful."

"You, too," Nicole said in an admonishing tone. "Now, please go back to the car. We're counting on you to honk the horn for us."

Alyx rolled her eyes, but did as Nicole requested. Nicole glanced around the room, quickly spotting the draperies that Scott said concealed the safe. She pulled them open. Sure enough, it was just where he said it was. Thankful something had finally gone right, Nicole pulled out the piece of paper with the dates on them. One of these had to be the combination . . . .

Quickly, she tried Mrs. Wyndham's birthday, then her husband's, and those of their three grown children. None of them worked. Finally, when she tried their anniversary, the safe clicked open.

She hadn't realized she'd been holding her breath until she saw the velvet boxes inside and released it in a whoosh. Elation filled her—it had worked. It had really worked!

In a flash, she took the fakes out of the safe and replaced them with the real jewels, then shut the safe. It was done, but it still wasn't over. First, she had to get out of here without being seen.

She zipped up the bag with the fake jewels in it, then twitched the drape covering the safe back into place and hurried toward the door. Only this time, she ran smack dab into Weatherwax.

As she bounced off the rotund butler, Nicole's heart pounded so hard, she was sure he could hear it. *Ohmigod, what should I do now?*

Deciding to attack before he did, she said, "You really ought to be more careful, Weatherwax."

Looking perplexed, he said, "I'm sorry, Miss—"

"Oh, there you are," Scott said in a hearty tone behind the butler. "I wondered where you'd gotten to."

Relief filled her. It might not be rational, but just knowing Scott was there to help her with this situation made her feel ten times better. Picking up on his cue, she said, "Yes, I got tired of waiting in the car so I thought I'd come in to see what was going on."

Weatherwax frowned. "How did you get in?"

"Through the front door," Nicole said, as if it were obvious. "I knocked, but no one answered, so I came in to see if I could find Scott."

"I didn't hear a knock," Weatherwax said.

"Obviously," Nicole said in a dry tone, trying to imply that he needed his hearing checked.

"But the door is locked."

Uh-oh. She gulped, her mind racing as she tried

to find a plausible explanation. She glanced at Scott for help, but he just grinned at her. "Of course," she said, playing for time. Then inspiration struck. "It is *now*. I locked it after I came in. You can never be too careful, you know." And she managed to make it sound as if she were accusing him of being somewhat less than conscientious.

As Weatherwax gave the door a questioning glance, Nicole said, "Scott, are you done? I'm late for my appointment."

"Sorry, honey," Scott said with a grin. "But the Wyndhams aren't here. I think they forgot about me."

Plastering a look of shock on her face, Nicole said, "Forgot . . . ?"

"Yes, but I don't think Weatherwax here believes me." He gave the butler such a challenging stare, Nicole wondered what had passed between them. "Do you, Weatherwax?"

Nicole watched in fascination as a number of emotions seemed to vie for dominance on Weatherwax's normally poker-faced countenance. Annoyance and disbelief fought it out with ingrained politeness. "Sir, I am quite sure the Wyndhams aren't expecting you—"

"Why else would we be here?" Scott demanded. He sounded angry, but she could see the devilry in his eyes. "You think we're here to crack their safe or steal their jewels or something?"

Before Weatherwax could answer, or Scott could say anything more outrageous, Nicole jumped into the conversation. "Of course they're expecting us." She pulled her planner out of the side flap on her bag and made a pretence of looking at it. "It says right here—"

She broke off, then flipped ostentatiously to the next page. Glancing at Scott with a stricken look, she said, "He's right. Your appointment wasn't today, it's next week. You're here a week early, Scott."

"I am?" Scott grabbed the planner from her and gave it a cursory inspection. "Why, so I am." He shut the book and gave it back to her then turned to Weatherwax. "Sorry about that. Seems I was mistaken about the time."

Looking a little mollified, the butler said, "Quite all right, sir." But he pointedly unlocked and opened the front door for them, saying, "I'll let the Wyndhams know you called and verify your appointment for next week."

Scott grabbed Nicole's hand and breezed through the door. "Oh, don't bother," he said casually. "They'll probably forget next week, too. I'll just cancel."

As Scott hurried up the walk, Nicole couldn't resist a look back. Weatherwax looked more than a little perplexed as he closed the door behind them. "Shame on you," she murmured. "Confusing the man like that."

"Me?" Scott said with a grin. "How about you? I've never seen anyone think so fast on their feet before." He hugged her arm tighter to his side and slowed their approach to the car and Alyx, who looked almost as confused as the butler by their appearance together. "You sure you've never done this before? You're a natural."

Feeling smug, Nicole said, "Yes I am, aren't I?"

She wanted to laugh, dance a jig, or throw her arms in the air, but she contented herself with a self-satisfied smile. *Damn, I'm good.*

"Tell you what," Scott whispered. "Let's celebrate by checking off one of those items on your list."

She slanted him a wary glance. "Which one?"

He laughed. "Well, I'm not planning on finding you a handsome stranger, so it'll have to be one of the others. You have tomorrow off, don't you?"

"Yes, the library is closed on Labor Day."

"Then I'll come by tomorrow morning and pick you up. Say, about five thirty?"

"Five thirty . . . in the *morning*?" Nicole said in disbelief. "Why so early?" And on her day off, too.

"To avoid Missy," Scott said with a grin. When Nicole gave him an annoyed glance, he said, "Well, that *is* a consideration, but the real reason is that we need an early start if we want to catch this adventure."

"What is it?"

"It's a surprise, but I guarantee you'll enjoy it."

Okay, she was willing to be surprised. But . . . "How should I dress? I mean, are we talking shorts or formal attire?"

"Neither. Jeans will do—just make sure you're comfortable and warm."

Warm, huh? He must be planning to take her into the mountains. "Okay," Nicole said. She was even looking forward to it. With Scott, anything could be an adventure.

Chapter Eleven

As good as his word, Scott picked Nicole up at five thirty A.M. She didn't press him for details at first, kind of liking the idea of a spontaneous adventure. But when he headed south on I-25 instead of going west toward the mountains as she'd expected, curiosity got the better of her. "Where are we going?"

"Colorado Springs."

"What's there?"

"Oh, lots of things. The Air Force Academy, the Olympic Training Center, Pikes Peak—"

She punched his arm lightly, halting his recital. "You know what I mean, where are we going today? Pikes Peak?"

"No, we're going to Memorial Park."

"Oh, that sounds exciting," she said, rolling her eyes.

"It will be," he promised with a grin. "Just wait."

They spent the hour-long trip in comfortable conversation, talking about everything under the sun. When they finally reached Memorial Park, there was a huge crowd at the open area. Towering above the milling spectators was a colorfully striped hot air balloon. As she watched, the balloon lifted off amidst cheering from the crowd. So that's why he'd brought her here. What fun.

"Oh, no, we missed it," Nicole said.

"Not to worry. That was only the pathfinder balloon. There are lots more." He parked the car and grinned at her. "Want to see?"

"Yes," Nicole said eagerly and scrambled out of the car.

At this time of the morning, the air was brisk and cold, and she was glad he'd told her to dress warmly. The grassy field was ringed with concession booths selling everything from food to sweatshirts advertising the Colorado Springs Balloon Classic.

Scott bought them both a hot chocolate and Nicole asked, "Is this an annual event?"

"Yes, every Labor Day weekend."

"I can't believe so many people are here so early in the morning."

"It's the best time to fly," Scott said. "And I thought you might like to see the whole process from the beginning. I've crewed for a friend here before, and asked if we could watch his balloon. Would you like that?"

Nicole grinned. "Sounds great."

They made their way through the crowd, and Scott introduced her as his fiancée to a lean, dark-haired man about his age named Eric.

"Are you going to be able to make it up today?" Scott asked.

Eric grinned. "Yes, the announcement came a few minutes ago. The sky's clear and the wind's below ten miles per hour, so it looks like we're going to be able to lift off with no problems." He turned to

Nicole. "You ever been to a balloon ascension before?"

"No, never."

"Then let me explain what's happening." He gestured proudly at the colorful cloth laid out next to them, a jumble of fiery shades ranging from yellow to orange to red. "I call her Flambeau. See that man standing in the mouth of the envelope, holding it open?"

Nicole nodded.

"We have to blow air into it with that fan to get it started, but once it's full, we'll use the burners on the top of the gondola to fill it with hot air and keep it moving."

He explained that the gondola was the basket-like contraption they rode in, and the colorful balloon secured to the gondola with strong lines was called the envelope.

"Hey, Eric," one of his crew called. "Can you come here a minute?"

Eric excused himself and went to see what he needed, so Nicole and Scott continued to observe Flambeau's inflation. Watching the balloon slowly billow open was interesting, but it seemed to be a lengthy process, so Nicole glanced around to see what else was going on. Fascinated, she watched as dozens of balloons puffed up all around the field, in hundreds of bright, vibrant colors. Most were shaped like the balloons she'd always seen in pictures, but there were balloons with other shapes as well.

"Look over there," Scott said, pointing to her left. "There's a champagne bottle rising. And there—I think that's Tweety Bird."

Nicole laughed. "Can they do that?"

"Sure, those are corporate-sponsored balloons. It's great advertising."

"Oh, look," Nicole exclaimed in delight. "That one looks like a rubber ducky. And I think that's a dinosaur."

As she watched, there was a flurry of activity behind them. The balloon there, striped in varying shades of blue, suddenly came upright.

Three people scrambled into the basket. A man with a radio gave them a signal and one of them yelled, "Let's go." The men holding it down backed off, and with a whoosh from the burners, they were suddenly aloft.

"How exciting," Nicole said as she watched the balloon soar into the cool morning air.

Then there was a shout from Eric and his crew. "Look," Scott said. "Flambeau is almost ready."

And now that the balloon was almost completely filled, she could see why it was named that way— bright tongues of flame swirled in spirals around the yellow balloon, making it look as if fire were leaping up from the bottom.

"Come on," Scott said, grabbing her hand. "Let's get closer."

The basket—no, gondola—tipped upright as the balloon rose in majestic splendor to bob lightly from side to side above them. Eric jumped in the gondola, and his crew and Scott leapt on the rim of the basket to hold it down.

Beaming, Eric beckoned to Nicole. "You ready to do this?"

"Me?" Nicole squeaked.

"Sure," Eric said. "Scott said you've always wanted to fly in a hot air balloon, so here's your chance."

Scott's grin was from ear to ear. "Oh, did I forget to tell you I arranged a ride?"

"Quickly, now," Eric said.

Hell, why not? When would she ever get a better chance? Not giving herself a chance to think or worry, Nicole scrambled into the gondola with Scott and Eric's help, then Scott slid in beside her.

After a few minutes, the man with the radio told Eric he could go. "Hands off," Eric yelled, and his crew jumped back.

Then, with a roar from the overhead burners, they lifted off the ground. The sensation was both exhilarating and a little frightening as they soared effortlessly into the air, following the other balloons that had taken off in a southeasterly direction. Eric's crew raced off the field.

"Where are they going?" Nicole asked.

"To the chase vehicle," Eric shouted above the noise of the burner. "They'll follow us by car so they can help retrieve the balloon when it comes down."

But Nicole could ask no more questions as they rose above the treetops. Her heart leapt into her throat as the trees dwindled rapidly. She gripped the edge of the gondola, shivering.

"Cold?" Scott asked, snaking his arms around her to bring her back snug against his chest.

Not knowing how to put her feelings into words, Nicole nodded. Her shivering was not only because of the cold, but also because of the sheer delight of their flight. She leaned back against him, grateful for his warmth and the stability of his presence.

Once her gaze was off the ground, she glanced around, gasping in appreciation. The view was breathtaking. The Rocky Mountains rose majestically to the west, then dipped to golden plains on the east, with the green-shaded crazy quilt of Colorado Springs spread out between them. They flew far above the splendor, wafting as light as a feather, racing as one with the breeze. It was glorious . . . magical.

And strangely quiet. The only sounds she heard came from the roar of their burners and those of the other balloons, Eric talking to his crew on the radio, and the occasional shouted greeting from other balloons.

Her heart lifted, buoyed by the experience and the feel of Scott's arms around her. Some people down below waved from their cars and she waved back, grinning foolishly. This was perfect and not as frightening as she had expected once she got used to it. *Why have I never done this before?*

Well, for one thing, she wouldn't know how to arrange it as neatly as Scott had, nor would she have been able to afford the cost of a commercial ride. Only Scott could have arranged this kind of surprise for her. She smiled just taking it all in.

Some of the balloons did what Eric called a "touch and go" by briefly touching the surface of the lake and taking off again, but she was glad they didn't try that. The "touch" worked every time, but the "go" afterward didn't always operate as planned and sometimes the gondolas got stuck in the water. That was a bit *too* much adventure, thank you very much.

Besides, she liked it high above the rooftops. Unfortunately after about twenty minutes they started to lose altitude.

"Are we coming down now?" she asked, feeling disappointed that it was happening so soon.

"Yes," Eric said. "I just need to find an open space to land in." He continued to talk with his crew on the radio as the balloon drifted toward the earth.

Then, abruptly, they were descending fast toward an open field. "Hold on," Eric cried. "We're going down."

Copying Scott's actions, Nicole grabbed a supporting strut. Eric manipulated various ropes and gadgets, and suddenly they hit the ground—harder than she expected. Nicole let out a little screech as they bounced, then bounced again until they came to a skidding stop.

"You okay?" Scott asked, holding her tight.

She nodded. She was fine, though a bit disappointed the ride was over.

"Okay, we're down," Eric said into the radio. "You have our position?"

An affirmative reply came from the radio. "We'll be there in two minutes."

Nicole glanced up. The balloon wavered in the light breeze, then dimpled on one side. Once the crew pulled up, Eric pulled one of the dangling lines and tugged open a hole in the top of the balloon. She watched in fascination as the envelope fluttered and deflated. It slowly fell in on itself, yellow, orange, and red dipping and swirling together in a mad whirl of dancing flames.

The crew members leaned on the basket to keep it from falling over, then helped the occupants onto the slightly muddy ground. As she watched, they unhooked the envelope from the gondola, then efficiently rolled the balloon into a ball about the size and shape of a beanbag chair.

As his crew loaded the envelope and gondola

into their trailer, Eric reached into the vehicle and pulled out a bottle of champagne. He popped it open with a flourish, saying, "It's traditional to end each flight with a glass of bubbly." He filled some plastic cups and handed one each to Scott and his crew members.

Eric grinned at Nicole. "How did you enjoy your first flight?"

"I loved it," Nicole said truthfully.

"We have a special tradition for first-timers . . . ." He glanced doubtfully at her. "But you'll have to kneel on the ground."

She glanced at Scott. His eyes were dancing with mischief, but he nodded encouragingly.

She gave the muddy ground a dubious look, but she was wearing jeans, so what the heck? Might as well have the full experience. She knelt down on the ground, feeling it squish slightly beneath her knees. "Now what?"

He filled her glass with champagne and placed it on the ground in front of her, saying, "Put your arms behind your back."

She did so, feeling a little silly.

"Now I'm going to recite the traditional poem. While I do that, you lean over, pick up the glass with your mouth, and drink."

Okay, it wouldn't be too humiliating so she'd play along. She barely heard the words of his poem as she concentrated on picking up the glass with her teeth. She somehow managed the feat, then wondered how she was going to drink it without dribbling it down her throat.

She started to tilt her head back anyway, but felt something cold and wet pouring over her head.

Sputtering, she snatched the glass out of her mouth and gaped up at the laughing faces of the men, who had all upended their glasses on her head.

I should have known . . . .

But she couldn't be angry with them. If they had all gone through this on their first time, so could she. Wiping a hank of champagne-drenched hair out of her face, she couldn't help but laugh. "Does that mean I'm officially baptized?"

"Absolutely," Eric declared as he handed her a towel, looking more than a little relieved that she wasn't angry. "You're one of us now, no longer a balloon flight virgin. You even get a prize."

As Scott helped her to her feet and she wiped off most of the wetness, Eric dug around in his pocket and pulled out a pin. "Here, this is for you."

The enameled pin was a representation of the Flambeau soaring in the sky. "Thank you," she said sincerely as she pinned it to her shirt. The small memento would always remind her of this wonderful experience. Well, wonderful except for the last few minutes.

"Let's go," one of his crew yelled, and they all piled into the chase vehicle and headed back to the park.

Once they were dropped off at the park, Scott said, "I'm hungry. How about you? Want to get something to eat?"

"I'm hungry, too," Nicole admitted as they headed across the park toward the car. "But I want some real food." Not the snacks they were selling at the park. "But I can't go anywhere looking like this—muddy and wet." The towel had helped remove some of the moisture, but the stickiness was still there.

He gave her a twisted grin. "Sorry—I'd forgotten about that part until Eric pulled out the champagne bottle, or I would've told you to bring an extra set of clothes. But I can make it up to you. How about we zip over to the mall, buy you a few things, then find somewhere for you to change before we have brunch?"

"Can I get a hot bath, too?" She felt totally grungy.

He laughed. "Absolutely. While you're shopping, I'll call around and find a hotel room with a tub."

"Sounds heavenly." He was so nice, so considerate, and so wonderful. Overcome by emotion, she threw her arms around him and gave him a brief, hard kiss.

Looking surprised, he said, "Gee, if I'd known that offering you a tub would generate this kind of response, I would have done it a long time ago."

Her arms still around him, her heart full, she said, "It wasn't just the tub, silly—it was everything. Thanks for one of the best times of my life."

The jubilation of crossing one item off her list made her throw caution to the winds. With any luck, maybe she could eliminate one or two more items today . . . .

Scott shook his head. Nicole was so easy to please. She seemed to enjoy anything. Why hadn't some man snatched her up long ago?

He didn't know and didn't care. Their loss meant his gain, and he was determined to pamper her. "You're welcome," he murmured. And since she was so conveniently in his arms, he leaned down to return her kiss . . . *his* way.

She tasted of sunshine and champagne, sweet yet earthy. It was a heady combination, and the noise of the crowd faded around him as he lost himself in her. Their lips met, parted, and met again . . . hungrily, as if they couldn't get enough of each other.

For the first time, Scott sensed that Nicole held nothing back, that she desired him as much as he desired her. But a lingering awareness of their surroundings brought him back down to earth. The carnival atmosphere of the balloon classic was no place for this.

He pulled away a little, just far enough to see her face. Her kiss-swollen lips and desire-filled eyes showed him that her need was as great as his. "How would you like to add another new experience to your list?" he asked, running his hands down her hips.

Her laugh was low and husky. "Perfect. Is this where we pretend to be total strangers?"

His heart leapt in his chest at her suggestive tone. He kissed her again, briefly. "I don't want any pretence with you." Only the real thing would do. "And I definitely don't want to be a stranger. But . . . have you ever stayed at a five-star hotel?"

Her eyes widened. "No, I haven't."

"Then it's an experience you shouldn't miss. Let's spend the rest of the day in total decadence, shall we?" Never mind the mall—they could find everything they needed at the Pourtales.

Nicole's smile was the only answer he needed. Quickly, they headed back to the car, and after he seated Nicole, he pulled out his cell phone and called the Pourtales to make reservations, along with a few special arrangements.

And, in no time at all, they were there at the beautiful historic building nestled in the foothills at the base of Pikes Peak.

Nicole glanced warily at the grandeur of the hotel, faced in local peachblow sandstone with white wrought-iron balconies studding the exterior. Fiddling with her still-wet hair, she said, "I don't think I'm dressed for this."

"Don't worry. They don't care how you look; they only care about the color of your money."

She looked doubtful, but as he escorted her from the car, he whispered, "Once you're in the room, no one will see you but me. And I think you're gorgeous." Though her expression showed she didn't believe him, it was the truth. Her glowing happiness and excitement were all she needed to clothe her in beauty.

He handed the car keys to the valet and escorted Nicole into the plush gold and white lobby. It looked the same as when he had spent that zany week with his sister, her two husbands, and all their attendant loonies last fall . . . right down to the same man at the desk.

"Hello, Billings," Scott said cheerfully as he handed the man his credit card. "We have a reservation under Richmond, Scott Richmond. Remember me?"

The tall, thin man's smile faded. "Only too well." His cool gaze skimmed over Nicole. "Will the rest of the circus be arriving later?"

"No, it's only me and my fiancée this time," Scott said, determined not to let this man destroy his good mood. "Don't worry. We're only here to clean up a bit, experience a few of your noted amenities, and relax. You won't even know we're here."

"Good, then I won't have to call in extra security." With one supercilious eyebrow raised, Billings deposited the key in Scott's hand with two fingers, as if he were afraid Scott were contagious.

"Thanks," Scott said, deliberately catching the man's hand in a hearty handshake. "I appreciate it." Then he ignored the manager's affronted expression as he led Nicole away from the desk.

Nicole glanced uncertainly back at Billings. "What was that all about?"

Scott grinned. "Oh, I spent a year here one week last fall. My sister got herself accidentally married to two men, and they duked it out for her heart in this hotel—figuratively speaking." And literally as well, if he remembered correctly. "Then Mother, Kelly's boss, Chaz's coworker, and her brothers showed up and they all had strong opinions as to what Kelly should do . . . and they made their opinions known in no uncertain terms. It was a crazy time." He led her toward the elevator, and they got on as the doors opened. "Billings was here then, and obviously he's never forgotten. I think we traumatized him."

"I see," Nicole said with a grin. "No wonder he was so unhappy to see you."

"Yes, he was right in the thick of it all. Caused some of the problems himself, too. I don't know how Kelly came out of it so well."

Nicole grinned. "I think I'd like to meet your sister."

"You two would get along great. But she's in

Turkey with her husband, Chaz, on an archaeological dig. If they come back for a visit, I'll be sure to introduce you."

"And her other husband?" Nicole asked with a quizzical look.

Scott laughed. "He's out of the picture now—the marriage was annulled, and a good thing, if you ask me." He led her out of the elevator and down the hall to the room.

As they entered, Scott glanced around in appreciation. They had done just as he asked and given him one of their more elegant suites, done in pink and white striped wallpaper that was edged with silver. The antique four-poster bed was decorated in gauzy white bed hangings and, as he had requested, someone had drawn the drapes against the sun, placed a dozen pink roses on the desk, and left fragrant candles flickering on all the flat surfaces.

The atmosphere was just as he ordered—romantic and perfect.

"Oh, it's wonderful," Nicole breathed, glancing around in delight.

With a flourish Scott opened the door to the bathroom. "Your tub awaits, Madame. While you bathe, I'll head down to the gift shop and find you something else to wear." He still remembered her sizes from their shopping expedition.

Nicole's eyes widened at the luxurious pink marble bathroom. She wandered in and checked out the bath oils and soaps invitingly displayed on the tub.

Before she got too caught up, Scott asked, "What would you like for brunch?"

"Oh, anything," Nicole said with a distracted air. He could see he had lost her to the siren call of a hot bath. For the moment, anyway. Leaving her to enjoy herself, he called room service to order a variety of dishes suitable for brunch, then made his way downstairs, gave the dour Billings a merry wave just to annoy him, and found everything he needed fairly quickly in the gift shop.

When Scott got back to the room, room service had just arrived, and he had the waiter lay everything out before he left on a table in the center of the room.

As Scott lit the candles on the table, he heard the door to the bathroom open. Nicole emerged with a gust of steam scented with lilacs, wearing a plush white robe with "Pourtales" stitched across the breast, her hair wet but combed and tucked behind her ears. She looked squeaky clean.

"Was that the food?" she asked.

"Yes, hungry?"

"Starved."

So was he. Soon, nothing but crumbs were left on the plates, and he was no longer hungry. At least, not for food. But Nicole looked decidedly delicious . . . .

Throughout the meal, her robe had teased him. Held together precariously with but a single belt, it gaped open in strategic places, providing tantalizing glimpses of the curve of her thigh, the fullness of her breasts.

Certain she had nothing on beneath all that white, he longed to loosen the belt and peel that robe off her, but wasn't sure how she'd react. Did she want him as much as he wanted her? He wouldn't push—she needed to set the pace.

Starting now. "What would you like to do the rest

of the day?" he asked. "The Pourtales has a wide range of activities available. Would you like to golf, swim, or go horseback riding?"

"No." Nicole stretched like a cat, revealing flashes of bare skin, and set his blood to pounding. "I'm feeling kind of lazy today."

"Well, we could soak in a hot tub, stroll through the gardens, or . . . get a massage." He tried to keep his voice even, not showing how much he wanted her to choose the latter.

"A massage," she said thoughtfully as she rubbed her shoulder. "That sounds wonderful. I think I pulled a couple of muscles when we landed. Besides, that's something I've never done before, either."

That's what he hoped she'd say. He moved around behind her and kneaded her shoulder through the thick robe. "Is this where it hurts?" he asked softly, the throbbing yearning between his legs making his voice husky.

"One of the places," she whispered.

All of a sudden, anticipation filled the air, as thick and heavy as his erection. "You know, I'm pretty good at massage myself," he said, trying to sound casual. He slipped his hand inside the robe to rub the bare skin of her shoulder, caressing more than massaging. "Would you like me to try?"

Her reply was soft and almost inaudible. "That sounds heavenly."

Desire surged through him, but he tamped it down firmly. He needed to go slow, not scare her away. But he couldn't resist placing a kiss on the velvety bend of her neck. She gave a soft gasp, and he said, "I'll be right back."

Gathering unused towels from the bathroom, he

spread them across the bed to keep the covers from being soiled, then grabbed the massage oil he had found downstairs. "I think the bed will be most comfortable," he said, his heart pounding so loud he was certain she could hear it.

"Probably," she agreed. But her eyes didn't meet his as she went to the side of the bed and hovered uncertainly. "How . . . ?"

Wanting to preserve her modesty, he said, "Let's do it this way. Loosen your belt, and lie down on your front. Then I can pull the robe out from under you . . . down to your waist."

"Okay." Trustingly, she did as he suggested. She loosened the belt and lay down, then tugged her arms free of the robe, crossing her arms beneath her head.

He pulled off his shirt so he wouldn't get oil on it, then slowly, so as not to frighten her, he pulled her robe down to her waist, revealing the smooth skin of her back and the swell of her breasts at her sides where they plumped against the bed.

Damn, she was fine.

His unruly cock strained against his pants, begging for release, but he firmly directed his senses to pay attention to what was happening *above* the waist. He opened the bottle and poured the slick vanilla-scented liquid into his hands, rubbing them together to warm the oil, then placed his hands on Nicole's shoulders.

She sighed in what sounded like pure pleasure as he rubbed the warm oil over her silken skin. She was a little tense, but he found her taut muscles and kneaded them into submission, enjoying the way she felt beneath his hands: soft and yielding.

Once she was fully relaxed, he let his hands roam a little farther afield. From the middle of her back, he stroked across her shoulder blades, then down her sides to graze the outer curve of her breasts as if it were an accident. She moaned a little, but didn't protest, so he did it again, wanting to feel her fullness in his hands, but letting this illicit touch suffice.

She shifted a little restlessly, so he trailed his hands down her sides to the dip of her waist and massaged her lower back for a few moments. She seemed to enjoy that, so he dipped a little lower, encroaching on yet another of her luscious curves.

When she didn't protest, he continued to caress the dimple at the top of her derriere with one hand as he slid the robe completely off her body with the other. Now, her naked backside was entirely exposed to his view . . . and what a view it was. Supple hills and valleys undulated delightfully, making him long to explore her landscape.

He couldn't stand it—he had to go adventuring. Boldly, he poured more oil into his hands and slid them both to cup her rear, rubbing the warm liquid over her tight, sassy ass.

She gasped, but it appeared to be more in surprise than dismay, so he continued massaging her there, letting the warm oil trickle down her cleft to the moist warmth he knew was waiting below.

"Oooh," she moaned, and her legs parted slightly. Taking it as an invitation, he slid one hand between her legs and spread more oil on the inside of her thighs, gently parting them until he could see the soft folds of her womanhood. Teasingly, he massaged all around that sensitive area, never touching it, until she was yearning toward him, clutching the bed sheets in fisted hands and almost whimpering with need.

Finally, when he could stand it no longer, he poured warm oil in that sensitive spot and dipped his finger inside. He almost lost it then and there as he felt her slick moisture blend with the oil and suck him inside. His cock throbbed, as if begging him to place it where his finger was, but Scott ignored it. He wanted Nicole to get her satisfaction first.

Quickly, he found her pleasure nub and stroked it. Almost instantly, he felt her come, spasming in waves around his finger as she arched her back and let out a little scream. Then she collapsed to the bed as if drained.

Satisfied that he had pleased her, Scott could wait no longer for his own satisfaction. Standing, he stripped off his pants and underwear then gently turned her over. She flowed up to meet him, then wrapped her arms around his neck and kissed him senseless.

His hands still full of oil, he ran them over her generous breasts. They were just as wondrous as he imagined. In return, she ran her hands down his chest until she clasped the aching center of his need.

Afraid he would lose it too soon, Scott jerked away. "No," he gasped. "It's too much. Wait a minute." He slid off the bed to retrieve a condom from the bag he had brought back from the gift shop.

After he put it on and knelt above her once more, Nicole murmured, "Come here," as she guided him between her legs.

He sank into her welcoming heat as if he were coming home. Dizzy with need, he had to move within her, had to feel the hot silk of her slide around him. He slid out then in again, repeating the motion until he was pumping as fast as he could, feeling waves of sensation pour over him, making him light-headed . . . yearning . . . almost there. Finally, he peaked and sailed over the edge, spilling his joy inside her, and crashed down in spiraling wonder.

Damn, that was good.

When he was finally able to open his eyes, he realized he was lying on top of her. He summoned the energy to roll off and gathered her to his side.

"Wow," Nicole said softly.

Wow, indeed. "I have something to tell you," Scott murmured. "I wasn't entirely honest with you."

"About what?"

"Well, I know you've never had a massage before. That part at the end?" He waved a hand limply. "That's not normally done."

She laughed. "Really? Too bad. I thought it was the best part."

"Me, too," he whispered. He hugged her to him, feeling emotion swell inside him for this wonderful woman, wishing she really were his fiancée. *Can I keep her?*

Chapter Twelve

As Nicole cuddled with Scott, naked and in broad daylight, she wondered what the heck she had done. Dumb question. She remembered exactly what they had done and exactly how they had done it . . . in every intimate, sensuous detail.

The why was pretty clear, too. When Scott set out to seduce a woman, he did a very thorough job of it. The real question was how should she react? Carefree sex was a new experience for her, and though she had certainly enjoyed this addition to her list, she couldn't help but feel a little . . . what?

Embarrassed was the only word she could come up with. This was so unlike the old Nicole, the Nicole she had been content with her whole life. She was a bit out of her comfort zone and didn't know how to get back inside.

Scott, holding her close, shook her a little. "Stop it."

"What?"

He propped up on his elbow to gaze down at her. "I can hear you thinking. It's not good for you."

His mussed hair, lidded gaze, and sexy mouth made her heart skip a beat—he was irresistible. She felt heat rush to the sensitive surface of her skin and averted her gaze. Maybe if she didn't look at him, she could react with her brain instead of her hormones. "Everyone thinks," she said defensively.

"Yes, but it's your second thoughts I'm worried about."

"That's natural, isn't it?"

He heaved an exaggerated sigh. "I knew it. You *are* having second thoughts."

He slid his free hand up to cup her breast, toying with her nipple. It pebbled immediately, responding to his caress and her instant flame of desire.

Reluctantly, she pulled his hand away. "I can't think when you do that."

He grinned. "That was the point."

She couldn't help but smile back at him. "But sooner or later, you won't be touching me and I'll be able to think again."

He nuzzled her neck. "Can we make that later instead of sooner?"

Very tempting, but that niggling little voice inside nagged at her, telling her there was something she should be worrying about. "No . . . ."

"Look," Scott said, pulling back to look at her face. "That was one of the best moments of my life. Didn't you enjoy it?"

"Yes, but—"

"That's what's important, isn't it? The new, madcap Nicole is emerging from the confining shell of the librarian."

True, it was what she *said* she wanted, but she was so mixed up. "Yes, I said that . . . ."

"I hear a 'but' there. But what? You can't enjoy yourself as well?"

"Of course I can." That was the whole point of

becoming someone new, to enjoy life as she never had before.

"Did you have fun on the balloon ride?"

"Yes, it was wonderful."

"Are you enjoying this luxurious hotel?"

"Very much." She'd never felt so pampered in her life.

"Then don't think, just feel." And, suiting action to words, Scott gathered her in his arms again and kissed her.

Dizziness assailed her as it always did when he pressed his mouth to hers. He was an expert at kissing and a master of seduction. But even as he made all her senses swim with his attentions, she couldn't help but wonder what was in store for them.

Scott pulled back and stared down at her with a sigh. "You're thinking again. Okay, let's talk it out."

He chivied her out of the bed and pulled back the covers so they could lie under them instead of on top. Once they were ensconced inside the warmth of the bed linens, Scott said, "You won't be happy until you worry it to death, so let's do it together."

"I don't know—"

"Let's see," he said, ignoring her. "What's the worst that could happen now that we have made love?" He snapped his fingers. "I know, you could catch a serious disease from me and die in agony."

He was being silly. "No—"

"Oh, that's right. I wore protection, so you're safe. Besides, I don't have a disease."

"That's not what I'm worried about."

He nodded thoughtfully. "Then what is the worst? I guess I could wait until you were sleeping, then bug out on you, stiffing you with the hotel bill and leaving you to find your own way home."

Amused now, she said, "You already paid the bill, and I know you wouldn't abandon me."

"So that's out. I guess my psychotic ex-wife could burst in here with a gun pointed at both of us."

Alarm filled her as she glanced askance at him. Was that really a possibility?

"No, wait," he said, slapping his hand to his forehead. "I've never been married. So, the worst could be that I'm so overcome with passion that my heart bursts and I die in your arms."

"That's ridicu—"

He ignored her interruption as he continued with his fantasy, weaving a grandiose scenario. "Then you'd have to call the police and the ambulance, and Billings would look down his long nose at you and kick you out, and reporters would show up and harass you, then you'd have to explain to Mother how I died, and—"

"Stop, stop," Nicole said, laughing. "That would be horrible, but I'm not worried about it. You proved you're extremely healthy a few minutes ago."

He sobered. "Then tell me, what *is* the worst that could happen?"

I could fall in love with you and have my heart broken when you move on. But she couldn't say that.

"You've thought of something," Scott persisted. "What is it?"

She decided to allude to her problem without actually coming out and saying it. "I could be just another notch on your bedpost."

He put on an affronted expression. "How tacky.

I don't do that. Besides, I'd be afraid someone would count them and scoff at how few there are."

Nicole frowned, wishing he wouldn't be so flippant.

Scott gazed down at her. "You're serious, aren't you?"

She nodded, not trusting herself to speak as tears pricked at her eyelids. This was important.

"I'm sorry, honey." Scott wrapped his arms around her. "I thought you realized I don't make love lightly or often." He waggled his eyebrows in a lascivious manner. "But I could make an exception about the 'often' part in your case."

She laughed, but it had a touch of sadness in it, too. "You see, that's part of the problem. The famous Scott Richmond charm."

"My 'charm' is a problem?" he repeated, looking surprised.

"Yes."

"How?"

"No one takes you seriously. No one believes you're really going to settle down, and they don't believe you're really going to go through with the wedding."

"I don't understand how their misconception is your problem."

She tucked the covers more securely around her. "Because they look at me with pity—the poor deluded librarian who actually believes she's marrying the elusive Scott Richmond."

"Don't let that bother you. It's more a comment on what they think of me than what they think of you."

She glanced down at the champagne-colored dia-

mond that represented their tie. "Yes, until the day
we call off the engagement." The inevitable smug,
knowing looks from some; the pity from others . . . .
She wasn't looking forward to it.

He sighed. "That again. I'm not sure why you
care. They're not even your friends."

It wasn't rational, but she did care what they
thought. Many of the people she'd met weren't the
self-centered snobs she'd expected. They were just
like everyone else . . . just with more money. And
she found herself liking them . . . even if they did
pity her.

"That's it?" Scott said when she remained silent.
"That's what you're worried about?" He sounded
annoyed.

"Yes." But when he opened his mouth again, she
said, "Don't try to fix it." Men didn't understand.
They always wanted to try to fix problems when all
women really wanted from them was comfort. "You
can't fix it." At least, not without marrying her, and
she wasn't even sure that was what she wanted.

"I don't get it. Calling off the engagement would
happen whether we made love or not. Why is it so
damned worrisome now?"

His voice was rising, and Nicole searched for an
explanation that wouldn't make him angry. She
shrugged. "I'm not sure." Trying to make a joke of
it, she asked, "Will you still respect me in the morning?" But it was no joke to her. His respect meant a
great deal, and she was afraid she'd lose it. She
wanted reassurance, wanted to know that he was
still going to be the same old Scott, teasing her, flirting with her, making her crazy.

Instead, he looked ticked. "What the hell does

that mean? You think I wanted nothing more than to get you in the sack? You think this meant nothing to me? That *you* mean nothing?"

Taken aback by his vehemence, she said, "That's not—"

His voice clipped, Scott said, "Never mind." He threw the covers off and got out of the bed, then yanked on his shorts. "Well, in that case, there's no sense pretending, is there? I've had my fun, so we might as well go."

Nicole watched in dismay as he continued to dress, his movements swift and angry. Damn. Now she'd made him mad, and she didn't know how to set it right.

By the time Scott saw Nicole again a few days later, he had calmed down. But he was still surprised at how much it hurt. He had thought she was the one person who saw through him, the one who could understand him no matter what. But Nicole had managed to prove him wrong. How could she know so much about his façade and not know when he was being sincere? It didn't make sense.

But he had to content himself with an inward sigh. He would continue to be himself and hope she could find a way to live with it.

He opened the door of his home, and there she was, looking a little startled that he had answered the door instead of Marta. He shrugged. "I was near the door so I answered it."

Nicole nodded and he gestured her inside. This whole thing was awkward. Not the usual fumbling embarrassment that came after making love the first time, but the kind of awkwardness that followed a fight.

"Thanks for coming," he said as he led her toward the drawing room.

Her reply was tentative, as if she wasn't quite sure how to respond to him. "Your mother thinks it's important."

"Yes, she's planned our engagement party and wants to let us know what she's decided."

"Oh."

Scott paused before opening the door to the drawing room. "Try to look a little less grim, won't you? It's supposed to be one of the happiest moments of your life."

"Yours, too," she countered with a snap in her voice. "I suppose that's why you're scowling at me."

"Okay, point taken." He forced a smile and offered her his arm. "Shall we?"

Her smile wasn't very convincing, but it would have to do. He opened the door and led her inside, seating her on a love seat. Gerald was there again, with Mother. Feeling testy for some reason, Scott said, "Good evening, Gerald. Making a habit of this, are you? Why don't you just move in?"

Mother gasped. "Scott, really."

But Gerald's answering look was bland and enigmatic. "I've been trying to convince Grace of that for weeks, but she keeps turning down my proposals."

"Sorry to hear that," Scott said. He was sincere. Gerald exercised a good influence on his mother. At least she hadn't hounded Scott for more money in a while.

Gerald's gaze flicked to Nicole then back to Scott again. "Maybe once you're married and gone, she'll say yes."

"Could be." That was, if he ever got married. *Don't count on it, Gerald.* Going toward the bar, Scott asked, "Would you like some wine, Nicole?"

She smiled wanly. "No, thanks. I have a headache, and alcohol usually makes it worse. Could I just have a soda?"

He nodded and fixed them both a soft drink. At least the headache might explain her lackluster attitude.

As Scott handed Nicole her drink and sat beside her, Grace looked back and forth between them. "Have you had another fight?" she asked without preamble.

Since it appeared obvious, Scott said, "Yes." But he wasn't about to elaborate on it.

"Pre-wedding jitters are normal," Grace said with a dismissive wave. "Nothing to worry about. You haven't done something silly like call off your engagement, have you?"

"No." He wouldn't humiliate Nicole that way, especially since it seemed to mean so much to her that she not be embarrassed by ending it so soon.

"Of course not," Nicole added feebly.

"Good," Grace declared. "Especially since your engagement party is this Friday and the invitations have already gone out."

"We'll be fine, Mother," Scott assured her.

She seemed to relax then. "Very good. Since you asked me to take care of the arrangements, I've made some plans and I hope you approve."

"I'm sure it will be wonderful," Nicole murmured. In an apparent attempt to look interested, she asked, "Where is it to be?"

Grace smiled. "We're having it at the library."

Nicole looked surprised. "The library?"

"Yes, the main library downtown has a lovely place—Schlessman Hall—that will hold up to three hundred people and will be just perfect for your party."

"Three hundred?" Nicole repeated faintly.

"Oh, don't worry. There aren't nearly that many people invited, but I have plans to fill up that open space. And everyone at the library has been very accommodating—they think very highly of you."

Scott was glad to see a genuine smile curve Nicole's mouth as she said, "How nice of you to think of it."

"Oh, it wasn't my idea," Grace said with an airy wave of her hand. "It was Scott's. He thought you and your friends might feel more comfortable in that kind of atmosphere."

Nicole turned that grateful smile on him. "Then I thank *you*. But what about your friends? What will they think about going to the library for a party?"

Grace beamed. "Oh, they'll enjoy the novelty of it. And I think some of them will be surprised at how nice the facilities are."

Scott hid a grin. Especially since he doubted many of them had actually set foot in a library before.

Gerald nodded approvingly. "Exactly right. Grace is well-known as a premier hostess. I'm sure everyone will be delighted."

Grace smiled at him with more warmth than Scott had seen her bestow on her previous admirers. Hmm, maybe Scott *would* have a new stepfather soon.

"Thank you, Gerald." Grace turned back to Nicole. "We'll have a band at one end playing soft music where people can dance, open bars and tables of hors d'oeuvres lining the sides, and lots of space for people to mingle in the middle. We'll use your pink and ivory color scheme, and Claire is lending us some of her miniature roses for the occasion . . . ."

Scott tuned his mother's voice out and watched Nicole. Her fascinated smile seemed to be all the encouragement Grace needed as she filled them in about the arrangements she had made. Throughout it all, Nicole nodded, appearing mesmerized. Scott hid a grin. She had never seen Mother in her element—and planning parties was definitely her forte.

When Grace finally ground to a halt, Nicole breathed, "It sounds perfect. I wouldn't change a thing. Even better, I didn't have to plan any of it."

"Of course not," Grace said with a genuine smile. "That's what you have me for." She glanced at her son. "Is it all right with you?"

"If Nicole's happy, I'm happy." And he was surprised to find it was true. His anger was all gone, and he wanted nothing more than to see her grateful expression turned his way.

"Good," Grace declared. "But I want you to stay by Nicole's side the entire time. This is liable to be a bit overwhelming, and you need to be there to help her."

"No problem."

Grace nodded approvingly. "At some point in the

evening, I'll have the band get everyone's attention
and I'll announce your engagement, then you can
say a few words."

Scott grimaced, but didn't say anything. Putting
himself on public display was his duty.

"If you need help finding a few words appropriate to the occasion, I can help you," Gerald offered
in a diffident tone.

Scott nodded a thanks, but he had no intention
of taking advantage of his offer. Gerald's style and
his were entirely different. *Thank heavens.*

"Do I have to speak, too?" Nicole asked in a small
voice.

"Only if you want to," Grace assured her.

Nicole made urgent negating motions. "Please,
no."

Scott grinned. "You mean this isn't on your list of
things you've always wanted to do?"

"Speak in front of a lot of people?" She looked
aghast. "No, thank you. That's not adventurous—
that's terrifying."

Grace patted Nicole's hand. "Then don't worry
about it. Scott will take care of it. He's used to this
sort of thing. All you have to do is stand there and
look beautiful."

Scott hugged her briefly, glad when she didn't
pull away. "She can do that without even trying."

"Good," Grace declared and rose. "Now, you two
go off and make up before dinner. I need to make
a couple of phone calls, and I'll see you in the dining room. Gerald, you're welcome to wait here."
And, having disposed of everyone to her satisfaction, Grace swept out the door.

Taking advantage of Nicole's stunned look, Scott

set his glass aside and gently did the same with hers, then led her upstairs to his office.

She followed him willingly enough, but wouldn't look at him once they were alone. Poor Nicole, she didn't know how to react. Taking pity on her, Scott said, "Do you think you'll be up to this?"

"Of course. Your mother has gone to such a lot of trouble, and has been so nice about the whole thing . . ."

"You're feeling guilty?"

"A little," she admitted. "All that expense for an engagement that isn't even real . . . ." She bit her lip, giving him a doubtful glance. "Do you think maybe we should call it off now, before it's too late?"

"No, I don't. For one thing, the expense doesn't matter. Mother loves any excuse to throw a party and we can afford it. Besides, backing out at this late date wouldn't save money anyway—she'd probably still have to pay for the food and it would just go to waste." He paused, quirking an eyebrow at her. "I thought you were afraid of people's reactions if we called it off."

She averted her eyes again and gazed down at her solitaire as she turned it around on her finger. "I know, and I'm sorry. That was very selfish of me."

"Not selfish," he said softly. "Human. And I'm sorry I got angry at you the other day. You were perfectly within your rights to feel as you do. I regret putting you in this position."

She shook her head. "I appreciate that, but . . . you were right. The engagement is a necessary deception. But I'm not sure it serves a purpose any longer."

"Actually, it does. Especially this party."

Her gaze flew to meet his. "What do you mean?"

"I'm sure the Larsons will be there, so maybe we'll have an opportunity to cadge an invitation to their house." Besides, he wanted to make their breakup as easy for her as possible. It seemed to mean a lot to her.

She shrugged. "Okay. Do you have any ideas—"

She broke off when a knock sounded at the door.

Scott opened it to find Gerald there. "Excuse me for interrupting," the lawyer said, "but I wanted to discuss something with you."

Odd, Gerald had never singled him out before. Scott opened the door wider to allow him in. "Sure, what's up?"

"I'm a little concerned about the insurance claim."

Uh-oh. Scott had a feeling he wasn't going to like this. "Why?"

"Because Mr. Digby has been asking Grace if he can take a look at the imitations in her safe, but she keeps stalling him." Gerald gave Scott a penetrating look. "Do you know of any reason why she would do that?"

"Not a clue," Scott lied.

Gerald nodded thoughtfully. "Then I'll see what I can do to put him off." He turned toward the door. "I'll see you downstairs."

Scott closed the door behind him and turned to face Nicole.

Looking upset, she asked, "Now what? If he opens her safe and sees some of those jewels are real, your mother is in big trouble."

"I know. Luckily, most of those are now the fake

ones, except for the ones we haven't replaced yet. The best I can do is take out the real ones so if he does get in, he won't find them."

"But won't that make him suspicious?"

"Probably, but I don't have a better idea. Do you?"

She bit her lip again. "No. You can delay him for a while by saying you sent them out to be cleaned, but not for long. We're going to have to find a way to replace those jewels soon."

"I know, but I still haven't had any luck in learning about the Larsons' security."

"Then talking to them Friday night at the party is going to have to be our top priority. We need a plan."

Another knock came at the door. It was Marta, letting them know dinner was about to be served.

"We'll be right down," Scott assured her. He waited for a moment until Marta was out of earshot, then said, "You're right, but what?"

Nicole smiled. "Oh, you'll think of something. You always do."

Scott swallowed hard. He was glad to hear she had so much confidence in his ideas. Unfortunately, he was fresh out.

Gerald excused himself for a few moments to make a phone call. "I'm at the Richmonds'. There's something odd going on with Scott."

His associate sighed. "I was afraid of that. What does he know?"

"When I told him his mother was stalling about the imitation jewels, he acted as though he didn't know what I was talking about."

"Well . . . maybe he doesn't."

"Or maybe he does and he lied to me," Gerald said grimly.

"What should we do?"

Gerald thought for a moment. "He has asked me for assistance in the past. Perhaps if the investigation heats up, he'll come to me again."

"Oh, I see. Then you can steer him in the wrong direction and keep him from finding out what's really going on."

"Exactly. I think it's the only safe choice we have at the moment."

Chapter Thirteen

To come up with a plan, Nicole had suggested they meet with Alyx. And while she did value her friend's opinion, she had suggested it more to have Alyx as a buffer between her and Scott. Nicole still felt a bit awkward around him, especially since he seemed to have changed toward her. To others, he might appear the same—friendly and flirtatious— but Nicole could tell the difference. She hadn't realized how constantly he'd found reasons to touch her until he stopped doing it. She missed it.

Now, she sat on the couch while he stood out on the balcony of Alyx's downtown Denver apartment, gazing eight stories down into the Sixteenth Street pedestrian mall. "What a great place."

Alyx moved out to join him on the small balcony. "I love it here in the heart of the city. There's always something happening down in the mall, no matter what time of the day or night. You should see it after the Broncos win."

Scott laughed. "Pretty wild, huh?"

"It can be. But it's a lot of fun to watch."

It gave Nicole a pang to see how comfortable Scott was with Alyx—far more comfortable than he seemed with her lately. She wanted to join them out on the balcony, but its small size made her hesitate. It was too close; too intimate.

Luckily, they came back inside.

Alyx grinned at Nicole. "Got my invite to the big do. I've never heard of anyone having an engagement party at the library before."

"You say that like we're going to have milk and cookies in the stacks," Nicole protested with a smile. "Actually, it was Scott's idea. He thought my friends might be more comfortable there."

Alyx turned to regard Scott with approval. "Good call. And I didn't mean to sound negative. Schlessman Hall is beautiful."

"That's what I hear," Scott said as he took a seat on the opposite end of the couch from Nicole. "Mother is taking care of the arrangements, so it's bound to be great. But, most importantly, the Larsons have said they're going to be there."

"The Larsons?" Alyx repeated with a puzzled look.

"They're the ones who have the fake sapphires."

"Oh, right."

"I assume you have some sort of plan?" Nicole asked.

"Of course."

Alyx perked up. "I know, we're going to break into their house while the party's going on."

Scott shook his head. "No, that wouldn't work. For one thing, it might look suspicious if Nicole and I went missing at our own party. For another, we haven't determined yet exactly where the jewels are."

"You don't think they're in the house?" Nicole asked.

"No, I do, but I don't know where in the house.

The other two were fairly easy to figure out, but the Larsons are too closed-mouthed about their security. We need to learn more before we can determine how to make the switch."

Alyx nodded, though she looked disappointed. "So what's the plan for the party?"

"I thought Nicole and I could corner the Larsons and pump them discreetly about their safety measures."

"Won't they get suspicious?" Nicole asked.

"Not if we do it right. Once we have them in sight, we can give Alyx the high sign and she can come over and start a conversation that will naturally lead to security."

"Like what?" Alyx asked eagerly.

Scott shrugged. "You could say your sister was just robbed, or maybe a neighbor. And since Nicole and I are thinking about moving in here after we're married, we'd naturally be concerned about the security of the building."

"We are?" That was news to Nicole.

Amusement danced in Scott's eyes. "Sure, why not? Would you rather live with Mother?"

Grace was nice but . . . live with her? "No," Nicole said as politely as she could, then frowned. "Wait a minute. We're not really getting married, so this whole question is moot."

Scott grinned. "Well, if the engagement and wedding are pretend, why not our future living arrangements?"

"You have a point, but none of my friends would believe it."

"She's right," Alyx said with a shrug. "Everyone knows how much Nicole loves her cozy little house with its peace and quiet. They wouldn't believe she'd agree to move here."

"Okay," Scott said. "Then you can say Missy got robbed and we're worried about the security at Nicole's house."

Alyx nodded decisively. "And Missy deserves it, too." She swerved her head abruptly to look at Nicole. "You didn't invite her to the party, did you?"

"Good Lord, no." Nicole didn't consider her neighbor a friend.

"Good," Alyx said. "If she came, she might try to hump Scott's leg or something."

Nicole grinned at the thought—rather like a Chihuahua making love to a Great Dane.

Scott laughed. "Mother would definitely not approve. Okay, we all agree—no Missy. But we can use her as an excuse to talk about security. We can ask the Larsons what they do to keep their valuables safe and ask for their advice. With any luck, they'll tell us exactly what we need to know."

Nicole nodded. "Sounds good to me." And it might even work.

"Yeah," Alyx agreed. "I like the part where I get to diss Missy."

Scott's cell phone rang then, and he moved off to the balcony to answer it.

Nicole smiled at her friend. "You just like being part of the plot."

"True," Alyx said with a raised eyebrow. "I *am* enjoying it—Scott's a lot of fun. In fact, I think I'm enjoying this engagement of yours more than you are."

Nicole was saved from answering when Scott came back into the room, putting his phone back in his pocket. "I'm sorry, I have to go. Mother has some sort of domestic crisis she insists she needs help with."

"That's okay," Nicole said. "I think we're done anyway."

"Good." He headed for the door. "I'll see you both at the party, then. Thanks for having us, Alyx."

"No problem," Alyx said as she let him out the door. She turned to give Nicole a penetrating look. "Okay, what's up?"

"Nothing much."

"Don't give me that. You know what I'm talking about. What's up with you and Scott?"

"Nothing." Unfortunately.

"Nothing?" Alyx repeated incredulously as she plopped down on the chair across from Nicole. "Yeah, I guess you're right. There was nothing going on between you two—and that's the problem."

"What do you mean?" Nicole hedged.

"Come on, it's so obvious. Every other time I've seen the two of you together, Scott has found any tiny little excuse to touch you, kiss you, rub your shoulders. Tonight, no touchy-feely. What happened? Did you have a fight?"

"Sort of."

"I knew it. What about?"

Nicole averted her gaze, not sure she wanted to talk about it even with her best friend. She shrugged, hoping Alyx would give up on the topic and move to something else. "It doesn't matter—"

"Oh, wow," Alyx interrupted. "I just figured it out. You did the deed, didn't you?"

"What deed?"

"You know—you got a little nookie, cookie." When Nicole stared blankly at her, not knowing whether to answer that or not, Alyx continued. "Did the horizontal mambo? Had hot monkey sex?"

Nicole held up her hands to ward off any more descriptions and felt her face heat. "I get it, I get it."

"I knew it," Alyx crowed. "You got it."

"That's not what I meant."

"I know, but it's true, isn't it? And I'll bet you a thousand bucks that you felt all guilty about it later and pissed him off."

"No bet," Nicole said, admitting the truth of Alyx's guess. Alyx would only harass her until she got it out of her anyway.

"Why?"

"Why did I do it, or why did I feel guilty?"

Alyx rolled her eyes. "Come on, it's obvious why you did it. Just look at Scott. And knowing you, I knew you'd feel guilty for doing something just for yourself for a change. No, the question is, why did you piss him off?"

"I didn't mean to . . . ." She paused, but the weight of Alyx's silence and her pointed stare made Nicole continue. "I don't know. I'm just afraid of looking like a fool, being dumped . . . getting hurt."

"And you told him so, I bet." Alyx looked exasperated. "Come on, what's the worst that could happen?"

Nicole had to smile. "Don't go there. Scott already did."

"Okay, then tell me." Alyx leaned in close, with a curious look on her face. "Was it good?"

"Oh, yes."

Her friend grinned. "Was it *real* good?"

"Fabulous," Nicole admitted.

"Ooh, tell me more."

"I will not. It was private."

"Oh, come on," Alyx said with a grimace. "Between the two of us, you're the only one getting any action. At least let me live vicariously through you." She paused as if suddenly realizing something. "Hey, was this the item he said he was going to help you check off your list?"

"No." Nicole smiled in memory. "He took me on a balloon ride in Colorado Springs."

"And you did it in a balloon?" Alyx asked, her eyes wide.

"No, of course not," Nicole said with a laugh. "It was cold up there, the pilot was in the basket, too, and it's not exactly private."

"Sounds like fun," Alyx said enviously.

"It was, up until the pilot dumped champagne on my head. Then Scott took me to a hotel to clean up."

Alyx wrinkled her nose. "A hotel? I thought Scott had more class than that."

"Oh, he does. He took me to the Pourtales."

"Really? Wow. I've never stayed in a five-star hotel. How was it?"

"Wonderful and decadent. Then he gave me a massage . . . ." She paused, knowing a dreamy expression filled her eyes as she remembered how good it had felt.

"Good Lord, girlfriend. Don't stop there. Tell Alyx aaaaall about it."

Nicole just smiled and shook her head.

"I knew it. You have that smug smile on your face. I'll bet it was the best sex of your life, wasn't it?"

Nicole just shrugged. She wasn't willing to confirm Alyx's guess, but she couldn't deny it, either.

Alyx nodded knowingly. "I figured he was great in the sack."

Nicole winced. Scott had used very similar words when he'd flung her fears back in her face. Hating the way that sounded, she said, "He is a wonderful lover." More tender and caring than she had ever expected.

"So what did you do to screw it up?"

Nicole sighed and gazed down at the engagement ring as she twisted it around her finger. "As you said, he figured I thought he only wanted to 'get me in the sack.'"

"Scott?" Alyx said in an incredulous tone. "He's not that type, Nicole."

"I know that. He misunderstood and wouldn't listen when I tried to set it right."

With compassion in her eyes, Alyx asked, "How do you feel now?"

"Upset, I guess."

"Upset that you had hot monkey sex or upset that you screwed up so badly you're not getting any more?"

Her mouth twisted in a rueful smile, Nicole asked, "Are those my only two choices?"

"Yep, that's it. Pick one."

Alyx was right. There were no other choices. "The latter, I guess."

Alyx nodded wisely. "Then what are you going to do about it?"

"Nothing." What could she do? Scott didn't want to hear an apology.

"You're just gonna let a guy like that get away from you?"

"He was never mine to begin with," Nicole reminded her. "This whole engagement is a sham, remember?"

"Yeah, sure. Pull the other one. Come on, Nicole. I've seen you two together. There's more to your relationship than just a pretend engagement."

"Maybe . . . but we've never acknowledged it."

"So acknowledge it."

"I can't." Especially now.

"Why not?" Alyx rolled her eyes. "Never mind, I know. You're afraid of getting dumped—yada, yada, yada. Who isn't? But if you don't put yourself out there, you'll never find that special guy. You've already found him—do you know how hard that is? How can you let him go?"

"You make it sound so easy." And maybe it was, for free-spirited Alyx.

Alyx shrugged. "I've been dumped a lot myself, so I know what I'm talking about."

"But *your* ego can take it." Nicole's, on the other hand, wasn't nearly so sturdy.

Alyx's expression turned rueful. "Not always. And it usually hurts. But you know what? Most of the time, the relationship was pretty darn good up until the breakup. I was never sorry I gave it a shot." She considered. "Well, maybe that once. But I should have known a used-car salesman was only taking me for a spin."

Nicole shook her head in amusement. "So what are you saying? That it's worth it?"

"Yes, sometimes. If *he's* worth it. And I think Scott is, isn't he?"

Definitely.

Now, where had that thought come from? Nicole hadn't even realized she felt that way until Alyx asked the question. She needed time to think about it, to explore how she really felt. "I suppose."

"Then go for the gusto. It might lead to something fabulous. And even if it doesn't, you'll still have a lot of fun along the way."

Maybe . . . . "But I'm not sure he feels the same way about me."

"Trust me, he does," Alyx assured her. "I see it in his eyes whenever he's near you. I see it in his hands whenever he touches you. Now you just gotta get it to come out of his mouth so you'll believe it, too."

"Assuming I wanted to do that, how would I go about it?"

"First, you gotta apologize—make it up to him."

"How, when he won't listen to my apologies?"

"Don't tell him. Show him. Hot monkey sex works wonders."

Nicole felt her cheeks warm. "I wish you'd stop saying that."

Alyx laughed. "But it's so much fun to watch you turn pink when I do. And don't change the subject. You know what you need to do—seduce him."

Actually, Alyx had a point. What better way to prove to Scott that she didn't think he was just trying to "get her in the sack" than to lead him to that very sack herself? Her heart raced just thinking about it. But . . . "I'm not sure I can do that."

"Sure you can. And, if nothing else, it'll be fun." Alyx's eyes widened. "Hey, that ought to be on your list, too. I bet you've never deliberately seduced a man, have you?"

"No, I haven't." Nicole had never thought of herself as the seductive type.

"Then live a little. Cross another item off your list. Seduce Scott." When Nicole didn't say anything, Alyx wheedled, "Come on, you know you want to."

She did indeed, but hated to admit it out loud. "I'll think about it."

"Good. You won't be sorry. You're halfway in love with him already."

With a sudden flash of comprehension, Nicole realized Alyx was wrong. *Not halfway—all the way.*

Several days later, on the night of the engagement party, Scott picked Nicole up, grateful that he had the good luck to avoid Missy once again.

"You look great," he said as he helped Nicole into the car. She wore that black dress he had helped her pick out, the one with the slit up the thigh and the low back. It made her look very classy and very sexy at the same time. He longed to stroke that soft skin, slip her dress off, and explore the wonders he knew were beneath it. Clearing his throat of an unexpected lump, Scott said, "I'll have to beat the other guys off with a stick."

"Thank you," she said vaguely, and Scott wasn't sure she'd actually heard him.

He figured he knew why, too. He settled himself in the driver's seat and started the engine. "Nervous?"

"A little."

As he pulled away from the curb, he said, "You'll be fine. You've met a lot of these people already. And some of them are your friends and coworkers."

"I know." She shrugged. "It just feels odd."

"Because we're making it official?" he guessed.

"Yes, it feels more dishonest somehow."

Would you rather make it real? Scott wanted to ask. But it was obvious she didn't. Not with the way she'd been acting lately. "I'm sorry, but it can't be helped."

"I realize that. Just . . . don't leave me alone with strangers, okay?"

"Why not?"

She wriggled in her seat, looking uncomfortable. "I know it's odd, but in a huge crowd like that, I sometimes panic when I talk to someone I don't know. Especially in a situation like this, when I'm afraid someone will find us out and denounce us or something. I don't know what to say, so the silence turns awkward and I end up looking like a fool."

He gave her a puzzled glance. She seemed so confident at times, then she would pop up with these odd insecurities. "But you did so well with Weatherwax the other day, and that was in an even more challenging situation."

"But that was one on one. It's the crowd thing that bothers me, knowing that I have to have endless conversations with people I don't know. Trying to sound witty or even mildly competent each time is a strain." She shot him a glance. "For me, anyway. I know you thrive on it."

"Then do what I do."

She rolled her eyes at him. "You're not going to

tell me to picture them naked, are you? That doesn't work."

"No." He gave a mock shudder. "That could scare the hell out of you. Out of me, even. Out of anyone, for that matter. No, what I do is pick something about their appearance and compliment them on it—hair, dress, jewelry, that sort of thing. They'll think you have good taste and you can ask them where they got it, and go from there."

"That doesn't always work, either."

"Really? Sounds like there's a story behind that comment."

"There is," Nicole said wryly. "I once complimented a woman on her hair and asked her where she had it done. I didn't know she was wearing a wig because she'd lost her hair to chemotherapy. She thought I was being nasty and insensitive, and never spoke to me again. Now I'm nervous about saying anything."

Scott winced. "Ouch. Okay, I'll try to stay by your side and warn you of any lurking dangers that might pop out at you."

"Thank you. I know you're kidding, but I always feel better when you're around."

Scott gave her a swift glance, wondering what she meant by that, but her expression was bland. She must mean he made her feel safe in a crowd. Well, that was something, anyway.

They chatted for the rest of the drive, and Scott entertained Nicole with some of his own social blunders. Rather than scaring her, knowing that he had messed up a few times himself seemed to help her relax.

When they arrived at the library, Scott escorted

her to Schlessman Hall, a beautiful three-story bridged atrium with lots of wide open space, beautiful arched wooden ceilings, and a large mural on the walls that depicted the history of the region. The vastness of the space could have dwarfed the relative smallness of the party, but his mother had wisely placed decorations on the walls at about eight feet above the floor, and strategically placed refreshment tables and bars to draw the eye's attention.

Nicole paused at the entrance, taking it all in. "It's beautiful."

Yes, his mother had outdone herself. The pink and ivory decorations were enhanced with touches of silver, the tables were covered with an abundance of food, and a band played softly at the other end of the hall near a dance floor where a few couples took advantage of the music.

"Were you worried it might look like our drawing room?" Scott asked with a grin.

"Something like that."

"Luckily, that's one of the few places Mother indulges her taste for the rococo." He reached into his pocket and pulled out a velvet jewelry box. "And, speaking of indulgences, I have something for you."

She gave the box an apprehensive look. "Did that come from your mother's safe?"

He laughed. "No, I picked it out all by myself. It's an engagement present, from me to you."

She looked at him with a helpless expression, whispering, "But the engagement isn't real . . . and I didn't get you anything."

"Don't worry about it. I figure you deserve some

kind of reward for putting up with this." When she continued to look indecisive, he said, "Open it."

She opened the box and the pleasure on her face when she stared down at the beaded blue glass necklace was all the present he needed. "It's my favorite—cobalt blue. How nice of you to remember. You know, I've collected some of the glass, but never any jewelry."

Happy that she was pleased, he added, "This is antique glass from Holland." And it had taken him a devil of a time to find it.

As he helped her put it on, she said, "Thank you so much, Scott. It's perfect."

Smiling, he said, "It looks good with that dress, too. Now we can go in."

She snuck her hand into his, and Scott looked at her in surprise. She had never deliberately touched him before—never initiated it, anyway. What was going through her mind? But her shy smile didn't reveal her feelings, so Scott was left to wonder if the gift had made her affectionate. Probably not, he knew he couldn't buy her affection. She probably just wanted their engagement to look real.

He gave her a reassuring smile and squeezed her hand, then led her fully into the room.

"Oh, there you are," his mother said, sailing majestically toward them.

"Hello, Mrs. Richmond," Nicole said. "The room looks stunning."

Grace beamed and appropriated Nicole's free arm, patting her hand. "Thank you. Now come with me, dear. There are some people I want you to meet."

Nicole flashed Scott a panicked look and her grip tightened on his hand.

Feeling like a knight to the rescue, Scott said, "I'll come, too. Don't you think we should present a united front as a couple tonight?"

He was rewarded with a grateful smile from Nicole as his mother said, "I suppose you can't let her out of your sight, can you? Ah, young love."

But she didn't appear to need an answer as she steered them firmly to a small knot of people and proudly introduced Nicole as her future daughter-in-law.

Nicole seemed to handle it well as they swept from person to person in his mother's wake, especially when they complimented her on her unusual necklace, but he could see the strain around her eyes. When she slid an arm around his waist and leaned into him, he could see she looked a little glassy-eyed as well.

Grace tried to draw them toward yet another group, but Scott said, "I think we need a break, Mother. Can you excuse us for a little while? I need something to drink and I think Nicole does, too."

"Oh, of course." Reluctantly, Grace relinquished Nicole's arm.

Scott nodded and steered Nicole toward the bar near the dance floor, hoping no one would stop them.

"Thank you," Nicole whispered.

But her gratitude was short-lived as a tall, thin man stopped her and said hello. Nicole smiled politely and introduced him to Scott as her library branch manager.

The man gave Scott a hearty handshake. "Congratulations on your engagement. Great idea, this party. Having it here, I mean. I've even had several people tell me they planned to make a donation. Isn't that great?"

"Yes, it is," Nicole agreed, but her smile looked wan.

"Glad to hear it," Scott said. "Now, if you'll excuse me, I think this is our dance."

And as the band struck up a slow tune, Scott whisked her onto the dance floor.

"I thought you wanted something to drink," Nicole said.

"No, it was just an excuse to get away." He smiled down at her. "I don't think anyone will follow you out here."

She sighed. "Good idea. Can we stay here the rest of the night?"

"Not *all* night. We have a couple of things we have to do, remember? Besides, your feet would be mad at you in the morning."

"I know, but it might be worth it." She snuggled close and laid her head on his shoulder as they swayed to the music.

Something within him melted. She was totally adorable, and her simple act of trust caught him off guard, making him feel as if she might even care for him.

No, that was wishful thinking. She was tired and he was just a convenient headrest, that was all.

But as they continued to move to the music and he held Nicole in his arms, love welled up inside him. At that moment, he knew he wanted to spend the rest of his life with this woman. He wanted to spend every day with her, make love with her, grow old with her. Nothing else mattered, if only she would be with him.

Now he just had to convince her . . . .

The dance came to an end, and she sighed when they stopped moving. Scott squeezed her lightly and murmured, "I wish we could stay here all night, but we have a plan to execute. Alyx is watching us and I see the Larsons over by the bar. You ready for this?"

Nicole pulled away. "I guess." She glanced toward the bar. "I remember what Mrs. Larson looks like, but I don't see her."

"She's behind her husband. He's the man passing an envelope to Gerald."

"I see." They started to leave the dance floor, but Nicole grabbed his arm to stop him. "Wait. Isn't that Digby next to him?"

So it was. "I wonder what he's doing here? He must have cadged an invite from Mother."

Gerald and Digby left then, and the Larsons were alone. "Looks like a good time to me," Nicole said. "Might as well get it over with."

Scott nodded and caught Alyx's eye, giving her a pointed look in the Larsons' direction. She nodded to indicate she got the message.

Scott led Nicole over and introduced her to Mr. Larson. They chatted for a moment before Alyx came barreling up, right on cue.

"Oh, Nicole," she squealed, throwing her arms around her friend. "I'm so happy for you."

Nicole smiled and thanked her, then introduced Alyx to the Larsons. "She's my best friend," Nicole added with a smile.

"And your maid of honor," Alyx insisted. "Don't forget that."

Nicole laughed. "How could I?"

"Oh, did you hear?" Alyx said, her eyes turning round. "Your neighbor Missy got robbed."

The Larsons made appropriate distressed noises as Alyx embellished her tale of dastardly deeds and stolen treasures. Scott raised his eyebrow at her, trying to let her know she was overdoing it a bit, but she just grinned at him.

"How horrible," Nicole said and slipped her arm around Scott's waist again, as if seeking comfort. She glanced up at him. "Do you think they'll come back to my neighborhood? I'd hate to have anyone pawing through my things."

"They might," Mr. Larson said. "Thieves sometimes work an entire neighborhood before they move on elsewhere."

Nicole did a creditable job of looking worried. "You think we should install a security system then?"

"Oh, yes," Mrs. Larson said. "It will make you feel much safer, believe me."

Nicole turned to Scott and he picked up on her cue. "Sorry, hon. I know nothing about them." He turned to Mr. Larson. "But I bet Mr. Larson does."

"Please, call me George," he said, then admitted, "I know a little. We recently had a new security system put in our house."

"Great," Scott declared. "Could you advise me, then, on what to look for?"

Appearing flattered that Scott had asked his opinion, George said, "Sure, if you'd like to come over to the house, I'd be glad to show you what we've done."

"Great." Exactly what he'd been hoping for. Scott made arrangements to meet them there, and the Larsons took their leave.

Scott grinned at Nicole and Alyx. "You two were perfect. Thanks."

"No problem," Alyx said with a wink. "Now, I think I'm gonna find me a cold glass of champagne and a hot bod. See you later . . . ." She waggled her fingers and strolled off in search of her prey.

Nicole chuckled. "I pity the poor man she has her eye on."

"Oh, I don't know. He might enjoy it." Scott wished Nicole was as free with her feelings as Alyx.

"He might at that."

They shared a smile, but their moment of understanding was ruined when Melinda wandered up. Great, just what he needed right now was for Nicole to be reminded of the woman who considered herself his old girlfriend.

"Hello, Scott," Melinda drawled, taking a sip of champagne. "So you're really going through with it?"

"With what?"

Melinda gestured vaguely around at the party. "All this. Getting married."

Nicole stiffened beside him and curved her arm around his waist again, as if branding him as hers. Scott didn't mind—he rather enjoyed her possessiveness. "Sure. Did you doubt it?"

She raised one perfectly arched eyebrow, ignoring Nicole. "I'll believe it when I see you walk down the aisle and say 'I do.'" She ran a manicured fingernail down his lapel. "How about a dance for old time's sake?"

It looked like Melinda had taken a few too many sips of champagne. Nicole's arm tightened around him, from possessiveness or a desire not to be left alone, he wasn't sure. Either way, he was enjoying it.

"No, thanks," Scott said with a smile to take the sting out of the rejection. "I plan to dance only with my fiancée tonight."

Melinda skimmed a derisive glance over Nicole that made Scott steam. "What's the matter? Can't get rid of the ball and chain?"

"Don't want to," he assured her with a tight smile and pulled Nicole closer. By now the two of them were plastered so tight together, Melinda had to get the message.

Nicole relaxed a little, but Melinda seemed oblivious to nonverbal communication this evening. Turning a fake smile on Nicole, she said, "You don't mind, do you? After all, you have his ring on your finger. I'm no threat."

"I know," Nicole said calmly.

Score one for Nicole. Looks like this was one conversation she wasn't having trouble with.

Nicole continued in a calm voice, "But not tonight, I think. Tonight he's all mine."

Melinda's eyes narrowed, but before she could say anything, the band struck up a flourish and Grace called for everyone's attention.

"That's our cue," Scott whispered and gratefully pulled Nicole away from Melinda and toward the band.

Grace took her place in front of the microphone

and thanked everyone for coming. Giving Scott a
fond glance, she said, "Like many of you, I despaired
of my son ever finding the right woman and settling
down. But he's done so at last, and I couldn't be hap-
pier. Please help me celebrate the engagement of
Scott Richmond to Nicole Dreyfuss."

Scott and Nicole became the center of attention
as his mother made a smooth movement that
turned the spotlight on him. Scott had no idea
what he was going to say, but as the applause faded,
he decided to wing it.

Glancing at Nicole, he said, "I would like to
thank everyone for helping us celebrate one of the
happiest moments of our lives. Second only to the
moment I place the wedding ring on her finger, of
course."

He grinned, and the crowd chuckled with him.

A man shouted from the back, "Yeah, sure. What
are the odds that'll happen?"

Another shouted, "Yeah, Scott. Where's the
punch line?"

Nicole looked stricken, and Scott felt like hitting
someone. Whose bright idea had it been to serve
liquor at the party?

"No joke," he assured everyone, then hastened to
do some damage control for Nicole's sake. "And I'd
say the odds are pretty good . . . unless she wises
up and dumps me before then."

Everyone laughed, but a glance at Nicole confirmed the damage had already been done. Damn
it.

Chapter Fourteen

Several days later as the Jag convertible sped through the night toward the Larsons' house, Nicole put her head back and enjoyed the sensation of the wind in her hair, hoping it would blow the wispy doubts and worries from her mind.

Unfortunately, it wasn't working very well. Scott's presence in the driver's seat made her hyper-aware of him, made her want to lean over and run her fingers through his windblown hair, place a kiss on his neck, caress his thigh . . . .

But wanting to act on Alyx's advice, wanting to seduce Scott, was a whole lot easier than actually doing it. Nicole wasn't quite brave enough for that yet, though she had tested the waters at the engagement party. They had been a little chilly at first, then turned a whole lot warmer when she had ventured to touch him and they'd danced that lovely dance. Unfortunately, Melinda's presence along with his friends' reaction to Scott's speech had made her feel doused in ice water.

She should have known some of them would detect the sham, no matter how hard Scott had tried to cover up. It had made her feel uneasy, like she

was an imposter. After that, it had been hard to re-
capture her willingness to be the aggressor.

She glanced at Scott, who was intent on driving.
It would be so much easier if he weren't so breezy
and so hard to read. If only she knew how he really
felt about her, this would be a whole lot less complicated.

Yeah, right. And if she were Alyx, she would have
just demanded to know his feelings about now. But
Nicole was nowhere near as comfortable with con-
frontation as her friend. Damn it, why didn't men
come with instruction manuals?

Impatient with her own thoughts, she asked,
"How are things going with your mother? Has
Digby let up on her?"

"Not yet. He keeps getting more insistent on seeing the fake jewels. Mother has been putting him
off, but I don't know how much longer that will
last." He glanced at Nicole. "But just in case, I had
to tell Mother I took the sapphires out for cleaning."

"Good idea." It would look even more suspicious
if they were missing without a good reason. Out of
curiosity, she asked, "Where did you put them?"

"In the glove compartment."

"The glove compartment?" she repeated incredulously. "Of *this* car?"

"Sure. Why, what's wrong with that?"

"It's a convertible."

He gave her a puzzled look. "You think the jewels object to having the top down?"

"No, I think it's easier to break in and steal them
in a convertible."

"I suppose it would be," Scott conceded, "if someone knew they were there. But no one does, so they're safe enough. And I locked the glove compartment."

Like that made it better? "But what if someone does break in? The lock won't stop them—it will only encourage them to believe there's something valuable there."

He shrugged. "I'll deal with that if it happens, but I won't worry about it."

And therein lay the difference between them. Nicole sighed. Well, this time she wasn't going to worry for him. Instead, she changed the subject. "Alyx didn't like being left behind."

"I know, but it couldn't be helped. George Larson didn't even invite *you*. I can explain you away, but your best friend? He would probably think something was up."

"I know." Alyx understood it, too, but didn't like it.

He stopped in front of a house. "You ready for this?"

She grinned. "You sure ask me that a lot."

"I guess I do."

And for good reason, she supposed. "One of these days, maybe we'll be able to show up at someone's house just to have a good time and not spy on them or try to figure out the best way to compromise their security."

Too late, Nicole realized he could interpret her comment as meaning she hoped they would be together afterward. Luckily, he didn't seem to take it that way.

"Ah, where would be the fun in that?"

"It would just be a nice change." But as he came

around to her door to help her out of the car, she realized she didn't feel the trepidation she'd expected as she gazed at the Larson house. She'd always had confidence in Scott's ability to smooth-talk his way into anything, but dealing with Weatherwax the other day had given her confidence in her own ability to wing it, too.

This so-called house was really a fabulous mansion, she realized as the butler showed them inside. But she didn't have time to take in its magnificence as Mr. Larson came toward them.

Looking surprised, he said, "I didn't know you'd have your lovely fiancée with you."

"I'm sorry," Scott said with a smile. "I thought you'd realize. After all, it is her house that needs the security and I thought she ought to have a say in how it is handled."

"Of course," the man said.

But he still looked doubtful, so Nicole decided to spread a little butter where it might do some good. "Thank you so much for having us," she gushed. "We feel so lucky to have someone with your expertise to talk to."

He preened a little, but said, "Oh, I'm not nearly as knowledgeable as all that. But won't you both come into the parlor where we can discuss it?"

They followed him in and refused refreshments as they seated themselves.

George rubbed his hands together. "So tell me, what is it you're trying to protect?"

"My house," Nicole said hesitantly. Was that what he meant?

"I mean what, specifically, is your purpose in

needing the security? What valuables are you trying to protect?"

"Well, I have a glass collection that has some value. It's spread throughout my house, mostly in the living room."

"She also has jewelry she inherited from her mother," Scott interjected.

I do? Well, maybe a few small pieces, but nothing valuable. Scott squeezed her hand warningly and she realized he wanted her to go along with it. Okay, she could do that. "Yes. And I'd hate to see it stolen—it has a lot of sentimental value."

Larson frowned. "The best place for that sort of thing is a safe-deposit box."

"But that would be so inconvenient," Nicole protested. "Especially since I like to wear it often." A sudden thought struck her. Did his wife keep her jewelry in a safe-deposit box? She hoped not; it would be impossible to replace them there if she did. Nicole wondered how to ask him that, but he answered it for her.

"That's what my wife says, too." He shook his head and shared an exasperated look with Scott as if commiserating with him on women's silly foibles. "So I had a safe installed just for her gewgaws."

"You have more than one?" Nicole asked, trying to sound like the dumb bunny he obviously thought she was.

"Yes, I often bring home important, confidential papers from the office and need a safe place to store them."

And she bet he handcuffed his briefcase to his wrist when he took them back. But she didn't care about that safe. She doubted he'd let his wife's "gewgaws" intermingle with his important papers. "I don't have anything like that," Nicole said. "But Scott might."

"Not much," he said with a smile. "We can share. But we would like to protect Nicole's collectibles, too."

"I understand," Mr. Larson said heavily. "Just look around at this place. My wife has so many antiques and collectibles, it looks like a damned showroom."

Nicole raised her eyebrows but didn't say anything. She rather liked the way his wife had decorated. Very understated and very classy.

"Then I assume you have a separate security system for the house in addition to your two safes?" Scott asked.

"I have to."

Scott nodded. "Would you mind showing us how it works? We'd like to see if it might be suitable for our needs."

"Sure," Larson said and took them around.

The more Nicole saw, the more depressed she became. The only bright spot was when they learned that Mrs. Larson's safe was in the bedroom. At least they wouldn't have to search for that. The only problem was, Nicole didn't see how they could possibly get past the alarm system since it required a recognized fingerprint to disengage it.

"Very impressive," Scott said. "Who installed it for you?"

"Jackson Security."

"I've heard of them—they have an excellent reputation."

"Yes, they do, and I've been very pleased with them so far," Larson said.

"Well, thank you very much for having us," Scott said as he shook Larson's hand.

"Glad to do it. Let me know if you need any more help."

"Thanks, I will." Scott escorted Nicole out the door and grinned at her.

"What are you smiling about?" she whispered fiercely as they walked toward the car. "And why are we leaving so early? We don't know how to get past their security yet."

"And we won't learn it from him."

"Oh, I see. You think his wife will blab?" But how were they going to find her to pump her for information?

"No, but he did tell us the one thing that might help us get in the door."

"What?"

"The name of the security company."

"How does that help?"

"Well, it just so happens that the owner, Boyd Jackson, is a good friend of mine."

"Mr. Digby is here again," Marta said in a disapproving tone.

Scott swore under his breath. It was bad enough that he had to entertain Gerald until his mother got home, but Digby, too? Especially when he'd invited Jackson, Nicole, and Alyx to dinner in an hour. But he supposed there was no choice. "Please show him in," Scott said.

Digby came in, looking belligerent. Figuring it

.

was better to go on the offense rather than defense, Scott asked, "You caught the thief yet?"

"I'm still working on it," Digby said, not at all perturbed that Scott had questioned his abilities. "These things take time."

Scott understood his game. Digby obviously wanted the credit for himself, which was why he hadn't called the police in yet. "I see."

"I'm sure you're doing your best," Gerald said.

Digby graced him with a grateful nod and addressed Scott. "One of the things that would help a great deal in the investigation is if I could get a good look at the copies your father had made. So I know exactly what it is I'm looking for."

"I'm sorry," Scott said, trying to look truly regretful. "But my mother isn't here, and they're in the safe in her bedroom."

"Surely you have the combination."

Scott toyed with the idea of disclaiming all knowledge of the combination, but Gerald shot him a warning look. "Of course he does."

Scott sighed inwardly, wondering why Gerald had chosen this moment to "help." "Yes, but Mother is finicky. She doesn't like people pawing through her things when she isn't there. It makes her very cranky." And that was no lie.

"She doesn't have to know."

"Oh, trust me, she'd know." Scott grimaced. "The servants know everything that's going on around here, and they'll be sure to let her know anything out of the ordinary."

Digby frowned. "Why won't you assist me in this simple request? Are you hiding something?"

"No, I'm just trying to avoid upsetting my mother. It's no fun being around her when she's angry."

"Is your mother trying to hide something?"

"Not that I know of."

"Then why is she keeping me from seeing the copies?"

"I don't know that she is."

"But she keeps stalling me when I ask to see them. Why?"

Scott shrugged. "You'll have to ask her that."

Digby shook his head with a sigh. "She's more slippery than you when she wants to be. Look, all I want to do is get a look at those jewels to see what I'm looking for in the stolen ones. Is that too much to ask?"

"I suppose not."

"Then why not help me? If we do it quickly before she returns, it will cause her—and you—less distress. Because one way or another, I intend to see those copies."

Gerald added his two cents' worth. "It seems a reasonable request. And it would help expedite the claim."

Scott sighed. Why not? He really had nothing to hide, though he didn't relish trying to explain why some of them were missing. "All right. But it'll be your head on the chopping block when she finds out, Gerald. And she will."

Gerald nodded in unruffled calm. "I have no problem with that."

"Then come with me."

Scott showed them to his mother's bedroom, and while Digby looked around curiously at the ornate gold and white furnishings, Gerald didn't seem curious at all, as if he were already familiar with the place. That was interesting. How much time had Gerald spent in his mother's bedroom? *Will I be calling you Daddy soon?*

Scott opened the safe and pulled out a few boxes and handed them to Digby. The investigator glanced down at the imitation ruby necklace. "It looks real."

"It's supposed to," Scott reminded him.

"Then how do you tell the real ones from the fake?"

"Several ways." He took a simple gold chain from the safe, then held it up to the necklace. "This chain is fourteen karat gold. The necklace you're holding is only plated. See how it looks brassier?"

Digby nodded, and even Gerald looked interested. Scott added, "The gems don't quite look like real rubies to those who know stones. They're man-made imitations, though very good ones. And the clincher is, my father had my mother's initials engraved on the clasp of each one of the imitations so anyone could tell them apart. See?"

Digby peered at the clasp. "Yes, I see the letters G and R."

"That's how you know they're the fakes."

"I see." He glanced at Scott. "Can I see all of them, please? I'd like to take pictures so I can have them on file."

Why not? Scott pulled all the boxes out of the safe, and Digby placed them on his mother's bed then took a small camera out of his pocket and snapped pictures of them. "Wait a minute. These aren't complete. Where are the sapphires?"

Damn. Scott had hoped he wouldn't notice that.

"When we were checking to make sure these were the copies, I noticed they were dingy, so I sent them for cleaning," he said casually.

"Just part of them?"

"Yes, I figured we needed a regular schedule to make sure they didn't get that way again, so I sent the sapphires out this quarter. The rubies will go next, then the emeralds and diamonds. That way I spread the cost over four quarters and not all the gems are gone at once." Realizing he was babbling, which could only look more suspicious, Scott shut up.

Digby nodded slowly. "But something else confuses me. Why did she keep the copies here instead of in the other room with the real ones?"

That was an easy one. "Because the bedroom safe isn't as secure. Mother sometimes forgets to close it, and the servants wander in and out while it's open. So, to avoid potential loss, she only keeps her less valuable pieces here. I had the safe put in the living room to house her more expensive ones."

"I see. Please let me know once the sapphires are returned."

"I'll do that," Scott promised with a tense smile.

"Good. What—"

Digby was cut off in mid-sentence by an icy voice from the doorway. "What is the meaning of this?" Grace demanded. She glanced at the jewels spread out on her bed, and her expression turned to outrage. "What are you all doing in my room? Explain yourselves at once."

Scott held up his hands in surrender, knowing there was no hope when Grace was on a tear. "They made me do it," he said plaintively.

But she was not lulled by his feeble attempt at a joke. "What is going on?"

Digby had the sense to look alarmed, but Gerald didn't lose his aplomb. In fact, the man was so full of aplomb, Scott doubted he ever lost enough to notice. Instead, Gerald soothed Grace, saying, "It's my fault. I was trying to save you some distress by showing Mr. Digby the jewels while you were gone, and I was hoping to expedite the claim and your money."

Wonder of wonders, it worked—Mother's feathers seemed to even out as he watched. Though Scott had a feeling her reaction was due less to Gerald's calming powers, and more to the mention of the money.

But as Gerald continued to soothe her, Scott and Digby shoveled jewelry boxes back into the safe as fast as they could. Digby even smoothed the bedspread when he was done.

Marta appeared in the doorway. "Your guests have arrived, Mr. Richmond."

"Guests?" Grace repeated. "What guests?"

"Remember, I asked Jackson to be my best man and invited him to dinner to meet Nicole and Alyx since he was unable to attend our engagement party."

"Oh, that's right," his mother said, checking her appearance in the mirror. "I suppose we should go down."

She turned to exit, and Scott muttered to Digby, "This might be a good time for you to leave, too."

"Yes, sir. Right away." And Digby managed to scurry out the door and out of the line of fire without ever coming near Grace.

Well, at least the investigator had finally gotten

what he wanted. Maybe he'd leave them alone for a while now.

Downstairs, Nicole and Alyx were already waiting for them in the drawing room, and Jackson had just showed up. Tall, dark, and rugged-looking with an impressive trust fund, Boyd Jackson had always attracted more than his share of the ladies when they roomed together in college.

Scott introduced them all, and Jackson bestowed a friendly smile on Nicole but when Alyx gave him a frankly admiring gaze and purred, "I'm very happy to meet you," Jackson responded with a mere baring of his teeth and a cold look, ignoring her outstretched hand entirely.

Uh-oh. Jackson was wary of women, having had many man-eaters chase after him and his trust fund before, but he had no way of knowing that, under that smart-aleck exterior, Alyx was a sweet marshmallow. Scott should have remembered Jackson's prejudices and clued him in to Alyx's true nature before he came. She didn't deserve to be treated this way.

Evidently she agreed because her gaze turned frosty and challenging.

"Drink anyone?" Scott asked before their animosity could escalate.

"Sure," Alyx said. "Something strong." She darted an annoyed glance at Jackson. "I think I'll need it."

Scott took drink orders from the others and when he came to Jackson, his best man said, "No thanks, I don't drink."

Alyx arched an eyebrow at him. "Oh?" she asked sweetly. "Is that why they call you Boy?"

Scott almost choked, and his mother looked aghast. But Jackson wasn't intimidated. In fact, he had a martial light in his eyes. "That's Boyd, not Boy. And I don't drink because I don't like the effect it has on me." He met her challenging gaze with one of his own and a slight smile. "Tell me, why do *you* drink? Having a man's name doesn't mean you have to drink like one."

Alyx shot an incredulous glance at Scott. "This is the 'best man' you could find?"

Sparks lit in Boyd's eyes. "I wouldn't go there if I were you . . . Miss 'maid of honor.'"

Now even Nicole looked alarmed, so Scott stepped in and glanced at the two combatants. "Okay, here are the rules. Both of you go to your own corner, and don't come out fighting until the bell rings. Got it?"

Alyx rolled her eyes. "You playing referee?"

"Someone has to." Besides, he wasn't at all sure who would come out on top in this contest. "And no hitting below the belt."

Alyx harrumphed and looked grumpy, but there was a light of interest in Boyd's eyes. It wasn't often that Boyd met a woman who would stand up to him, and Scott got the impression he rather liked the experience.

Jackson evidently decided to play nice. "Have you set the date yet?" he asked.

"Not yet," Scott said in relief. "But I thought my best man ought to meet my fiancée and her maid of honor sometime before the wedding." *My mistake.*

The talk turned to the wedding and other innocuous topics as they finished their drinks and went in to dinner.

Scott caught Alyx by the elbow and murmured, "Be nice. We need his help."

"Oh, all right," she said ungraciously. "I'll be nice if he will."

Scott sighed. It looked like it was going to be a long dinner . . . .

And it was. Boyd and Alyx continually tried to one-up each other throughout the meal. They seemed to enjoy themselves, but they were the only ones who did. Nicole gamely tried to get Jackson to talk about his security company, and Grace kept trying to steer the conversation into calmer waters, but those boats just wouldn't float. Gerald ignored it all as if nothing out of the ordinary were happening, and Scott just watched it all in resignation.

Finally, dinner was over and after Grace and Gerald escaped, Scott led the others back into the drawing room.

As they all seated themselves again, he wondered how he could bring the conversation around to the security company and convince Jackson to help them. "How's business?"

"Fine," Jackson said, then leaned back in his chair and gave Scott a shrewd look. "Why do you ask?"

"Just curious."

"Uh huh." Jackson looked sardonic. "And I'm curious about when you're going to tell me the real reason why you invited me here."

Chapter Fifteen

Nicole almost choked. Boyd Jackson was a heck of a lot smarter than Alyx gave him credit for. Nicole couldn't help but like him. Not many men knew how to give as good as they got when it came to dealing with Alyx. It was a new experience for her friend, and once Alyx got over her annoyance, maybe she'd see it for the rarity it was. Instead, she seemed to see him only as a challenge.

Scott stared at Boyd for a moment, then his mouth quirked into a smile. "Okay, you got me. We need your help."

"Scott," Alyx protested, "what are you *doing*?"

Scott shrugged. "If we want his help, we need to tell him everything."

"Yes, you do," Boyd said firmly. "I take it this means you don't really need a best man?"

Alyx opened her mouth to reply, but Nicole stopped her with a hand on her arm. "Let Scott explain."

"Yes and no," Scott said. "If I really needed a best man, you'd be the one I asked. But I don't."

Nicole relaxed. If Scott meant to tell his friend the truth, it would be a lot easier to explain what they were trying to do.

Boyd glanced at Nicole with a grin. "Does that mean you're available?"

Nicole couldn't help but smile back. He was really a nice guy, and under other circumstances, she would really like to get to know him better.

Though she didn't answer, Scott did, looking annoyed. "Not while she's engaged to me."

"But you just said you *weren't* engaged."

"Not really, but the world thinks we are."

"Ooookay." Boyd leered engagingly at Nicole with humor dancing in his eyes. "Let me know when it's over, and maybe we can get together."

Nicole hid her amusement, knowing Boyd was only yanking Scott's chain. Besides, she kind of liked Scott's reaction. "I'll do that."

"Only a few people know it's not real," Alyx snapped, looking as annoyed as Scott.

Hmm, maybe Alyx wasn't as indifferent to Boyd as she pretended.

"That's right," Scott said. "Only the people in this room. And I'd like to keep it that way, so no flirting with my fiancée until we call it off, okay?"

Interesting. Scott's tone was more serious than joking. How did he mean that?

Boyd grinned. "You got it. But you have to tell me the story."

"Okay." Scott held out his hands in a warding gesture. "But I know how you are about honesty. Just wait and hear me out all the way through before you comment, all right?"

Boyd nodded, though his slight frown didn't bode well for Scott's chances of convincing him.

"Wait a minute." Alyx stood, looking indignant.

"What is he, some kind of cop? You think he'll turn you in or something?"

"I doubt it," Scott said.

Boyd's expression didn't lighten any. "I'm not a cop, but I am in the security business. And I won't lie to you or to the police. If you've done something wrong, keep it to yourself. I don't want to hear it."

Scott shook his head. "We can't. We need your help."

Nicole added, "And we aren't the ones who did something wrong."

"Just hear me out," Scott said in a wheedling tone.

Boyd closed his eyes momentarily and shook his head. "I'm sure I don't want to hear this, but go ahead."

"The reason Nicole and I got engaged is because her sister stole my mother's jewels."

Boyd rolled his eyes. "That makes sense. I always get engaged to the relatives of people who stole from me."

Nicole swallowed a chuckle, but Scott and Alyx didn't look so amused.

"She's only seventeen," Scott said. "Nicole's sister, I mean. She needed the money to attend college, and my family owed her."

"So she stole it from you?" Boyd shook his head in disbelief. "And you condone this? Where is this felon now?" His tone was light, but the expression on his face showed he didn't find this funny at all.

"She's safe in another state," Nicole said in soothing tones.

Boyd looked back and forth between them. "And you let her get away with it?"

"Let her?" Alyx exclaimed. "Hell, Scott helped her."

Nicole shot her friend an annoyed glance. "You're not helping."

"What?" Boyd looked confused, and Nicole didn't blame him. "You helped her?"

"Yes," Scott said impatiently, then told him the story. "I didn't realize she had already set up buyers for the jewels. I figured I'd catch her before she fenced them and buy them back from her."

Boyd seemed a little mollified by Scott's explanation, but the stealing part obviously still didn't go over well with him. Hell, it hadn't gone over well with Nicole either, so she couldn't blame him. "Chrissie told us who she sold the jewels to, but we couldn't report them to the police or they'd put her in jail."

"Okay, I get that." Boyd turned a puzzled glance on Scott. "What I don't get is why *you* got involved or why you need a pretend engagement because of it."

Scott sighed. "Because my father had copies made of the jewels, and that's what Chrissie took by mistake. But before I could stop her, Mother reported the real ones stolen to the insurance company."

Boyd's mouth dropped open. "Are you saying your mother deliberately committed fraud?"

"I'm afraid so."

"Then I don't know what you expect me to do except go to the police." He ran an impatient hand through his hair. "You've just made me an accessory. I can't afford that in my business."

Nicole winced. He was right, but she couldn't allow him to jeopardize Chrissie's future. "We can't send my sister and Scott's mother to jail. Surely you can see that."

"But what they did was wrong."

Obviously annoyed by Boyd's attitude, Alyx snapped, "The world isn't all black and white, you know. Ever heard of gray and maybe a little pink or purple?"

Ignoring her, Scott spoke directly to Boyd. "We know they screwed up, but they haven't hurt anyone. Just listen to the rest."

Boyd nodded for Scott to continue.

"The people who bought the jewels from Chrissie are friends of my mother."

"You have *got* to be kidding." Boyd glanced around in bewilderment. "This is a joke, right? I'm on 'Candid Camera' or something?"

Nicole grimaced. It did sound rather fantastic, told that way.

"No, it's not a joke," Scott said firmly. "And I'm afraid that if they learn the jewels they bought are fake, they'll find a way to ruin Mother's reputation."

"Wait. Let me get this straight. You're worried that these thieves will ruin your *mother's* reputation?"

"Yes. They wouldn't say it was because of the jewels, of course. But if they find out the jewels are fake, they'll find another way to ruin her. It's the way that crowd works."

"Maybe she deserves it," Boyd said bluntly.

"What if it was your mother in the same situation?" Scott asked. "Would you feel the same way?"

"My mother died years ago." But when Scott

raised an eyebrow, Boyd said, "Okay, okay, I get your point. But what do you intend to do about it?"

Seeing that Scott didn't seem to be getting far with him, Nicole said, "We figured if we switch the jewels and give them the real ones, they'll never be the wiser and the problem would never come up."

Boyd shook his head in disbelief. "And the engagement?"

Nicole grimaced. "I don't exactly run in the same circles Scott does, so he figured this would get me into their homes with him, to help him check out their security systems and figure out how to replace the jewels."

"Bad idea," Boyd said. "Do you have any idea how hard it would be to get past one security system, let alone three?"

"We already did two," Alyx shot back.

"We?" Boyd repeated, looking back and forth between Alyx and Nicole.

"Well, Scott did the first one and Nicole did the second," Alyx admitted. "I only got to drive." And she still sounded miffed about it.

When Boyd's incredulous gaze settled on Nicole, she felt herself flush. She didn't like the feeling of being diminished in his eyes.

"How did you manage that?" Boyd asked.

Scott explained, then said, "The only problem is, we haven't been able to figure out how to replace the third set of jewels yet. That's where you come in—it's one of your systems."

"Mine? And . . . what? You expect me to tell you how to circumvent it to get into the safe?"

That was the general idea . . . .

"Yes, please," Nicole said politely. "If you wouldn't mind."

"I would mind. Forget it."

Alyx made a noise of disgust. "I knew he wouldn't do it."

Boyd snorted. "That's the first sensible thing you've said all day. What sane man *would* go along with this harebrained scheme?"

"A friend, maybe?" Scott said in hopeful tones. At Boyd's exasperated glance, he added, "I've never asked you for a favor before."

"And this one's a doozy," Boyd countered. "You can't just ask someone to crack a safe for you, especially someone in my business, no matter how good a friend he is."

"Come on," Alyx said. "You know it's exactly the kind of thing Scott would ask someone."

Scott acknowledged the jibe with a rueful grin. "Okay, guilty as charged. But remember, we're not stealing anything. We want to take the worthless fakes out of the safe and put in the real jewels. Not only so they won't notice the substitution, but also to make sure the insurance company doesn't find out Mother reported the fakes stolen."

Boyd shook his head. "I don't care what you say. Any way you look at it, breaking into someone else's safe is wrong."

Nicole couldn't hold still any longer. "So is what the Larsons have done. In fact, they're worse than we are, because all we're trying to do is protect people. But didn't they commit grand larceny or something by buying stolen jewels?"

He seemed struck by that, but said, "The Larsons? You're sure it's them?"

"Positive," Nicole said. "Chrissie was right about the other two who had the jewels—I don't see why she'd lie about the third."

"That's hard to believe . . . ." Boyd shrugged. "In any case, you should go to the police."

Scott sighed. "We told you why we can't do that."

"Then I'm sorry, but I can't help you."

Boyd truly did seem sorry. But had she seen a little wavering there?

Scott stood abruptly. "Then we'll have to ask you to leave so we can discuss it. Wouldn't want to make you an accessory."

Boyd stayed seated and stared at Scott. "You mean you're still going through with it?"

"Yes."

"You'll never get past *my* system."

Scott shrugged. "We have to. And we'll do it with or without you." His expression softened. "But it would be a whole lot easier with you."

Nicole saw signs of Boyd's internal struggle before he finally sighed and shook his head. "I can't believe I'm saying this, but okay. I'll help you."

"Why?" Alyx asked in a suspicious tone.

"Because Scott's my friend. Because if I don't help you, you're bound to get caught and go to jail." Boyd grinned. "And because the sooner you get this over with, the sooner the engagement is called off and I can put the move on Nicole."

Nicole laughed, but Scott didn't seem to think it was funny. All he said was, "Thanks. We appreciate it. Now, if you'll just tell us how—"

"No can do." Boyd shook his head, looking stubborn. "If I'm going to help you, we're going to do it my way."

* * *

Several days later, Scott drove toward the Larsons' house again, with Nicole, Alyx, and Jackson packed in the Mercedes. One part of him felt relief that they were finally going to have this over and done with, but a much larger part didn't want it ended. Once they replaced the last set of jewels, he would have no reason to stay engaged to Nicole.

Jackson's comments the other night had brought that home to Scott. He knew his friend was only joking about pursuing Nicole after the engagement was over—at least, Scott *thought* he was joking—but it had reminded him that soon they would have no claim on each other.

And after seeing her tonight in a soft pink sweater that dipped down to reveal some truly magnificent cleavage, Scott was reminded even more of how wonderful it felt to hold her naked body, stroke that soft skin. It made him even more anxious to stake his claim, especially since Jackson had very obviously noticed Nicole's charms as well.

Unfortunately, if Scott let her break off the engagement too soon, he feared he'd never win her back. Their budding relationship was still too tentative and too new to survive that kind of severance. He had hopes that she might feel the way he did, but needed a little more time to overcome her fears.

Besides, if they broke it off too early and Nicole felt publicly humiliated, he wasn't sure she would agree to continue seeing him. But he didn't want to scare her away, either, by being too aggressive. Maybe he could convince her a delay was in both their interests . . . .

He pulled up in front of the Larsons' house and turned the engine off.

Jackson, in the front passenger seat, threw a glance toward the backseat. "Tell me again why the whole gang is here?"

"Because Nicole wants it that way," Scott answered honestly.

Jackson glanced back at Nicole, his gaze lingering with admiration on her chest. "Hmmm."

"It's your fault," Alyx snapped. "If you won't let us participate, we at least want to be in on the end."

"You have to stay in the car," Jackson reminded her.

Alyx rolled her eyes. "Yeah, well, I'm getting used to being the wheelman."

"I'll be here, too," Nicole said.

"Well, I guess that's something," Alyx muttered. "But I should be the one who gets to go inside with Jackson. The servants have seen Scott and Nicole."

"I told you," Jackson said, only a little impatience coloring his voice. "They're less likely to suspect anything out of the ordinary if my assistant is a man."

True, plus Scott couldn't imagine what would happen if Jackson and Alyx were let loose in a house together with no referee. There might be no house standing by the time they were done.

"Besides," Scott said cheerfully, "I have a disguise." He pulled a ball cap on his head and slid on a pair of tinted glasses.

"*That's* a disguise?" Alyx asked in a derisive tone.

"What did you expect?" Jackson asked. "Plastic surgery and shoe lifts?" He shook his head. "The simple ones are the best. Besides, dressed in jeans and a Broncos sweatshirt with that hat and glasses, he looks nothing like Scott Richmond, society's darling."

"Society's darling?" Scott repeated in disbelief.

Jackson shrugged in seeming embarrassment. "I read it somewhere . . ."

"They're right," Nicole said. "This way all the attention will be focused on Boyd."

Alyx threw him a resentful glance. "I still don't see why we have to do it his way."

"Because he's the only one who can get entrée to the house without looking suspicious." Scott wasn't sure if Alyx was complaining because she wasn't involved, or because Jackson, whom she had taken an instant dislike to, *was.* Probably a bit of both.

"I'll explain it again," Jackson said, his voice a little too condescending. "Breaking in is too risky—"

"Not when you know how to get past the security," Alyx snapped.

Scott shook his head. He liked them both, but Jackson and Alyx definitely brought out the worst in each other.

"*And* it's illegal," Jackson continued as if Alyx hadn't spoken. "So that's why I called the Larsons and told them I was offering a complimentary six-month checkup on the system."

Personally, Scott thought it was brilliant. And the Larsons had eagerly taken him up on his offer. "The best part is he managed to set up a time when they aren't home. The butler, Peterson, will show us through."

Alyx scowled. "Yeah, I know. But it seems so . . . tame."

Jackson rolled his eyes, but Nicole jumped in before he could say anything. "Well, I'm glad. This way we don't have to worry so much about them getting caught."

"There's still an element of chance," Jackson said. He slanted a glance at Alyx. "A little danger if Peterson insists on following us too closely. That's why Scott's going in as my assistant—to distract him if need be."

"I don't understand," Nicole said. "If the safe will only open to a fingerprint, how can you get in?"

"Because I can program up to three prints, and mine is one of them. It's a precaution in case something happens to the Larsons and their heirs need to get into the safe."

"I see."

Scott glanced at his watch. "It's just about time now."

Jackson nodded. "Where are the jewels?"

Nicole handed them to Jackson, and he placed them inside the silvery oversized briefcase, then pulled out a couple of small black objects and handed one to Alyx. "But just in case we need your help, here's a beeper."

Alyx gave it a dubious glance. "What do I do with this?"

Snapping the case shut, Jackson said, "If we need more distraction, we'll beep you and you can ring the doorbell to get the butler off our back and keep him occupied long enough for us to replace the sapphires."

Alyx looked a little mollified, but obviously couldn't resist challenging him. "What do I say when he opens the door?"

"Tell him you're selling Girl Scout cookies," Jackson suggested with a grimace. "Hell, I don't know. You can wing it, can't you?"

"Of course she can," Nicole said soothingly. "You'd better go now."

Scott and Jackson exited the car. Scott grinned at his friend as they walked toward the door. "Nice of you to give Alyx something to do."

Jackson shrugged, though Scott could tell he looked a little embarrassed. "Nice, hell. I was just trying to get her off my back. Besides, we might need her." He handed the device's twin to Scott. "Here, hold onto this. If we need Alyx, just press the button in the middle and it will beep on her end."

Scott nodded and stuck it in his pocket as Jackson rang the doorbell. The man who answered could only be the butler. Unlike Weatherwax, Peterson looked kind and genial. Scott relaxed a little. Maybe this plan would even work.

Jackson introduced himself, referring to Scott only as his assistant, and explained he was there to check the security. The butler let them in without reservation.

Jackson had given Scott a crash course in how to help him test the system, which primarily meant Scott held the case and the equipment while Jackson fiddled with the security panel.

"No need to watch," Jackson told Peterson casually. "This will take a little while."

"I don't mind, sir," the butler said, peering over Jackson's shoulder. But there was a thread of steel in that genial voice and Scott suspected he either had instructions from the Larsons to keep a close eye on them, or had decided to do it on his own.

Jackson shot him a suspicious glance. "Well, I'll have to ask you to step back a little. The inner workings of my system is proprietary information."

Peterson smiled. "Oh, I assure you, I'm no threat. I don't understand a thing you're doing."

"Then you don't need to be so close, do you?" Jackson asked pointedly. "Besides, I don't even let my clients see how it works. They only need to know it will protect their valuables."

And, in the face of Jackson's stern look, Peterson backed off, looking annoyed. Well, Jackson had gained himself a little distance from the butler, but the man would probably dog their footsteps throughout the house. Immediately, Scott's mind began whirling with possible plans to draw the butler away.

Unfortunately, replacing the jewels wasn't simply a matter of slipping one box in and taking another out. If so, they might still be able to get away with it. But they had taken the real jewels out of their boxes and left them loose in the briefcase, so it was necessary to physically remove each piece of fake jewelry from its box and replace it with the real one.

As they checked the perimeter of the house and its security, it looked like Jackson was trying to draw out the process and make it look extremely tedious and unremarkable. Unfortunately Peterson seemed to have vast stores of patience and resolve.

When he could stall no more, Jackson said, "I need to see the safe in the study now."

Peterson bowed slightly and led them to the study, filled with law books and decorated in dark leather and wood. The rest of the house was so light and airy, Scott suspected George Larson had re-

belled against his wife's decorating scheme and insisted on the ultimate in macho decorating at least
in this room.

Scott watched closely as Jackson fiddled with the
safe. There was always the possibility that the jewels
were in here, too. But with a slight shake of his
head, Jackson indicated they weren't.

He closed the safe and glanced at Peterson. "One
more safe, and we'll be done. I need to see Mrs.
Larson's now."

Scott didn't need Jackson's significant look to
know that's where the jewels had to be. As they
headed toward the master bedroom upstairs, Scott
faked a cough. Then when they arrived in the room
and Jackson headed toward the safe, Scott turned
his false cough into a racking one.

Grabbing Peterson's sleeve, Scott said, "Can I"—
he coughed—"have a drink"—cough, cough—"of
water?" With the kitchen downstairs, it would give
Jackson some extra time to replace the jewels, if
he worked fast. Remembering the jewels were in
the briefcase, Scott casually dumped it in Jackson's
arms.

Peterson cast a glance at Jackson and frowned,
obviously torn between supervising the security and
seeing to a guest's comfort. Jackson slowed his
movements, evidently giving Scott time to find a
way to remove Peterson. Not knowing what else to
do, Scott bent over, hacking as much as he could.

Luckily, the man's training kicked in. "Just a moment," he murmured.

Scott hid a grin and prepared to follow the butler down to the kitchen to keep him occupied. But
Peterson fooled him by swerving into the master

bathroom. Still pretending to cough, Scott shared a disgusted look with Jackson when he heard the taps running, then Peterson came out carrying a glass of water. Damn, the man was too clever.

As Scott drank the water, his mind whirled with other ways to distract the butler, but suspected Peterson would be on to them if he wasn't careful. Surreptitiously, he slid his hand in his pocket and pressed the beeper button. Alyx would be thrilled, knowing they needed her help.

The doorbell rang almost immediately. He should have known Alyx wouldn't sit calmly by, waiting for them to call on her. It was a good thing he had beeped her. No telling what she would have done otherwise.

Peterson frowned, but it was his duty to answer the door. He had to go. He gave one last glance at Jackson who had just opened the safe, then headed out the door with a sigh.

Immediately, Jackson opened the safe wider and rummaged around inside. Scott went over to the door to watch for Peterson's return, but it came much faster than he expected.

"—get the door for me," Peterson said to someone down the hall.

A woman murmured assent and Scott suddenly realized that meant Peterson was heading back *here. Now.*

As Peterson appeared in the doorway, Scott went into another paroxysm of coughing to alert Jackson. Jackson glanced up as Peterson returned, then calmly closed the safe.

Jackson gave Peterson a tight smile. "That should do it. Thank you for your time."

What the hell was going on? No way would Jackson have been able to replace the jewels in that short a period of time. Had he given up? "Is that it?" Scott asked probingly.

"That's it," Jackson said in clipped tones.

"Are you sure?" Scott asked. "No more tests to run?" *Come on, Jackson, work with me here.*

But Jackson wasn't playing. "We're done," he said in final tones.

Scott had no choice but to follow him and Peterson out the door and down the stairs, all the while wondering why his friend was acting this way.

When they reached the front door, he heard Alyx say, "But wait—" as a maid firmly closed the door in Alyx's face.

"Is everything all right?" Peterson asked the maid.

She shook her head in disgust. "Just a saleswoman who won't give up."

The doorbell rang again. Peterson raised an eyebrow. "She certainly is persistent."

"I think I can help with that," Jackson said with a smile.

He opened the door and stepped outside, then grabbed Alyx's elbow and turned her around, whispering in low, urgent tones.

To keep Peterson from watching, Scott nodded at him. "Thanks for your help . . . and the water."

"You're quite welcome, sir."

He obviously wanted to see what Jackson and Alyx were doing, but Scott stepped in front of them and continued to watch Peterson with a fixed stare, as if wondering what the man wanted. Apparently uncomfortable with Scott's gaze, Peterson finally closed the door.

Scott hurried to catch up with Jackson and Alyx as Nicole watched anxiously from the driver's seat.

"Get in quick," Jackson said with a glance back at the house. "We need to get out of here before he sees we're together."

As soon as they were in the car, Nicole peeled out of there like the hounds of hell were nipping at their back tires.

"What's going on?" Scott demanded. "You didn't have time to replace the jewels."

"No, I didn't . . . because they weren't there."

Chapter Sixteen

Scott was taken aback at first. "Oh, I get it. You're kidding, right?" Jackson was probably trying to get Scott back for all the jokes over the years.

"No, I'm not. The jewels weren't there."

"But they have to be there," Scott protested. "Where else could they be?"

Now that they were out of the neighborhood, Nicole slowed down. "Maybe they're in the other safe," she suggested.

Jackson shook his head. "We looked there. All he had inside were some papers and securities."

"Are you sure?" Alyx asked. "Maybe they were hidden under the papers or something."

"I'm sure," Jackson said in a curt tone.

Nicole nodded. "From what Mr. Larson said the other night, I doubt he'd let his wife use his safe at all."

"The sapphires have to be in her safe then," Alyx insisted. She glared at Jackson. "Are you sure you didn't see them? They're dark blue stones—"

"I know what sapphires look like," Jackson all but growled. "They weren't there. She didn't even have her jewelry in boxes, just a few loose pieces—the more expensive stuff—and none of them held sapphires."

He opened his case and pulled out the padded envelope with Grace's jewels. Handing it to Scott, Jackson added, "Here, take these. I don't want them in my possession."

Scott couldn't really blame him. "I'm sorry to put you through this, but we really did think the jewels were there. Chrissie told us the Larsons have them, and I see no reason to doubt her." He thought for a moment. "Let's go back to the house and we can figure this out on the way."

Nicole nodded and turned onto the correct road. "Is it possible they have another safe you don't know about?"

"I doubt it," Jackson said. "All my systems are tied in together. It wouldn't make sense to have a safe that wasn't included."

"Maybe the jewels aren't in a safe," Alyx suggested. "Maybe they're in a jewelry box or something."

"I doubt that, too," Jackson said. "She had the good stuff locked up. If she had the sapphires, she would have put them there as well."

"What about somewhere outside the home?" Alyx persisted. "Like at his office or a bank?"

"That's possible," Nicole said. "But the way Mr. Larson talked the other night, there's no way he'd keep his wife's 'gewgaws' at the office, and though he'd like her to keep her jewelry in a safe-deposit box, his wife won't do it."

"Then where else could they be?" Alyx asked.

Yep, that was the question. Scott shook his head. "I don't know, but we have to find them—for Mother and Chrissie's sake."

They continued speculating about where they might be the rest of the way to the house. Scott's mind raced furiously, but he couldn't come up with a definitive answer. Nothing made sense.

As they pulled up in the garage, Jackson said, "We have no way of knowing where the jewelry is or what they're going to do with it. They're probably being broken up even as we speak, to make them into different pieces so they'll never be recognized."

"I hope not," Scott exclaimed. "Any jeweler worth his salt will know immediately that they aren't real. Then we'll really be in trouble." As he went around to help Nicole out of the car, he added, "We have another problem, too. I told Digby I'd sent the fake sapphires for cleaning and promised him I'd let him know when they came back so he could photograph them."

Jackson shrugged. "So let him see the real ones. You're fast enough on your feet to convince him they're the fakes."

"Not *that* fast," Scott said with a grimace. "I showed him how to tell the fakes from the real ones last time he was here."

Alyx, who had exited the car under her own steam, placed her hands on her hips and rolled her eyes. "Why did you do that?"

Good question. "To prove to him that the ones in the safe weren't the real ones. I figured we'd be able to replace the sapphires, just like the first two sets, so I'd have the fakes to show him with no problem."

"Well, there's no sense in worrying about might-have-beens," Nicole said quietly. "Instead, we need to talk about what we can do. And maybe we could do it inside the house?"

"Very sensible," Jackson said in an approving tone, smiling down at Nicole and, not incidentally, ogling her cleavage.

A spark of jealousy lit within Scott. *I'm the only one entitled to drool over that cleavage.*

But he tried not to show his annoyance as he opened the door to the house and invited them in. At least one good thing had come out of this mess. He and Nicole would have to stay engaged until they cleared it all up.

He ought to feel guilty about putting his own desires before his mother's and Chrissie's, but he didn't. He and Nicole had gone far out of the way to cover their relatives' butts—more than anyone could reasonably expect—and the two of them deserved some quality time to themselves. He was determined to see that they'd get it—one way or another.

First, however, they had to figure out where the Larsons had hidden the sapphires.

As they came through the front hall, Scott spotted the housekeeper. "Hello, Marta. Is my mother at home?"

"No, sir." And before he could ask, she added, "Neither is Mr. Wainwright."

Scott tried not to grimace. It was a strange reflection on his mother's relationship that their housekeeper accepted the fact that Gerald might be in Grace's home without her. "Thank you. We'll be in the drawing room."

Once he closed the door behind them, Alyx said, "Okay, what are we going to do?"

Scott thought for a moment. "First, we need to buy some time with Digby."

"How?"

Good question. "I'm not sure. Mother has put him off too many times, and I don't think he'd accept any more delays from me."

"Maybe Gerald could help," Nicole suggested. "He seems really good at finding legal ways to stall people."

"You'd have to tell him the story," Jackson said. "Part of it, anyway."

Alyx frowned. "Do you think that's wise?"

Damn, why did everything have to be so complicated? Scott thought for a moment, then said, "I think Jackson's right. Gerald seems to love my mother, so I don't think he'd cause any problems. Even if he doesn't, client confidentiality ought to cover it." Besides, the man needed to know what he was getting into before he took the final matrimonial plunge. "I'll call him."

Scott appropriated his mother's address book from her study and brought it back with him to the drawing room. He tried Gerald's home number, but he wasn't home. The housekeeper thought he might be at the office, so Scott called the number he found in his mother's book.

A recording clicked on. "You have reached the law offices of Wainwright, Harding, Larson, and Wyndham. We are sorry we are unable to take your call—"

But Scott heard no more as he dropped the receiver in the cradle, feeling stunned.

"What's wrong?" Nicole asked.

More grimly now, Scott called the number again

and put the speaker phone on. Once more, the recording said, "You have reached the law offices of Wainwright, Harding, Larson, and Wyndham—"

Nicole gasped and Scott hung up again before the recording could capture their voices.

"I don't get it," Alyx said, looking back and forth between them. Jackson looked equally clueless.

"Those names . . ." Nicole murmured.

Scott gave a bitter smile. "Yes, they sound familiar, don't they? Gerald's last name is Wainwright . . . and the Hardings, Larsons, and Wyndhams all bought my mother's stolen jewels."

He should have known, should have realized. The clues were all there—law books at the Wyndhams' and Larsons' houses, someone's request for a legal opinion at the Hardings . . . Hell, he'd even seen Larson pass an envelope to Gerald at the engagement party. An overabundance of lawyers should have clued him in to the fact that they were all working together.

Jackson frowned. "You mean Wainwright's partners all bought his girlfriend's stolen jewels. Why?"

"Sounds like they have quite a scam going," Alyx said. "I'll bet they fleece every rich widow in town."

"I doubt that," Scott said. "But they certainly did it to my mother."

Nicole looked stricken. "But Gerald is so nice."

"And so are the others," Scott said. "But he's done nothing but play us for fools. He's in on it. He has to be."

"But why?" Nicole wanted to know.

So did Scott. "I don't know yet, but I do know he must have taken advantage of my mother. She admitted he has the code to the house. She probably gave him the combination to the safe in the living room as well." He turned a grim smile on Nicole as realization dawned. "Well, that explains how Chrissie got in so easily. He must have had one of the women give Chrissie the numbers." One mystery solved.

Nicole looked sick. "Yes, that would explain it."

Scott seethed. He'd liked Gerald, had trusted him, and had even hoped the man would marry his mother. Betrayal tasted awfully bitter.

"What are you going to do about it?" Jackson asked.

Scott's mind worked furiously. "I'll bet he has the sapphires. Somehow we need to get them from him."

Nicole looked confused. "Why would he take the sapphires from the Larsons?"

"I don't know, but my gut tells me I'm right. And he's got them in his house, I'm sure of it."

Jackson nodded. "That makes more sense than anything else we've come up with."

"Now we just need to get ourselves invited to his house. Mother mentioned the other day that he's having a dinner with some people from his office at his house in a few days—and she's playing hostess."

"I don't get it," Alyx said. "Isn't it too late to exchange the jewels? I mean, he has to have figured out they're fakes by now. Why give him the real ones?"

"Oh, we're not going to replace them for his benefit," Scott said with a mocking grin. "We'll do it for ours. After we exchange them, we'll let Digby find them."

Jackson nodded slowly. "Good idea."

"One way or another, we'll expose Gerald for the thief he is." Scott glanced at all of them. "You with me?"

They all nodded, even Jackson. Scott knew Jackson didn't like a liar and a thief any more than Scott did.

"Good. Let's make plans, then." And when Scott was done with him, Gerald would regret the day he decided to mess with the Richmonds.

Scott put the first part of his plan in place the next night when he invited Nicole to dinner and asked Mother to keep it to just the three of them. He didn't want to make Gerald suspicious with the questions he planned to ask.

Mother seemed pleased to have them with her, and after the soup was served, she asked Nicole, "Have you set a date for your wedding yet, dear?"

Nicole looked uncomfortable so Scott intervened. "Not yet, Mother. We're still getting used to the fact of being engaged. We need a little time to figure out what we're going to do before we jump into wedding preparations."

Nicole shot him a grateful look, but Grace looked puzzled. "What do you need to figure out?"

"Oh, you know. Where to go on the honeymoon, where to live afterward, that sort of thing."

"You're not going to live here?" his mother asked in surprise.

"That's what we have to decide," Scott said with a smile. Though he didn't know why she'd think a new wife would want to live with her mother-in-law. "Nicole has her own house in Aurora so we could live there, or maybe find something of our own somewhere else around Denver."

"I see," his mother said and waved for the cook to serve the main entree.

Her thoughtful tone and dismayed look made Scott realize that Grace would probably be lonely if he left so soon after his sister moved out. "But nothing's decided yet," Scott hurried to assure her.

"That's right," Nicole added. "We haven't even come close to any sort of decision. And we do like this Capitol Hill area. It has so many lovely and historical mansions. Like yours . . . and Mr. Wainwright's."

Scott took a bite to hide his grin. Nicole was getting very good at this—she'd slipped that in like a pro. And Mother perked up at the possibility they might be living somewhere nearby. To take advantage of that, Scott added, "I told Nicole that Gerald's house was built in the 1880s and how he's kept it historically accurate. She'd really like to see it."

"Oh, could I?" Nicole asked with a smile.

"I'm sure Gerald would be happy to give you a tour some time," Grace said. "Oh, that reminds me. Gerald asked me to give you a message, Scott. He said Mr. Digby is satisfied with the information he has now and is no longer asking to see the sapphires you sent out for cleaning. I should get my check soon."

Scott exchanged a disbelieving glance with Nicole. Yeah, right. He didn't trust this new piece of information at all—or Gerald. "That's good to know," he told his mother. But to get back to the point . . . "Maybe Friday would be good? You mentioned Gerald was having a dinner party then."

Mother looked taken aback. "Well, yes, but you weren't invited, dear."

"Oh, I'm sure Gerald won't mind," Scott said. "He's spent enough time here, I'm sure he wouldn't mind reciprocating the hospitality. We'd love to see as much of the inside of his house as he's seen of ours."

When Grace seemed to hesitate again, Nicole jumped in. "It would be wonderful if we could join you."

She gaped at both of them. "I—I don't know."

"You're the hostess, aren't you?" Scott asked. "I'm sure he wouldn't mind if you brought us along . . . and Jackson and Alyx, too."

Nicole shot him a warning glance. Okay, maybe he'd overdone it a bit, but Mother couldn't refute the facts.

Grace placed her silverware very carefully on the table. "I'm sorry, but it simply isn't appropriate to invite yourself. I'll arrange for you to view the house some other time."

And the tone of her voice let Scott know she considered the subject closed. Fine. He'd just find some other way to get in. He shook his head slightly at Nicole's despairing expression to let her know he wasn't defeated yet. Out loud, he said, "That's too bad. I heard he wanted to keep it as authentic as possible. Does that mean there's no electricity or central heating?"

His mother relaxed a little and picked up her fork again. "Of course there is. Some of the earlier owners had it put in, though Gerald has done his best to ensure any improvements don't ruin the structural integrity or original character of the mansion."

"So he has indoor plumbing and a security system?"

"Well, the plumbing is a little dated," she admitted. "But it's very quaint. Though he doesn't really have a security system."

Nicole nodded, evidently seeing where he was going with this. "That makes sense. Electronics would destroy the historical ambiance. I bet he even has one of those old-fashioned floor safes so he didn't have to cut into the walls."

Grace shook her head. "No, and please don't suggest it to him. Those things are so heavy, if he had one put in his study, it would probably crash through to the floor below."

Nicole grimaced along with her. "I see what you mean. Too bad he had to cut into the walls, then."

"Oh, he didn't," Grace said with a wave of her hand. "He installed sensors outside the house to discourage vandals and protect his antiques, but he actually keeps very little in the way of small valuables in the house, so he decided not to have a safe. He keeps those locked in his desk."

Nicole shot Scott a triumphant glance and elation surged through him. Perfect. A simple lock should be easy to get past, and the jewels had to be there—he just knew it.

Nicole continued to probe for information. "Is it one of those charming roll-top desks?"

"No, actually it's an old British mahogany and leather desk, quite beautiful."

"I'm sure it is," Nicole said. "And I'd love to see it and the rest of the house sometime."

Grace smiled at her. "And so you shall." Then she turned the conversation to another subject and they spoke of innocuous things until dinner was over and Grace took her leave of them.

As Scott drove Nicole home, she asked, "How do you plan to get us invited to Gerald's house? I know you—you don't give up that easily."

He shrugged. "I'll figure out something." Even if he had to show up on Gerald's doorstep to do it. "And we'll invite Digby along for the ride, too, so he can get credit for the arrest."

"Is that wise?" Nicole asked, anxiety in her voice. "What if Gerald tells Digby that Chrissie stole the jewels and your mother knew the stolen jewels were fake?"

"By the time Gerald gets a chance to say anything, we will have already proven his guilt. All we have to do is deny everything he says. With the evidence in front of him, who's Digby gonna believe?"

"I hope you're right," Nicole said doubtfully.

"Don't worry. It'll all work out." Digby wasn't much of a challenge—Scott was sure he could fast-talk him into believing what he wanted him to believe.

For the rest of the ride, Scott entertained her with wilder and wilder plans as to how they might get access to Gerald's house, but in reality, he wasn't quite sure how he was going to accomplish it without Gerald becoming suspicious.

When they arrived at Nicole's house, she rummaged through her purse. "Wait—I brought my garage door opener so you won't show up on Missy's radar."

Scott laughed, but drove in to the opened garage and watched as the door closed behind him.

But Nicole made no move to get out of the car. "I can't believe the end is almost in sight," she said in a voice that sounded almost wistful.

Wishing it was over . . . or wishing it wasn't? Hoping she meant the latter, Scott said, "That doesn't mean we have to end our engagement right away . . . ." When she didn't answer, he added hurriedly, "You know, so it doesn't look bad. We'll do it whenever you're ready." Then cursed himself for sounding like a fool.

"We can't keep on with the lie if we're not planning on getting married . . . ." But Nicole's tentative voice made it sound as if she were willing to be convinced otherwise.

"Why not? I was kind of enjoying it."

The courtesy light that had come on when the garage door opened suddenly went out, plunging them into darkness. Silence stretched. Why didn't she say something? Had he blown it? Was she even now trying to find a way to let him down easy? The tension ratchetted up as they continued to sit there silently, in the dark.

"You were?" Nicole finally said.

Relief filled him. "Yes, I was. I thought maybe we could still . . . date. Or something." Anything.

"With a broken engagement? Wouldn't that look . . . odd?"

"No, I mean keep it going. We don't need to end it right away since it bothers you so much. And I'd kind of like to get to know you when we're not sneaking into someone else's house or worrying about what's going to happen to Chrissie or my mother."

The silence was full of tension as he waited to hear how she would react.

Finally, when Nicole did answer, her voice sounded shy. "Would you like to . . . come over for dinner tomorrow night?"

"Wow. You mean you can cook, too?"

She laughed. "Well, I'm no gourmet chef, but I can throw a meal together."

"That sounds great," Scott said.

"I'll see you tomorrow at seven, then." Nicole exited the car and opened the garage door again.

Scott sighed. *I guess a kiss is out of the question.*

He grinned to himself as he started the car and shifted into reverse. But tomorrow night, all bets were off.

Chapter Seventeen

Nicole glanced around her living room, checking to make sure everything was in order. Tonight Scott was coming over for their date and she wanted to make sure everything was perfect. True, they had been out together before, but this was the first time they had acknowledged that it was a real "date." It made her a little nervous, especially since she had decided to take Alyx's advice and try to seduce him.

That resolution had given her a few qualms, but if she was successful, she hoped it might tell her something about how Scott felt about her. The fact that he wanted to continue their engagement was a good sign, but she wasn't sure why. Was it only because she had made such a fuss about being dumped?

Then again, he said he wanted to get to know her better . . . but he'd stopped touching her. It was very confusing, and she hoped for some sort of resolution tonight.

She sighed. But what if she found out he didn't care after all? *After* she took him to bed?

Either way it didn't matter. *She* cared and that's what counted.

Nicole finished her walk-through. Everything in

the living room was as clean and neat as she could get it, the dining room was spotless, wine was chilling in the refrigerator, and dinner was simmering on the stove.

She put on soft music and debated whether to light the slender candles on the table. She set the matches down, deciding not to. It would look too romantic, too needy . . . as if she were trying too hard. She already felt as if she were overdoing it with the way she was dressed.

But Scott had seemed so fascinated with her low-cut sweater yesterday that she'd found one in her closet that was even lower. Normally, she didn't wear this one without a blouse underneath, but the hot pink sweater and the form-fitting black pants she wore beneath them made her feel sexy.

Too sexy, maybe? Was it too obvious? Damn. She should change. She turned toward the bedroom, but halted when the doorbell rang. Too late.

She glanced down at her cleavage and tugged the sweater up a bit, trying to hide the blatant advertisement of her intentions. It didn't work. She still looked like she was posing for a Victoria's Secret catalog or something. Oh, well. She couldn't change now.

She opened the door and smiled at Scott. He stood stock-still in the doorway, clutching a bouquet of flowers, as his gaze slowly ranged from her head to her feet, snagging momentarily on her chest.

He swallowed visibly. "Wow. You're certainly looking your breast this evening." Surprisingly, Scott turned red. "Best. I mean you're looking your best this evening."

Suddenly, Nicole felt a whole lot more confident. She'd thought he'd made the joke deliberately. But knowing her appearance had made Scott's Freudian slip show made her feel self-assured . . . powerful even.

It also made her breasts tighten in response. And, from Scott's fascinated gaze in that direction, evidently the sheer fabric of her bra and the fine knit of the sweater did nothing to hide her anticipation. She resisted the urge to glance down at the front of his pants to see if he'd had a similar reaction. There was plenty of time for that later.

But if he didn't get out of that doorway, nothing was going to happen tonight. "Would you like to come inside and have something to nibble on?"

His eyes widened as he took another furtive glance at the crinkled tips of her breasts. "Wha-at?"

"*Nibble,*" she said more distinctly, hiding an urge to laugh. "Would you like something to nibble on—crackers and cheese or something?"

He shook his head as if to regain his composure. "No, I'm fine." But he didn't move.

"Are the flowers for me?" she asked, trying to give him a hint.

He dragged his gaze away from her chest, seeming surprised to see the yellow roses in his hand. "Uh, yeah." He thrust them at her.

She accepted them, gesturing him into the house so she could shut the door and close out the rest of the world. She leaned down to inhale the distinctive scent of the roses, feeling a little disappointed. Red roses meant passion. Even pink roses might indicate some interest in touching her again. But yellow—what did that mean? "Thank you for the roses—it's very sweet of you."

Scott gestured vaguely around at the living room. "I remembered your blue and yellow color scheme and thought it would go well."

Her smile widened. Matching her decor wasn't quite as good as expressing undying passion, but she gave him points for putting some thought into his choice. "Come in and have a seat. I'll just put these in water and check on dinner."

Instead, Scott followed her into the kitchen, sniffing the air. "Smells great. What is it?"

"Chicken marsala with pasta and salad. Is that okay?" She hoped so—it was one of the few dishes she knew how to make well.

"If it tastes as good as it smells, I'm sure it will be. Anything I can do?"

She smiled as she pulled a vase out of the cupboard and filled it with water. "Not really. It's almost ready. Unless you'd like to pour the wine? It's in the refrigerator, and the glasses and corkscrew are on the table." And the wine might help calm her suddenly nervous stomach.

He made a sweeping bow. "Your wish is my command."

He opened and poured the wine while she found a spot for the roses in the living room. When she came back into the kitchen, he handed her a glass with a flourish and held his up in a toast. "To . . . good friends and good times."

Nicole smiled. *Very good times, I hope.* She repeated his toast and clinked her glass with his, then took a sip. Their eyes met over the rim of the glasses, and

Nicole felt her stomach lurch again. Better feed it soon.

Holding her glass out to him, she asked, "Would you mind taking this out to the dining room table for me? I'll bring the salad and rolls so we can start eating."

"Sure."

When she brought out the first course, she found that Scott had lit the candles on the table and turned the lights down low. Her heart thumped a little faster, and she was glad that he had been the one to choose the romantic ambiance. Smiling, she set the food on the table and asked him to be seated.

As they ate, her stomach calmed as they spoke of normal date things—books, movies, sports—and she found they had a lot more in common than she realized. Seeing how right they were for each other made her even more determined to see this through. After dinner she abandoned the dishes in the sink and mentally promised to do them later. For now she wanted to spend more time with Scott.

She found him in the living room, sitting on the couch with only one lamp on low. She kicked off her shoes and curled up next to him.

He leaned back with a sigh, his left arm along the back of the couch. "That was great."

She settled back beneath his outstretched arm, hoping he'd get the hint. "Thank you, but I know I'm nowhere near as good as your cook."

"But she does it for a living. That makes your meal all the more impressive." And, as she had hoped, he dropped his arm around her shoulders.

With a relieved sigh, she snuggled up to him.

She'd been wanting an excuse all evening to touch him and to have him touch her. With the side of one breast squashed up against him, her cleavage had deepened, making her breasts look full and the valley between them even more pronounced with her nipples clearly outlined against the soft fabric of her sweater.

Scott's gaze lingered there, and she smiled even as her breasts tightened again. "Thank you for noticing," she said with a touch of humor. "Would you like something to . . . nibble on?"

Scott's gaze darted to her eyes. "We're not talking food anymore, are we?"

"No, we're not," Nicole confirmed as she boldly laid a hand on his thigh.

Scott's indrawn breath was encouraging. At least he didn't run away screaming.

"You know," he said casually, "if I didn't know better, I'd think you were trying to seduce me."

Her heart thumping rapidly at her own daring, Nicole kissed his neck, then murmured, "What makes you think you know better?"

He froze for a moment. Taking advantage of his speechlessness, Nicole pressed her lips to his.

His response was all she could have hoped for. He hauled her onto his lap and kissed her thoroughly. Hot . . . wild . . . sweet. His hands kneaded and squeezed as hers coaxed and caressed. *Yum.* Her panties flooded with moisture, and she could feel a satisfyingly hard lump pressing into her buttocks. It looked like the seduction was working.

"Just a moment," she said. Standing, she pulled her sweater off with one swift move and tossed it on the floor. At Scott's surprised look, she explained, "I was getting hot."

"Good," he said with a chuckle. "Then I'm doing it right."

Still seated, he grasped her hips and tugged her toward him, then unclasped the front hook of her bra and let her breasts spill into his hands. "Hmm, I think I'll nipple on these . . . ."

Her chuckle was short-lived as he drew one pebbled breast into his mouth, licking and sucking it as he rolled the tip of the other between his fingers. A cascade of sensuous sensations washed through Nicole, warm and wonderful. She gasped with the sheer pleasure of it, her knees weakening.

Need blossomed within her, settling between her legs. And suddenly, Scott's hand was there, caressing her intimately through the fabric of her slacks, making her moan with the intensity of it.

He stopped suckling to whisper, "My God, you're soaking wet."

With hurried fingers she helped him pull off the rest of her clothes until she stood naked and trembling before him.

Going down on his knees, he didn't bother with preliminaries as he licked her hot, private place.

Ohmigod. She'd never experienced anything quite like this heady, hedonistic sensation. Standing nude before him while he was fully clothed . . . watching his head bent to taste her so intimately . . . It was incredibly erotic. The wickedness of it soon blotted out all coherent thought, and she exploded in shuddering waves of dizzying nirvana.

Her knees buckled and Scott had to grab her before she lost her balance totally. "Are you all right?" he asked with a grin.

She waited for a moment until the tremors ceased and she could speak again. "Very all right." She stared down at him and smoothed his hair. "But this wasn't how it was supposed to happen."

"It wasn't?"

"Oh, I'm not complaining, but I had plans . . ."

He rose and held her to him, quirking an eyebrow as he stroked her naked backside. "What kind of plans?"

"I was going to lure you to my bedroom and have my way with you."

"So what's stopping you?" He released her and stepped back a pace, holding his arms out to his side in a surrendering motion. "I'm all yours."

And that one part of him that she was most interested in at the moment strained at the seam of his fly, obviously very eager to begin.

Smiling, she tugged him into her bedroom, leaving only the bedside table light on. It seemed odd to have a man in here. It had been such a long time since she'd had any sort of sexual relationship, and with Chrissie always around before, she'd never invited men to her bed. But being here with Scott seemed right.

He grinned down at her. "What am I supposed to do now?"

"Take your shoes and socks off."

He did so, and she said, "Now leave the rest to me." Slowly, she pulled his shirt out of his pants and unbuttoned it, savoring the fact that he was watching her so closely, intent on her fingers.

She pulled the shirt off down his arms and let it

fall to the floor, then ran her hands across his chest. She loved the way a man felt so different from a woman—his broad chest, the crisp curling hair, the flat nipples.

And there was another way a man was different from a woman . . . . She unhooked his belt and unzipped his pants, then pulled his pants and underwear down together in one swift movement. His sex sprang forth, proud and strong, and she wrapped her fingers around him, stroking his velvety hardness.

Scott moaned and Nicole released him, remembering her plans.

"Don't stop," he said softly, caressing her breasts.

"Just for a moment," she promised. "Let's go over to the bed."

On the way over, she picked up a bottle of massage oil she had left on the dresser. Buying it had been one of the most embarrassing things she'd ever done in her life, but she wanted to repay Scott in kind.

He raised his eyebrows and grinned. "That looks promising."

She smiled. "One good massage deserves another, don't you think?"

"Absolutely. Where do you want me? On the bed?"

His eagerness made her smile wider. "Yes, please."

He started to lie down on his stomach, but she stopped him. "No, on your back." She had a feeling the other way might be a little painful for him.

He stretched out on the bed, totally comfortable in his own skin as he pillowed his head on his hands and watched her closely. How did men do that so easily? Though he'd seen her unclothed twice now, Nicole still couldn't help but feel a little self-conscious in her nudity. True, Scott seemed pleased enough when he looked at her, but she thanked heaven the light was low enough to hide her many imperfections.

And to keep him from spotting those flaws, she needed to distract him. She opened the bottle and poured the spicy scented oil into her hand then rubbed her hands together to warm it. Since Scott was obviously ready for anything Nicole had in mind, she went straight to business. Using both hands, she smoothed the oil up his inner thighs then ran them over his soft sacs and hard shaft.

He bucked in response and let out a moan. Smiling, she squirted more oil on his genital area and stroked his full length with the slick substance, running her fingers up and over his sensitive tip. As she moved her hand on him, he clutched the bed-clothes in both hands and his face contorted in pleasure.

But after a few moments, Scott gasped, "Stop, stop, stop."

She halted. "What's wrong?"

He took a shuddering breath. "Don't want it to end now. Want inside you."

"We can arrange that," Nicole said.

She reached over to the bedside table and pulled out a condom, which she slowly unrolled over him. As she did so, he poured oil on his hands and spread it on her breasts, kneading and plucking.

Damn, that felt good. She wanted him inside her. Now.

Straddling him, she positioned his shaft at her opening then sank down on him. He slid in, fitting as perfectly as if he were constructed especially for the purpose. They gasped in unison. It felt so perfect, so right.

She moved up and down on him, slowly at first, then more rapidly. He grabbed her hips and held on tight as she rode him like she owned him.

Having already been satisfied once, Nicole had intended to do this primarily for his benefit, but soon realized this position felt remarkably . . . good. Remarkably . . . wonderful. Remarkably . . . *ohmigod*.

She peaked, convulsing around him in surges of pure carnal sensation. As if it were the trigger to set him off, he pumped into her furiously, shuddering with release.

When he let his arms fall to his sides, Nicole collapsed on top of him. *Wow*.

They lay there like the dead for a few moments, then Scott stirred. "Let me up a moment. Do you have a trash basket?"

She summoned enough energy to roll off him and point toward the side of the bed.

He sat up and moved to the side of the bed to toss the used condom in the trash. A rustling noise sounded beneath him as he rolled back toward her. Looking puzzled, he pushed down on the mattress. "What do you have under here?"

She felt her face heat. "The money."

"What money?"

"The money Chrissie got for the jewels."

He laughed. "You hid it under your mattress?"

"I know it's terribly unoriginal, but I didn't know where else to put it . . . ."

He lay back down on the bed and cuddled her to him. "That's okay—I'd forgotten about it. We need to take care of it at the same time we take care of Gerald."

"You have a plan, then?"

"Not a great one, but I do have a plan. We'll just show up on Gerald's doorstep and surprise him."

Nicole laid her head on Scott's shoulder and sighed. "Okay." She was too depleted to even think about things like that right now.

Scott squeezed her. "You really did have your way with me, didn't you?"

"Uh-huh," she agreed lazily. "Thank you for helping me check that off my list. I've never seduced anyone before."

He stiffened. "Is that all this was?"

Oh, no. She was *not* going to let him misunderstand this time. "Of course not, silly. I could have had any man for that. Instead, I wanted you."

But his voice was still stiff as he asked, "Does this mean we're still engaged?"

"Only if you want to be," she said tentatively. Did he? From the sound of his voice, it didn't sound like it.

"I just want to spare you pain."

That again. She wished she'd never said it. Now she didn't know whether he wanted to stay engaged because of her silly getting-dumped phobia or because he wanted to be with her.

Ask him, a small voice urged her.

No, she couldn't. What if he said he didn't want her? It would be the most embarrassing moment of her life.

But if she didn't ask, she wouldn't know. She

opened her mouth to do so, but instead, curt words emerged. "I'll survive. I have to, don't I?"

He sighed. "I guess." He released her and rolled to his side. "Well, thank you for a great evening, but I'd better be going."

As he scooted off the bed, she watched in dismay. *Damn, I got my answer.* Unfortunately, it wasn't the one she wanted.

"Don't get up," he said with a kiss to her forehead. "I can let myself out." And, dressing quickly, he did just that.

As she heard the door close behind him, Nicole buried her face in her pillow and tried not to cry.

Scott closed Nicole's front door behind him and leaned back against it with his eyes closed, fighting back despair. Leaving her bed was one of the hardest things he'd ever done, but he couldn't stay. It was obvious she wanted out of the engagement, wanted to get on with her new, adventurous life without the disadvantage of a man holding her back.

Their goals were incompatible and would never mesh. He feared if he stayed too long, it would just hurt more. He had to leave now.

But when he opened his eyes, he groaned at the sight clearly detailed in the street lamp near his Jag. He hadn't locked it, and someone was sitting in the driver's seat now, watching him.

Missy.

Damn. He didn't want to deal with her, didn't want to even see the woman's face, but he had no choice if he wanted to use his car to get home. He stalked over to the Jag and yanked open the door. "Get out. Please." He only added the please to make it more likely she'd remove herself.

She emerged slowly, and the sight that met his eyes almost made him shove her back inside. She wore something provocative and sheer that clearly revealed her small breasts in all their nonexistent glory. And, just in case he hadn't noticed, she licked her lips and ran her hands over her tiny chest.

"Thanks," he said curtly and tried to get past her into his car, but she forestalled him by stretching her arms in front of the doorway. If he wanted to get past her, he was going to have to touch her.

Forget it. "Would you please move?" he asked through gritted teeth.

Her smile was predatory, her voice breathy. "I'd be happy to, stud. Just tell me where and when."

Good Lord, did she think this was sexy? "'Where' is away from my car and 'when' is now."

"Oh, no," she murmured. "I'm not going anywhere until you recognize that I'm *not* a lesbian and *not* a man in drag."

She reached for him, but Scott backed away. "Okay, I get it. You don't like women and you're not a man." He gazed dismissively at her near-naked body. "Then you must be a little girl."

Sparks fired in her eyes. "On the contrary, I'm very much a woman. And I'll prove it to you."

She reached for him again, but he grabbed her wrists and held her off. Obviously, his insulting jokes weren't working. It looked like he was going to have to tell her the truth. "No, thanks. I prefer to think of you as a child."

"Why?" Her annoyed look turned to one of amused speculation. "Oh, I get it. You like them young. Okay, I can do that. Shall I be Daddy's little girl?"

"No, *you* don't understand," Scott said, his tone implacable. "Your behavior might be understandable in a young girl just trying out her femininity. But the same behavior in a grown woman who is not only married but trying to seduce her neighbor's fiancé is unforgivable. Worse, it makes her look cheap, slutty, and extremely desperate." He glared down at her for a moment, so she would know he was completely serious. "Which would *you* rather be?"

Angry now, she jerked her wrists out of his hands. She rubbed them, staring at him with hate in her eyes for a few moments, then raised her chin and said, "Go to hell."

She turned to walk away and Scott asked, "Where are you going?" Not that he cared, but he worried that she might take her ire out on Nicole.

She tossed her head. "To play with my fucking dolls."

Chapter Eighteen

Scott stared up at Gerald's front door, flanked by Nicole, Jackson, and Alyx. *This is it.* Finally, they'd replace the last of the jewels, expose Gerald for what he was, and there would no longer be a need for the pretend engagement.

His upbringing told him he shouldn't be here, that it was extremely uncouth to crash a party, but he didn't care. He wasn't here to be polite. He was here to get justice for his mother.

And for himself. It was all Gerald's fault that Scott was about to lose the woman he loved because of this whole mess. Okay, so it wasn't entirely rational, but he didn't care. It was the way he felt. Someone had to pay.

He glanced at Nicole. "Do you have the money?"

She patted her bag. "Yes, right next to the sapphires you gave me earlier." She glanced around. "But where is Digby? I thought you were going to invite him."

"I did, but he won't be here until later. We need proof of the theft first, then once we have it, we can expose the lot of them to Digby and Mother."

He glanced at Jackson and Alyx. "You guys sure you want to do this?" He had invited them to be at the finish, figuring they deserved to be present if they wanted to. He knew Alyx would, but he was surprised when Jackson agreed as well.

They both nodded, so Scott looked for a doorbell. Not finding one, he used the knocker. Soon, a woman who could only be Gerald's housekeeper opened the door.

"We've come to see Mr. Wainwright," Scott said without preamble. And, before she could deny them entrance, he shoved past her.

The others followed him in, making the housekeeper flustered. Trying to shoo them back out the door like an unruly flock of chickens, she said, "Mr. Wainwright can't see you now. He's entertaining."

"Nonsense," Scott said with brittle humor. "I know Mr. Wainwright. He's not at all entertaining. The man's as dull as a butter knife."

The poor woman looked confused. "Excuse me?"

"Never mind. Just tell him we're here."

"I can't do that, sir. He has guests."

"We're guests, too. In fact, we're bound to be very noisy guests unless we get to see Mr. Wainwright."

Alyx grinned and clutched her throat. "I feel a scream coming on . . . ."

The housekeeper waved her hands frantically. "No, no, don't do that. I'll get him."

She hurried off. The others chuckled, and glanced around the foyer where she had left them. Scott was impressed despite himself. Regardless of what the man had done to Grace, Scott had to admit Gerald had impeccable taste. The area he could see was done very much in period mode. If the rest of the house was like this, it must be truly impressive.

The housekeeper came back, wringing her hands. Gerald hurried in behind her, a frown marring his brow. "Is there an emergency? Did something happen to your sister? There's so much unrest in that part of the world . . . ."

"No, Kelly's fine, so far as I know. We just came for a tour."

Gerald looked taken aback. "I beg your pardon?"

"A tour," Scott repeated. "Of your house. We've been wanting to see it."

"Now?" The lawyer glanced incredulously between the four of them. Alyx grinned at him, but Nicole and Jackson's smiles were a little sick.

"Sure, why not?" Scott said. "We were free and knew you were home, so thought it would be a good time."

"Well, it's not," Gerald said with a frown. "I thought you knew I was entertaining your mother and my coworkers."

"Oh yeah, she did say something about that," Scott admitted. "Don't worry, we won't bother you."

Gerald frowned. "Come back tomorrow and I can give you a proper tour. I don't have time right now."

"Oh, don't worry about that," Scott said with a smile. "I'm sure your housekeeper can show us around. Then we won't disturb you or your guests."

Gerald's expression turned suspicious. "Have you been drinking?"

"Stone cold sober," Scott assured him. "We just want to see your house."

Scott could tell Gerald thought he was a raving

lunatic, but he still managed to retain his politeness. "Oh, all right. But make it quick." He turned to the housekeeper. "Eloise, you go with them."

"But the dinner . . ."

"Don't worry about dinner," Gerald said curtly. "Rhonda can handle it. I need to return to my guests."

Now that he had gotten what he wanted, Scott could afford to be gracious. "Thank you. We'll be quiet—I promise."

Gerald nodded in a distracted manner and hurried off. Eloise turned to them with a frown. "I'm sorry I can't show you the dining room right now because it's in use. But if you'd like to see the living room . . . ."

She led them through the rooms downstairs, giving the history of the house, its renovations, and its owners. Unwilling to give the woman anything to complain about, Scott was a model tourist as they followed her upstairs, and the others followed his lead. They asked pertinent questions, murmured appreciation for the furnishings, and complimented the owner.

When they reached the study, Scott grasped Nicole by the elbow and whispered, "Get rid of her."

She looked stumped for a moment, and Scott said aloud, "Are you feeling all right, Nicole?"

She shot him an irritated glance, then said, "Not really. It's so hot in here . . ." And, indeed, she did look wan and pale as she slumped into a chair. "Eloise, could I trouble you for a glass of ice water?"

Smart lady. Eloise wouldn't be able to get that

from the bathroom. Nicole had learned from his mistakes.

"Of course," Eloise said, looking concerned. "I'll be right back."

Once the housekeeper was out of the room, Scott darted over to the massive mahogany and leather desk. It had to be the one. He tried the center drawer. "Locked. Jackson, can you—"

But his friend was already ahead of him. Getting down on his knees, Jackson went to work on the lock.

Alyx planted her hand on her hips. "And how did Mr. Honesty learn how to pick a lock?"

"You learn a lot of things in the security business," he muttered. Then, with a satisfied smile, he pulled the drawer open.

"Good job," Scott declared and searched it. Nothing in the top drawer. Nothing of interest in any of the drawers. "The jewels aren't here," he said, disappointed. "In fact, there's nothing valuable here."

"That's odd," Alyx said. "Maybe they're somewhere else in the room?"

"Shouldn't be," Jackson said with a frown. "Why would he lock it when there's nothing to hide?"

Nicole came over to peer down into a drawer. "Some of these old desks have hidden compartments. Maybe this one does, too?"

"Good point," Jackson declared. "Let's look."

He opened a drawer, and everyone grabbed a different one, pulling them out completely to check behind them, and tapping on them to look for hollow spots. Finally, Scott noticed that the deep drawer he held was heavier than he expected for the few papers in them. And it didn't seem as deep as it should be.

He probed at it, then crowed with success. "This one has a false bottom."

Eager now, he pried it open as the others watched him. Inside were a few familiar jewelry cases. He opened one and, as he expected, found his mother's false sapphires. He held the necklace up in triumph. "Success."

Finding proof of Gerald's perfidy was bittersweet. Scott had known they had to be here, yet had hoped the man would be innocent. Now they just needed to replace the jewels and find a way to get Digby to see what Gerald had hidden in his desk.

Quickly, Nicole pulled the real jewels out of her purse and they replaced the fakes.

Just as they finished, Alyx said, "Uh-oh."

Scott glanced up to see Gerald standing in the doorway, looking thunderous. "What the hell are you doing in my desk?"

Nicole couldn't help it—she let out a squeak of surprise. *Oh, no. We're caught.*

But Scott appeared totally unruffled. Holding up the bracelet, he said, "Recovering stolen property."

Nicole had never seen Gerald move so fast as he did now. Crossing the room in an instant, he grabbed the bracelet out of Scott's hand and shoved it back in the false bottom of the drawer, then slammed it shut. "You fool," he said through clenched teeth. "You'll ruin everything."

Scott returned his stare, glare for glare. "Well, yeah. That was the point."

Nicole saw a movement in the doorway. The housekeeper and . . . "Mr. Digby," she exclaimed in surprise. Oh, no, he was here too soon.

But the investigator appeared even more astonished as he stared around the room. "What's going on here?"

"Ah, Digby," Scott said in triumph. "Just the man I want. Come in, come in."

Digby entered the room tentatively, as if he expected something might explode in his face.

Gerald scowled. "What the devil are you doing here?"

Eloise gestured helplessly with the glass of water Nicole had sent her for. "He knocked and said he was expected . . . ."

"It's okay, Eloise," Gerald said. "You can leave now." Once the housekeeper was gone, Gerald turned a questioning look on Digby.

The investigator nodded at Scott. "He asked me to come. Said he had an important break in the case."

Gerald turned back to Scott. "Look, you have no idea—"

But he was interrupted by Grace, who breezed in, saying, "Gerald, your guests—" She stopped dead, glancing around the room in confusion.

Nicole winced, then realized it might be for the best. At least this would save them from sending for her.

"What's going on here?" Grace demanded. "Scott, did you push your way in for a tour when I expressly told you not to?"

Scott frowned. "That's not—"

"It's all right," Gerald assured her. "I had Eloise

show them around. In fact, they've finished and were just leaving."

He gave Scott a warning look, which Scott ignored. "Sorry, Gerald. The jig is up. You might as well come clean."

Grace frowned at Gerald. "What does he mean by that?"

"Nothing, nothing," Gerald assured her. "Just a little misunderstanding." He glared at Scott again. "One I can clear up with very little effort if we can speak in private."

Scott crossed his arms across his chest, looking stubborn. "Is that what you call it? A misunderstanding? Sorry, I'm afraid I understand all too well. And I think Mother needs to hear this, too."

"No, she wouldn't be interested," Gerald said, sounding desperate now. "Grace, if you would be so kind as to let our guests know—"

"No way," Scott said, then smiled wolfishly when Boyd closed the door and stood in front of it like a guard. "She's staying."

And it was obvious no one else wanted to miss a word of this. Except maybe Digby. He made an abortive move toward the desk. "This is highly irregular . . . ."

"Maybe," Scott said. "But it gets the job done." He pointed dramatically at Gerald. "There's your thief."

But his pronouncement fell flat. Nicole didn't know what she had expected, but Gerald's look of disgust wasn't it.

Digby's response was surprising, too. "I'm sure there's been some mistake . . . ."

"I should hope so," Grace said indignantly. "Gerald is no thief. Why, he's being considered for a position on the bench. Scott, why would you say such a thing?"

She looked so bewildered and lost, Nicole moved to her side and put a supportive arm around her. Grace needed to hear this, but it wasn't going to be easy for the older woman.

Alyx huffed. "He says it because it's true."

Nicole gave Alyx a warning shake of her head. It was better to let Scott handle this.

Alyx grimaced, and Scott said, "Yes, it's true. Look at what we found." He pulled the drawer open again and dislodged the false bottom to show Grace and Digby the sapphires.

Digby gave Gerald an uncertain glance, then frowned at Scott. "How do I know you didn't plant these?"

"Why would I do that?" Scott asked.

"Well, you did open the desk before I got here," Digby said. "You could have."

Why was Digby acting this way? It was as if he didn't want to believe Scott. Suddenly, Nicole felt very conscious of the fake sapphires and money burning a hole in her purse.

"If I were going to plant evidence, don't you think I'd put *all* the jewels here?" Scott asked. "These are only the sapphires. I'll bet if you check the safes of the people downstairs, you'll find the rest of the missing jewels. The whole law firm is in on it."

"But that's not possible," Grace said in disbelief. "That young girl stole the jewels."

Stunned silence filled the study as everyone turned to stare at her.

Ohmigod, Grace knows about Chrissie. Nicole threw a frantic glance in Scott's direction, but he ignored it, intent on his suddenly flustered mother. "What did you say?"

"She didn't mean it," Gerald said quickly. "Really, she knows nothing about this."

Digby nodded. "Quite right, quite right."

Scott stared at the investigator in disbelief. "What do *you* know about this?"

The man's guilty expression was at odds with his quick, "Nothing. I know nothing. Isn't that why you invited me? To tell me what's going on?" He darted a nervous glance at Gerald, as if for reassurance.

"I think it's obvious," Boyd drawled from the doorway. "Those two are in it together, along with the rest of them downstairs. What's *your* position in the firm?" he asked Digby. "Law clerk?"

Digby looked at Gerald once again, who shook his head in resignation and made a gesture as if to tell him to answer as he wished.

"I'm a junior associate," Digby admitted.

Nicole gasped. How could it be? *I don't understand . . . .*

"You slimy weasel," Alyx exclaimed. "Pretending to be an insurance investigator when you're nothing but a scummy lawyer. I'm gonna call the police right now."

Scott forestalled her. "No, don't. I smell something fishy here, and it isn't what Eloise served for dinner." He turned to Grace. "What did you mean, a young girl stole them?"

Fear for her sister sliced through Nicole, then abruptly subsided. *Wait a minute.* If Digby wasn't really an investigator, maybe they didn't have anything to fear. She turned to hear Grace's response.

"I—I don't know what I meant," Grace said. "I was confused, that's all."

But Scott obviously didn't believe her. "Did you *arrange* this, Mother?"

"No, of course not," Gerald said before she could answer. "I did."

Grace sighed and moved beside Gerald to pat his hand. "No, dear. I won't let you pay for my mistakes. Yes, I'm the one who hired the girl to steal my jewels."

Alyx shook her head. "Unbelievable."

Nicole was inclined to agree with her, though it made perfect sense. "But why would you hire Chrissie of all people?"

"Chrissie?" Grace said vaguely. "Is that her name? I don't recall. I just remember her coming to me and asking for money, saying we owed her a college education for letting her father go. I felt bad for her, and this way we helped each other. She got the money from selling those ugly jewels, and I was supposed to get the money for the villa."

Well, knowing Chrissie had stolen the jewels at their owner's request made Nicole feel ten times better. But talk about the blind leading the clueless . . . .

Grace gave Nicole an odd look. "How did you know her name?"

Might as well tell all. From the expressions on Gerald and Digby's faces, they seemed to know already. "She's my sister."

"Your sister?" Grace repeated, then dropped into the desk chair as if in shock. "But how—"

"I met Nicole when she came to stop her sister from stealing the jewels," Scott explained. "We've been working together ever since to save the two of you from your folly."

"Yeah," Alyx said. "And there's a tale in itself. Ask him sometime what happened when Chrissie stole the jewels."

Scott shot her a warning glance. "Never mind about that."

"How did you know I was involved?" Grace asked faintly. "The girl swore she'd never tell."

"She didn't," Scott said in a curt tone. "In fact, we didn't know you were involved until just now. But when we found you had committed insurance fraud, we knew we had to cover for you."

"But it wasn't fraud," Grace insisted. "My jewels *were* stolen—by Nicole's sister."

Since Grace didn't seem to understand, Nicole said gently, "It was fraud when you reported the real jewels stolen, knowing it was the fakes that were really missing."

Grace looked puzzled. "No, I didn't."

Nicole exchanged equally confused glances with Scott.

Gerald heaved a sigh. "I think I can clear all this up."

"Please do," Scott said sarcastically.

"I meant it earlier when I said I arranged it." He gave Grace an uncertain glance. "I inadvertently overheard Grace talking to Miss Dreyfuss, arranging for her to steal the jewels. I feared for the consequences of such an act, so I . . . intervened."

"You intervened?" Scott repeated. "How? And

why didn't you just put a stop to this ridiculous scheme?"

Gerald shook his head. "I wish I had, now. I thought this would be a way to help your mother get the money without her knowing—she wouldn't let me give it to her."

"Of course not," Grace protested. "I couldn't accept a gift like that from a man who isn't my husband."

Gerald smiled at her. "Well, I asked you to marry me often enough . . . ."

"So what *did* you do?" Scott asked, sounding impatient.

The attorney looked embarrassed. "I wanted to make sure neither of them got into trouble, so I made slightly different arrangements . . . after I switched the jewels."

"You switched them?" Grace said. "But how? I never gave you the combinations to our safes."

He looked sheepish. "I'm afraid I lifted them from your purse. I know you always keep your combinations there." He gave Scott an apologetic glance and shrug. "Anyway, I switched them so Miss Dreyfuss would steal the fakes and leave you the real ones—I didn't want to deprive you of them. Then I pretended to call the insurance company, but really called Mr. Digby."

"You see?" Grace said to Scott. "I didn't commit fraud. I can't believe you thought it of me."

Though Boyd looked relieved, Scott was obviously uncomfortable, saying, "When I found the real jewels in your safe, the ones you had reported stolen, what else was I to think?"

"But why did you call Mr. Digby?" Nicole asked Gerald. It didn't make sense.

"I wanted him to pretend to be an insurance investigator so I could pay the insurance claim myself, thinking no one would be the wiser. That way Grace could have the villa she's had her heart set on."

"You did that for me?" Grace asked, looking flattered.

Nicole supposed it was sort of romantic, in a strange kind of way.

While Gerald looked abashed, Scott asked, "So why did the Larsons, Wyndhams, and Hardings buy the stolen jewels?"

Once again, Grace looked confused, but Gerald explained. "I couldn't offer to buy the stolen merchandise myself, or Miss Dreyfuss might have recognized me. So, I arranged for the three wives of my partners to drop heavy hints at the club. Your sister fell for it, and I gave them the money to pay her on delivery of the stolen merchandise." His mouth twisted wryly. "They even enjoyed it, and liked being able to help me give such a gift to Grace."

Grace looked less pleased at that, but said nothing.

"So *you're* the mastermind," Nicole said wonderingly. She knew Chrissie couldn't have come up with this scheme on her own. And no wonder the police never got involved. "Well, at least now I know who this belongs to." She opened her purse and shoved the sheaf of bills into Gerald's hands.

"What's this?" he asked.

"The money you paid Chrissie for the jewels. I wouldn't let her keep it."

"But you said your sister was away at college . . . ?"

"Yes, because Scott loaned me the cash. I didn't want to use tainted money."

Boyd nodded approval, but Gerald made a move as if to give it back to her. Nicole crossed her arms across her chest and scowled at him. He got the hint and dropped it on the desk.

"There's one thing I don't understand," Grace said.

Alyx rolled her eyes. "Only one?"

Ignoring her, Grace continued, "If the insurance report wasn't real, then why did Mr. Digby go through with the investigation?" She left unsaid the fact that she hadn't gotten the money yet, either, but it was there in her voice.

"Because Scott started nosing around," Gerald complained. "I don't know how he figured it out, but when he started acting suspiciously by going upstairs at the Hardings' party, I suspected he knew part of the scheme anyway."

"I'm no fool," Scott said, obviously stung.

Gerald raised an eyebrow. "Really? And yet you take such pains to make people think you are . . . ."

Bingo. It was what Nicole had told Scott all along.

Scott winced. "Ouch."

"And if I had known of your cleverness to begin with, I would have let you in on the scheme. As it was, I feared you were too much of a playboy to take it—or anything else—seriously."

Scott winced again. "I guess I deserve that."

Gerald didn't argue with him. "I couldn't figure out why you were replacing the fake jewels with the real ones, but I tried to scare you off by pretending your mother was being reluctant and Digby was too insistent."

Briefly, Scott explained why they felt it necessary to switch the jewels.

"I see," Gerald said. "But when you wouldn't scare, I tried to stop you by telling you Digby had given up."

The light dawned and Nicole pointed at Digby. "That's why you asked those probing questions— you were trying to scare us." It had worked, too. "But why were you so insistent on seeing the sapphires?"

He looked embarrassed. "I was trying to pressure Mr. Richmond into confiding in Mr. Wainwright so he could steer him in another direction."

Scott nodded admiringly. "I almost did. I tried to call him—at home, then the office. That's when I learned the names of his partners."

It was Gerald's turn to wince. "So that's how you caught me. I wondered."

"Yeah," Scott said. "But I still didn't figure out what really happened. I feel like such an idiot. If only I hadn't acted the fool, none of this would have happened."

True, but then Nicole would have never met Scott, either. She wondered how she felt about that. Would it have been better to have never met him? Never lost the man she loved?

She didn't know, but she did know she felt relief that Gerald had turned out to be one of the good guys after all.

Grace looked back and forth between Scott and Nicole with a dismayed look. "Does this mean your engagement isn't real?"

I wish it was. But Nicole deferred to Scott to answer.

"No, Mother, it's not," Scott said gently. "And, now that this is all over, Nicole wants to break it off as soon as possible."

No, I don't, Nicole wailed inside.

Grace looked as unhappy as Nicole felt. "All right, then. Just let me know what to tell my friends."

"You won't need to tell them anything," Scott assured her. "When we attend the benefit next week, it will be very clear why we're no longer engaged . . . ."

Chapter Nineteen

The night of the benefit, Nicole sat alone in her living room, waiting for Scott to pick her up, feeling nothing but dread. She stared down at the engagement ring, the beautiful champagne-colored diamond solitaire Scott's father had saved for his wife-to-be. She had just gotten used to wearing the thing, and tonight she was going to have to give it back.

She blinked back tears at the thought of never seeing Scott again. She loved his wacky humor, his sharp intelligence, the way he found excuses to touch her, his thoughtfulness . . . . He was a true prince in a world of wannabes, yet everyone saw him as the jester. Even his own mother.

It saddened her that once their engagement was broken, no one in his social circle would ever understand and appreciate the real Scott Richmond. He was truly special.

Unfortunately, she was about to lose him. Alyx had been very impatient with her, urging Nicole to tell Scott how she felt about him, but Nicole couldn't bring herself to do it. True, he had indicated an interest in dating her, but after being engaged to him, that wasn't enough for Nicole. If he couldn't envision them spending the rest of their lives together, as she could so easily, then it would hurt too much to date him casually. She wanted all or nothing. And nothing was what she got.

The doorbell rang and she rose, smoothing her dress down. This was one of the dresses Scott had bought her—a subdued sheath in silvery gray that matched her mood.

She opened the door and Scott regarded her with appreciation. "You look great, as always."

But Nicole was in no mood to hear it, so she just nodded and indicated that she was ready to leave.

After she closed the door behind her, Scott waved to someone next door. She glanced in that direction and realized he was waving at Missy, who did nothing but wave back briefly and go inside.

Surprised, Nicole said, "Was that Missy or did an alien take over her body?"

Scott chuckled. "No, it was Missy. I saw her after I left here the other night and we came to . . . an understanding."

Very mysterious. But if it kept the woman from bothering Scott, Nicole didn't care what had happened.

They got into the car, and as they pulled away from the curb, Nicole asked, "What's the plan for tonight?" He'd never really told her.

He didn't pretend to misunderstand her. "The plan is for me to act like a jerk so you can jilt me publicly. That way there will be no doubt in anyone's mind who is the dumper and who is the dumpee."

Emotions clogged her throat—too many to even

identify. Even now, Scott was trying to make her look good, trying to calm her fears. So why in hell wasn't he trying to keep her?

"Is—" She paused to clear her throat. "Is that really necessary?"

"It is if you don't want everyone to think I dumped you. I thought that's what you wanted."

And there was the answer to her question. Obviously, the reason he wasn't trying to keep her was because he didn't want her. Resigned to the inevitable, Nicole stared out the window. "How do you plan to do it, then?"

"I'm not sure. Just watch for your cue."

Nicole rode the rest of the way in silence, trying to fortify herself for the ordeal to come.

The dinner wasn't much better. They sat at a round table with Grace and Gerald and six of their friends, including Melinda and her brother. It was painful to watch Scott pretend to get drunker and drunker—and flirt outrageously with Melinda. Nicole was probably the only one who noticed he didn't really imbibe much. The others seemed to take it as a matter of course that Scott would make a fool of himself. And Melinda was downright smug.

Finally, once the speeches were all done, Gerald called for everyone's attention at the table. Standing, he smiled at them. "I want you all to be the first to know. Grace has finally agreed to be my wife."

Nicole rose from her chair to hug Grace. "I'm so happy for you," she murmured as everyone exclaimed their congratulations. "You deserve it. What made you finally say yes?"

Grace lowered her voice so only Nicole could

hear. "After he went to such lengths to get me what I wanted, I realized he really loved me."

"Good," Nicole said, grinning. "I hope he gives you the villa as a wedding present."

"He already did," Grace confided, then had to turn back to the table to receive everyone else's congratulations.

Nicole blinked back tears. She was genuinely happy for the two of them. Too bad her story wouldn't have an equally happy ending.

And it looked like the end was now in sight. Scott squeezed her knee in an obvious signal and stood. Nicole fortified herself for what she had to do.

Scott swayed slightly and raised his glass to Gerald and Grace. "Congrashulashuns, Gerald," he said with a sloppy gesture that sent the wine sloshing over the rim of his glass. "Lesh just hope your fiancée isn't as mush of a nag as mine ish." Then he took a sip of wine as everyone gasped.

Annoyed, Nicole wondered how these people, who had known Scott all his life, could possibly believe he would really act this way.

Appearing to be oblivious of everyone's reaction, Scott gave a bark of laugher. "Nag, hag, bag, sag. Funny how they all rhyme, ishn't it?"

It would have hurt terribly, if Nicole didn't realize it was all an act . . . and if she weren't hurting so badly already.

"That's enough," Grace said, sounding outraged. "Sit down and be quiet. You've had too much to drink."

"Oh, no," Scott said cheerfully. "Not nearly enough, have I, old girl?"

He nudged Nicole as if to ask for her response, but she knew he was urging her to take the cue.

No, not this way. I don't want it to end this way.

Who was she kidding? She didn't want it to end at all.

But, seeing her reluctance to respond, Scott gave her one last goad. "Oh, I shee. You're too tipshy to say anything. But I bet Melinda would have lotsh to say." And he swatted her on the rear.

Melinda gasped and Nicole shot to her feet. This had to end, now, before Scott made more of a fool of himself. "On the contrary," Nicole spat out. "I'm not drunk, and I have a great deal to say."

She had been avoiding his gaze all night, but as her eyes met his in fury, she couldn't help but notice the pain there, hidden behind the facade. She froze. *My Lord, he's hurting as much as I am.*

But why? Why would he go through this? Then the answer hit her—just like Gerald, he was going to these great lengths to give Nicole what he thought she wanted.

Her heart lifted. Did that mean he loved her as much as Gerald loved Grace? As much as Nicole loved Scott? How could she know?

Scott jeered at her. "Well, lesh hear it, then."

But his eyes had turned compassionate, urging her to do what they had agreed upon. *I can't.* Unfortunately, the only alternative was to put her heart on the line . . . in public, for everyone to see. Could she face the humiliation if she was wrong?

Hell, yes. Scott was worth it.

"All right." Taking a deep breath, she turned to face the rest of the table. "I've been meaning to say this for a long time. You're all wrong about Scott. Dead wrong."

Their shocked expressions showed this wasn't what they expected to hear. And Scott's antics had drawn the attention of other diners at nearby tables, so Nicole suddenly had a much bigger audience than she had expected.

Her heart pounding, she went on to say firmly, "Scott isn't a fool, he isn't a playboy, and he isn't a silly little boy who never grew up. He's witty, charming, intelligent, and very much an adult."

Several of them cast doubtful gazes at Scott as if to say, "Yeah, right." Only Gerald gave her an encouraging nod.

"But he knows that none of you expect better of him, so he's always been your court jester, acting the fool for your entertainment." Now some of their expressions turned speculative. "Think about it," Nicole urged. "If he was really the fool you thought him, would he have graduated third in his class? Would he have been able to repair the family fortunes?" She took a deep breath as she went out on a limb. "And would he have been able to pull off this act tonight?"

"Act?" Melinda repeated, confusion on her face.

Scott stopped swaying and put down his glass, watching Nicole soberly. Good—he wasn't going to fight her in this.

"Yes, act," Nicole confirmed. "For reasons I'd rather not discuss, we decided to end our engagement. But I was so worried that people would think he dumped me that Scott staged this little play for me."

Slowly, Nicole removed her ring, then gazed into

Scott's eyes. "I'm sorry, Scott, but I can't let you do that."

All traces of his former drunken appearance had disappeared. Nicole tried to read his expression, but couldn't, though a small light in his eyes gave her hope.

Melinda spoke up. "But your engagement is still off, right?"

"That's up to Scott," Nicole said. Taking a deep breath, she said to hell with the embarrassment and dove in. Holding out the ring, she said, "Scott, you gave me this once before, when we both knew it wouldn't last. But I'd like you to offer it to me again now."

"Why?" he asked softly.

"Because I love you. Because I want to spend the rest of my life with you. Because marrying you is now at the very top of my list."

He stared at her for a moment. Her heart pounded and her stomach churned as she waited for his answer. What would he say?

Gently, he took the ring from her, then dropped to one knee and held the ring up, his expression and pose uncharacteristically serious. "Nicole, will you marry me?"

Joy surged through her, but she had to know . . . . "Why?" she asked softly.

"Because you understand the real me. Because I love you more than I ever thought possible. And because I am so humbled that you were willing to take this huge risk to ensure our happiness." He held up the ring. "Will you marry me?"

Perfect. "Yes!" she shouted, throwing her arms wide in exultation.

And as he grabbed her into his arms for a fierce kiss, the room exploded in applause. Well-wishers pounded them on the back, but the only person Nicole had eyes for was Scott.

"I warn you," he said with a twinkle in his eye. "I don't want a long engagement."

"Neither do I, but you know we'll have to let your mother plan it, then make sure my sister and yours can be there."

He groaned. "Can't we just elope?"

She shook her head. "Boyd and Alyx would never forgive us, not to mention your mother."

"Hmm, Jackson and Alyx together in the same wedding, having to be nice to each other . . . ." He laughed. "Okay, seeing that might be worth the wait—especially since Jackson won't be able to put the move on you now." Wagging a finger in her face, he said, "But I warn you, I'm not waiting a moment longer than necessary."

"Neither am I," she assured him. "I can't wait for us to begin the rest of our life together. Just promise me I'll never have to wear your mother's jewels."

He laughed. "Done." Gently, he took her hand and poised the solitaire at the end of her ring finger. "Are you sure you want a piece of jewelry that spent time in my mother's safe?"

"Yes—this is the only one I want." Though it was one of the few pieces Scott hadn't caught Chrissie in the act of stealing, it would always remind Nicole of the way he had stolen her heart. She slid it firmly back on her finger where it belonged.

About the Author

Pam McCutcheon is the award-winning author of ten romance novels, one novella, two how-to books for writers, and four fantasy short stories (the latter written as Pamela Luzier). She loves romance, screwball comedies, and the wyrd stuff, so most of her stories include some humor or the paranormal. To find out more, visit her on the web at www.pammc.com.